Praise for Rachel Howzell Hall

"A fresh voice in crime fiction."

—Lee Child

"Devilishly clever . . . Hall's writing sizzles and pops."

—Meg Gardiner

"Hall slips from funny to darkly frightening with elegant ease."

—*Publishers Weekly*

Praise for *Fog And Fury*

"This captivating blend of angst, mystery, and page-turning suspense delivers a top-notch reading experience."

—*Kirkus Reviews* (starred review)

"Enough nuance and complexity to make things feel fresh. Readers will be eager to return to this series soon."

—*Publishers Weekly*

"A gripping series debut."

—*Booklist*

"Of immense appeal for readers with an interest in mysteries and thrillers featuring a female sleuth, a myriad of unexpected plot twists, and a memorably 'big reveal' finale. Unreservedly recommended."

—*Midwest Book Review*

"A new Rachel Howzell Hall thriller is always call for celebration, and this one may be her very best. *Fog and Fury* is a PI page-turner, full of investigative twists, deeply rendered characters, and lush, evocative writing that could come from no one else. Pick this book up now."

—Jess Lourey, Edgar Award–nominated author of *The Taken Ones*

"Rachel Howzell Hall once again proves why she's one of the best crime fiction authors writing today. *Fog and Fury* combines whip-smart observations about race and class with a twisty mystery and cliff-hanger ending that'll have you already wanting to put the next book on your TBR list. It's a must read for noir fans, especially if you loved her Lou Norton series."

—Kellye Garrett, award-winning author of *Missing White Woman*

"Rachel Howzell Hall has done it again with *Fog and Fury*. This is a story with depth, heart, and terror, and it cements her as one of the strongest voices in crime fiction today. Newly minted PI Alyson 'Sonny' Rush is a character to root for. Add in her extended family, the dark secrets in the town of Haven, the messy relationships and social growing pains, all at once familiar and frightening, and you have the recipe for a stellar thriller. Don't miss it!"

—J.T. Ellison, *New York Times* bestselling author of *A Very Bad Thing*

Praise for *What Fire Brings*

"Rachel Howzell Hall is a master of the psychological-suspense thriller. *What Fire Brings* delivers shocking secrets, surprises on every page, and a killer twist that will leave you breathless. A must-read!"

—Melinda Leigh, #1 *Wall Street Journal* bestselling author

"This one will keep you guessing! Hall's considerable talent is on full display as she expertly deploys misdirection and subterfuge in a riveting tale of intrigue and suspense where nothing is as it seems. The past collides with the present to forever alter the future while the twists keep coming until the final shocking reveal. If you love an intricate plot with well-crafted prose, incisive insight, and complex characters, do not miss this propulsive mystery by a superb storyteller!"

—Isabella Maldonado, *Wall Street Journal* bestselling author

"Crackling wildfires, dark secrets, and a serial killer on the loose. Rachel Howzell Hall's *What Fire Brings* is a captivating and creepy thrill ride through the California canyons, right up to the final and fiery twisty end."

—Wanda M. Morris, award-winning author of *All Her Little Secrets* and *Anywhere You Run*

"Rachel Howzell Hall is simply one of the finest crime writers of her generation, and *What Fire Brings* is her most assured novel yet . . . and one that hits a little close to home for everyone who puts pen to paper or finger to keyboard. Tense, illuminating, and filled with surprises on every page. A masterwork that will leave you flipping pages to see what you might have missed."

—Tod Goldberg, *New York Times* bestselling author

Praise for *What Never Happened*

"Rachel Howzell Hall does it again. *What Never Happened* blends blade-sharp writing and indelible characters with a suspenseful story that pulls you in and won't let go, as a seeming paradise grows dark with storms, suspicion, and murder. I couldn't put it down."

—Meg Gardiner, #1 *New York Times* bestselling author

"*What Never Happened* opens with a gut punch and doesn't let up from there. Rachel Howzell Hall's twist on the you-can't-go-home-again story is smart, dizzying, and thrilling. She not only handles the mystery elements expertly, but she honors the grief and rage of our past and present."

—Paul Tremblay, bestselling author of *The Cabin at the End of the World* and *The Pallbearers Club*

"Rachel Howzell Hall has crafted her own genre of slow-boiling, powerfully emotional thrillers. Her realistic characters are ordinary people, haunted by past horrors that won't stay buried, forcing them to face pure evil to find their own redemption."

—Lee Goldberg, #1 *New York Times* bestselling author

"In *What Never Happened*, Rachel Howzell Hall seamlessly weaves together the past and the present, decorating her breakneck plot with dark secrets and unexpected reveals that glitter like jewels. I couldn't turn the pages fast enough."

—Jess Lourey, Amazon Charts bestselling author of *The Quarry Girls*

"*What Never Happened* is superb. Beautifully and smartly written, it is an engrossing thriller with an ending that will leave your head spinning. It is deliciously creepy and perfectly crafted. In a word, stunning! Don't miss this one!"

—Lisa Regan, *USA Today* and *Wall Street Journal* bestselling author

"Rachel Howzell Hall's *What Never Happened* is a spine-tingling twist of a roller coaster that keeps you on the edge of your seat to the very last page and will have you saying 'Thanks a lot, Rachel, for my lack of sleep.'"

—Yasmin Angoe, award-winning author of the critically acclaimed Nena Knight series, *Her Name Is Knight* and *They Come at Knight*

"Rachel Howzell Hall continues to prove why she's one of crime fiction's leading writers. *We Lie Here* is a psychological-suspense fan's dream with both a heroine you'll want to root for and a story you'll want to keep reading late into the night. A must-read!"
—Kellye Garrett, Agatha, Anthony, and Lefty Award–winning author of *Like a Sister*

Praise for *These Toxic Things*

An Amazon Best Book of the Month: Mystery, Thriller & Suspense

"This cleverly plotted, surprise-filled novel offers well-drawn and original characters, lively dialogue, and a refreshing take on the serial killer theme. Hall continues to impress."
—*Publishers Weekly* (starred review)

"A mystery/thriller/coming-of-age story you won't be able to put down till the final revelation."
—*Kirkus Reviews*

"Tense and pacey, with an appealing central character, this is a coming-of-age story as well as a gripping mystery."
—*The Guardian*

"The mystery plots are twisty and grabby, but also worth noting is the realistic rendering of a Black LA neighborhood locked in a battle over gentrification."
—*Los Angeles Times*

"Rachel Howzell Hall . . . just gets better and better with each book."
—CrimeReads

"Rachel Howzell Hall continues to shatter the boundaries of crime fiction through the sheer force of her indomitable talent. *These Toxic Things* is a master class in tension and suspense. You think you are ready for it. But. You. Are. Not."

—S. A. Cosby, author of Blacktop Wasteland

"*These Toxic Things* is taut and terrifying, packed with page-turning suspense and breathtaking reveals. But what I loved most is the mother-daughter relationship at the heart of this gripping thriller. Plan on reading it twice: once because you won't be able to stop, and the second time to savor the razor's edge balance of plot and poetry that only Rachel Howzell Hall can pull off."

—Jess Lourey, Amazon Charts bestselling author of Unspeakable Things

"The brilliant Rachel Howzell Hall becomes the queen of mind games with this twisty and thought-provoking cat-and-mouse thriller. Where memories are weaponized, keepsakes are deadly, and the past gets ugly when you disturb it. As original, compelling, and sinister as a story can be, with a message that will haunt you long after you race through the pages."

—Hank Phillippi Ryan, USA Today bestselling author of Her Perfect Life

Praise for *And Now She's Gone*

"It's a feat to keep high humor and crushing sorrow in plausible equilibrium in a mystery novel, and few writers are as adept at it as Rachel Howzell Hall."

—Washington Post

"One of the best books of the year . . . whip-smart and emotionally deep, *And Now She's Gone* is a deceptively straightforward mystery, blending a fledgling PI's first 'woman is missing' case with underlying stories about racial identity, domestic abuse, and rank evil."
—*Los Angeles Times*

"Smart, razor-sharp . . . Full of wry, dark humor, this nuanced tale of two extraordinary women is un-put-downable."
—*Publishers Weekly* (starred review)

"Smart, packed with dialogue that sings on the page, Hall's novel turns the tables on our expectations at every turn, bringing us closer to truth than if it were forced on us in school."
—Walter Mosley

"A fierce PI running from her own dark past chases a missing woman around buzzy LA. Breathlessly suspenseful, as glamorous as the city itself, *And Now She's Gone* should be at the top of your must-read list."
—Michele Campbell, bestselling author of *A Stranger on the Beach*

"One of crime fiction's leading writers at her very best. The final twist will make you want to immediately turn back to page one and read it all over again. *And Now She's Gone* is a perfect blend of PI novel and psychological suspense that will have readers wanting more."
—Kellye Garrett, Anthony, Agatha, and Lefty Award–winning author of *Hollywood Homicide* and *Hollywood Ending*

"Sharp, witty, and perfectly paced, *And Now She's Gone* is one hell of a read!"
—Wendy Walker, bestselling author of *The Night Before*

"Hall once again proves to be an accomplished maestro who has composed a symphony of increasing tension and near-unbearable suspense. Rachel brilliantly reveals the bone and soul of our shared humanity and the struggle to contain the nightmares of human faults and failings. I am a fan, pure and simple."

—Stephen Mack Jones, award-winning author of the August Snow thrillers

"Heartfelt and gripping . . . I'm a perennial member of the Rachel Howzell Hall fan club, and her latest is a winning display of her wit and compassion and mastery of suspense."

—Steph Cha, award-winning author of *Your House Will Pay*

"An entertainingly twisty plot, a rich and layered sense of place, and most of all, a main character who pops off the page. Gray Sykes is hugely engaging and deeply complex, a descendant of Philip Marlowe and Easy Rawlins who is also definitely, absolutely her own woman."

—Lou Berney, award-winning author of *November Road*

"A deeply human protagonist, an intricate and twisty plot, and sentences that make me swoon with jealousy . . . Rachel Howzell Hall will flip every expectation you have—this is a magic trick of a book."

—Rob Hart, author of *The Warehouse*

"*And Now She's Gone* has all the mystery of a classic whodunit, with an undeniably fresh and clever voice. Hall exemplifies the best of the modern PI novel."

—Alafair Burke, *New York Times* bestselling author

PRAISE FOR *THEY ALL FALL DOWN*

"A riotous and wild ride."

—Attica Locke

"Dramatic, thrilling, and even compulsive."

—James Patterson

"An intense, feverish novel with riveting plot twists."

—Sara Paretsky

"Hall is beyond able and ready to take her place among the ranks of contemporary crime fiction's best and brightest."

—*Strand Magazine*

THE VIEW FROM HERE

OTHER TITLES BY RACHEL HOWZELL HALL

Haven Thrillers

Mist and Malice

Fog and Fury

Vallendor

The Cruel Dawn

The Last One

Detective Elouise Norton

City of Saviors

Trail of Echoes

Skies of Ash

Land of Shadows

Stand-Alones

What Fire Brings

What Never Happened

We Lie Here

These Toxic Things

And Now She's Gone

They All Fall Down

No One Knows You're Here

THE VIEW FROM HERE

RACHEL HOWZELL HALL

Published by Thomas & Mercer, Seattle

www.apub.com

Amazon, the Amazon logo, and Thomas & Mercer are trademarks of Amazon.com, Inc., or its affiliates.

EU product safety contact:
Amazon Media EU S. à r.l.
38, avenue John F. Kennedy, L-1855 Luxembourg
amazonpublishing-gpsr@amazon.com

ISBN-13: 9781662538971 (paperback)
ISBN-13: 9781662538988 (digital)

Cover design by Lisa Amoroso
· Cover image: © olga Yastremska / Alamy; © asharkyu / Shutterstock

Printed in the United States of America

Then you will know the truth, and

the truth will set you free.

John 8:32

Don't know how I got here . . .

It's so dark in this house, even with every light burning bright. It's always worse at night, when you're alone.

But I'm not alone.

My shoulders ache, exhausted from holding my breath, exhausted from waiting for the next time . . . Gravel in my eyes because I haven't slept in six, seven, eight days . . . Can't even cry anymore. My sobs sound like coughs—

What's that?

He's standing behind me, but that's impossible . . . Right?

I'm not sure what's possible. I can't explain this. I can't explain anything anymore.

"Nicole."

He calls me, but I don't answer. Because if I answer, then I discount everything I believe.

I hunker on the couch, silent, eyes glued to the television, clutching the machete, waiting to slash at phantoms or friends or thin air. The full moon peeks through the curtains. Six hours before the sun cracks over the horizon. Can I last that long?

My teeth click, my nerves tighten, my trust in praying and guardian angels and God rips into tiny, tiny pieces . . .

Six hours . . .

"Nicole!"

I close my eyes, clamp my jaw, refuse to answer.

He'll go away. Just wait a few minutes more . . . I could leave the house, and stay somewhere else. But I'm not safe anywhere. Not from him. Not anymore . . . I am alone.

Somewhere in the house, a door gently closes. My breathing quickens because no one else is here. Or someone is here, but I don't know who . . . or what . . . I grip the machete tighter, hoping that it will be enough.

Will you kill someone you love? Yes. Or . . .

A footstep.

I jump up from the couch and spin around to see . . . No one. Adrenaline tastes like metal and lemons, and I swallow to make the bitterness go away. The machete, now high over my head, wobbles in my grasp and my eyes scan the room . . . No one. But that can't be true . . . can it?

Please, God.

No more.

Please, God. Make it stop.

How did I get here?

PART I

CHAPTER 1

I sat in the waiting room of Orleigh Tremaine Newman—a Whole Person Corporation. The space stank of old coffee, onions, and lavender perfume. The receptionist—a goth girl named Piper—sat at a messy desk and polished her nails shiny black as the ringing telephone rolled to voicemail. Boxes of copy paper and toner towered near a dusty, plastic fichus. A crumpled Burger King bag sat atop an abandoned computer monitor.

This space was nothing like my former shrink's clean, bright, and clutter-free waiting room. There, Kimmy, the receptionist, answered the telephone after the first ring and never ate obnoxious foods at her desk. She had remembered each patient's name and most important, each of our prescription needs.

Nervous, I kept my eyes on Angelina Jolie's picture in *People* magazine because I didn't want to chat with the other patients seated around me.

The blonde sitting across the room tore at a napkin until tiny bits of paper settled at her feet like snowflakes. A morbidly obese pink-skinned man rocked back and forth in his chair. I didn't know his problem, but I'm sure eating played a role. Another woman—a redhead—sat next to the fat man. She rubbed a blue satiny square cut from an old baby blanket.

I was the ordinary, always-anxious Black girl wearing antiqued Levi's and Gucci loafers. I had a house, a husband, a Volvo, and a job writing about groundbreaking drug therapies developed by CelluTech, one of the leading biotechnology firms in the country. Unlike the blonde across from me, I tore my tiny bits of paper internally—mounds of confetti piled near my gallbladder. I never thought that at thirty-seven years old, I'd still need therapy.

During the spring of my fifth-grade year, my great-aunt Beryl had noticed that I had "retreated inside" of myself. No matter how many tablets of vitamin C and Saint-John's-wort she forced me to take, I still wasn't "actin' right."

"Your momma and daddy been dead for eight years," she said. "Why you all strange now?"

I shrugged, then retreated to the pages of *Anne of Green Gables*. Strange? I had never talked much. Had always picked at my food. Preferred the company of fictional characters in books and on television over Aunt Beryl, her ten cats, and her nosy church friends.

Out of ideas, she took me to see Simon Daniels, PhD. Once a week, I'd expressed my anguish through journal entries, word searches, and collages made from cut-out pictures out of *Ebony* magazine.

After session ten, Aunt Beryl marched into Dr. Daniels's office to say, "You still ain't fixed her."

Dr. Daniels cast a worried glance at me, then said, "Miss Porter, she's lost both of her parents. That's a painful ordeal, even for adults. There's no pill for grief, and it doesn't have a timetable. It doesn't show up like the number three bus, rumbling at each stop—anger, denial, acceptance—until it reaches the terminal at the end of the day."

Aunt Beryl clucked her tongue and hoisted her purse onto her lap.

"Nicole's bus has just taken an eight-year journey," Dr. Daniels explained. "It may be years before she reaches the end. She needs your patience and understanding. You are the only person she has left in the world."

Aunt Beryl glanced at me, then, her brown eyes—Dad's eyes, my eyes—softer than before. "You sure she don't need to take nothing? I hear gingerroot—"

"She'll be fine," Dr. Daniels had assured her. "She's young. She'll bounce back."

I stopped seeing psychiatrists during college because college women often resisted advice from people with wrinkles and W-4 forms. We ignored The Man and embraced Oppression, stumbled around campus hungover from weed or Boone's Farm Strawberry Hill, zoned out during French lit, but incredibly alert back in the dorm for *General Hospital.* Angry, moody, and high for four years—who had the time or the desire to see a shrink?

Besides, Doctors Daniels, Handler, and Grinstein had fixed me. Yes: Each had suggested that I continue seeing a psychiatrist throughout my life, but those had been suggestions. I'd *suggest* that all women consult a personal dietician and a genetics counselor, and to hire a maid. No harm if they didn't. Merely a *suggestion.* And I considered therapy like that—an elective like metals or home ec class.

Truman and I married, and all was fine until our eleventh anniversary. As we spent less time together, I became more insecure and Truman became less communicative. Once we started bickering over trivial things—*you didn't put gas in the car, why didn't you put gas in the car?*—I thought, *Maybe it's me. Maybe I should get help.*

I didn't perform a comprehensive search for a psychiatrist. Instead, I called my HMO's customer service line, and asked for an African American woman who specialized in death, grief, and marriage. Gayle Clark, MD, a wee Black woman with a small gray Afro, made pots of hot peppermint tea at each of our sessions. She had listened, nodded, and prodded me about my parents, my aunt, my insecurities and abandonment issues, and how all of this was affecting my marriage. She had also prescribed Paxil to combat my anxiety, and Valium to help me sleep.

Truman knew about Dr. Clark, but he never asked what we talked about. Instead, he said, "Glad you're talking to someone," then returned to playing *World of Warcraft*.

"Someone" used to be him.

One afternoon, after discussing Truman's late nights at work, and my sense of being ignored, Dr. Clark announced her departure. Her husband, an Adventist pastor, had agreed to build a church in Bolivia. Dr. Clark would follow him and provide family counseling for the soon-to-be-converted. She had already selected my rebound relationship. "Her name's Lori Tremaine," she had said. "And she is a *jewel*. A wonderful, warm human being."

I studied Dr. Tremaine's profile on the Find-a-Therapist, Inc. website. The white woman in the picture posed with a golden retriever beneath a giant oak. Her long auburn hair piled atop her head like autumn leaves. *Do you feel detached from your life, from who you are? Do confusion and dread haunt you day-to-day? Are you exhausted by the secrets you keep? I can help you find inner peace.*

As I entered the office, Lori Tremaine, MD, stood from her high-backed leather chair to shake my hand. "Nice to meet you, Nicole. Glad you could come."

I forced a smile and assessed the woman's handshake: limp. And: *glad you could come?* As though she was hosting a Tupperware party. Or a wake.

She sported a pixie haircut now, and wore a denim Be Dazzled blouse separated from the denim skirt by a wide snakeskin belt the color of mangoes. Her hazel eyes, rimmed with green liner, sparkled as though she had just finished a bottle of white Zinfandel. She looked more like Reba McEntire than a member of the American Psychiatric Association.

Her office smelled of cinnamon and chocolate-scented candles. A large cup of coffee sat near the computer keyboard, coral lipstick prints around its rim. Every flat surface hid beneath stacks of papers, elephant figurines, and pictures of the doctor and her life partner on their sailboat. There were no chaises like you see in movies and television sitcoms. Just regular leather chairs placed before her massive wood desk.

I settled into a guest chair.

Dr. Tremaine said, "Water?"

"No, thank you." Out the picture window, I glimpsed a blue ribbon of ocean twinkling with sunshine.

"So, Nicole," Dr. Tremaine said, sitting behind her desk. She opened a manila folder that contained two sheets of paper, then glanced at me. "Why are we here today?"

"Well," I said. "Umm . . . I thought Dr. Clark . . . You know . . . Did she, like, forward my file?"

"Let's see . . ." The psychiatrist returned her attention to the folder's contents. She pulled out the second sheet, then slipped on a pair of emerald-colored reading glasses. "It says here . . ." She read in silence for a few moments, then said, "Nothing much. Just a note that says, *Talk about the house.*" She peered at me over the top of her frames. "Does that mean anything to you?"

I shivered, then offered a curt nod.

Dr. Tremaine closed the folder, and said, "Don't feel pressured to talk about that, though. We can discuss other issues first to become better acquainted. Tell me about your family life."

"I'm here *because* of my family life." I paused, then added, "Kind of. And it's related to the house." I scratched my nose and stared at the wrinkled lip prints on Dr. Tremaine's cup. "Not just my family life now, but also my childhood . . . Not that my life *now* isn't affected. Because it is. But my life *then*—that's not the primary reason I'm here. Although . . ." Lost and nervous, my right foot bobbed up and down as though it generated electricity for the lights and computer.

"Okay." The woman slipped off her glasses, then sat back in her chair.

She wasn't taking notes. Why wasn't she taking notes?

"We can talk about whatever you want." She reached for her coffee cup and sipped.

"I'm not much for chatter," I said, fighting the desire to slap the cup from the shrink's hand because people in need of help don't like seeing their care providers taking it easy like retirees on a Carnival cruise. "So, if you don't mind, I'd like to start on the house. If you don't mind."

"I don't mind at—" Dr. Tremaine took another sip of coffee, but didn't place the cup back on the desk. She smiled at me with coffee-stained teeth and lips uneven with color. "You start then."

I nodded, then shifted my leg so that the other foot could pump. "This will sound weird out of context, but . . ." I swallowed, then said, "My house is haunted . . . I think."

I think.

As though those two words of uncertainty negated the heretical "house is haunted." Because hadn't I learned in church? The dead can't haunt. They lay in their graves, awaiting the return of Christ so that they could either be caught up in the clouds or banished to hell. *For the living know that they will die, but the dead know nothing. Nada. Zilch.*

Truman and I had visited a so-called haunted house—an antebellum mansion wasting away in the bayous of Louisiana. We had listened to the Cajun tour guide whisper about the souls of runaway slaves trapped there, and about cold spots and mysterious crying, about pictures that, when developed, came out as blurry spots. "Ghosts," the Cajun had said with a certain nod. And we had shivered in those cold spots and had heard the crying of tortured slaves and had taken pictures of creepy Spanish moss hanging from moaning oaks and had glimpsed the empty bedrooms where little white children and their mothers had died from consumption, and we had had our film developed and had noticed the blurry spots in each shot.

"They's ghosts," Truman had said in a Southern accent. Then, we had laughed and had placed those photographs in our travel diary alongside pictures of the Eiffel Tower and the Mayan ruins.

Saying "haunted" to Dr. Tremaine discounted everything I religiously believed. Aunt Beryl had never wavered from her strict understanding about the dead's state, never telling me once that my mom and dad were watching over me in heaven—even though the heaven story could've offered a lonely child comfort, and kept her from visiting the dungeons of her imagination. But my aunt didn't play that. She had scolded me the one time I had joked, "My mom is rolling over in her grave." And now, to utter this "haunted" heresy aloud, and to a stranger?

Aunt Beryl was probably rolling over in her grave.

In my profession, I showed restraint in the words I chose. *Sorafenib* may *help prevent* some *kinds of kidney cancer.* Because my writing had to remain hyperbole-free, my natural inclination to overexaggerate and overstate eked out in other ways.

My house is haunted.

Not: *My house is noisy.*

Not: *My house is too cold and makes strange sounds.*

Again: not that I believed (religiously) in "haunted" anything. And no one had died in our house. The previous owners had suffered a huge loss once their dot.com fortune dwindled and the bank foreclosed. Their American Dream had died, but Carl hadn't hung himself from a ceiling beam in the living room, and Yvette hadn't slit her wrists in the primary bathroom's sunken tub. They had moved to Miami to teach graphic design to senior citizens.

But once we had moved in, I realized that the house was too big, and had too many hallways, doors, and walls. My voice echoed in the quiet on one day, and on the next, it didn't carry at all. The stale stink of cigarettes inhabited the guest bedroom, even though neither Yvette nor Carl had smoked. Long shadows in the living room threatened to swallow me if I wandered too close. And the grumble of the foundation steadying itself on the hill sounded too deep—as though construction had originated in hell.

A month after moving in, I walked back from the village coffee shop at the base of the canyon and stood before my new home. Why did my skin crawl? The house hadn't done anything to me except . . . *exist*. And it didn't resemble a jack-o'-lantern or evil incarnate like Shirley Jackson's Hill House. The two-story Mediterranean sat on a hillside in Beachwood Canyon, its facade partially covered by pink bougainvillea. It boasted a flagstone walkway that meandered between bushes of fragrant wild rosemary. Harmless. Even . . . *pleasant*.

"Newsflash: Houses make sounds and sometimes, they even smell weird," Truman (a son of the suburbs) had said. "You're used to living in apartments."

He was right about that. After my parents' deaths, I had moved into Aunt Beryl's three-bedroom apartment condo in Culver City. Her house was never quiet. She owned ten cats: Moonlight, Phinneas, LaLuz, Cooper, Sheldon, Olive, Peanut, Benito, Rambo, and Orson Welles. Constant movement, constant mewing, the ever-present glow of amber-colored cat eyes in the dark.

Then, Truman and I married, and had lived in apartments where our neighbors blasted Wu-Tang Clan at one thirty in the morning; where the aromas of bok choy and garlic spirited through the corridors; where carpeted floors held the footprints of people we would never meet.

But in the canyons of the Hollywood Hills, the howls of coyotes and the wind rustling through chaparral drowned out a woman's screams. The earth overpowered all man-made scents with its rotting sweetness, and I held my breath every time I stepped outside. Smelled like someone had dumped a hooker out there in the coarse grass. That stink just didn't seem normal. Also not normal: opalescent mist creeping across the canyon's face from sunrise to sunset.

The thick aroma of evergreen sap drying on the asphalt, and in the soles of your shoes. Sharp wild sage scorched by past brush fires. Wildflowers that smelled like cinnamon, cheese, and peppermint combined—nothing like their domesticated cousins in shops and stands, flowers that smelled like . . . *flowers*. The canyon's version of nature seemed heavy, aggressive . . . primal.

For months, I had left most of the moving boxes packed and stacked in the guest room. I had restricted my living to my bedroom and to the upstairs den. The house didn't want me there, just as Aunt Beryl hadn't wanted my books and pens and childhood all over her (and the cats') condo.

"What do you wanna do?" Truman had asked once. "Move?"

Yes, let's get something smaller, something less isolated, I longed to say. But moving would have been impossible. The bank had given us the last honest home loan in Los Angeles, and we would have had to sell at a tremendous loss. And Truman doesn't lose. Also, I could not scientifically prove to my husband why the house gave me the heebie-jeebies. Not that I needed to produce a vat of phosphorescent ectoplasm, but it would've helped.

With nowhere to go, I swallowed my anxieties about the drafty cupola at the end of the hallway that shrank if I peeked out its window. I ignored my bedroom ceiling that lowered an inch every night as well as the slow-spinning ceiling fan that would, one day, chop me up as I slept. I reasoned away the weird scratching at the window screens, and disregarded the strange flashes of prismatic light in the sky right above the hilltop. I ignored all of this (unsuccessfully) because lint and spontaneous combustion, open metal cans and lockjaw, also freaked me out. I ignored all of this because my earliest childhood memories featured me nightmaring every time I closed my eyes, the boogeyman, Satan, and Dracula hiding beneath my bed, perching on my shoulder, and tapping at my window. For me, having the heebie-jeebies was as natural as having the hiccups.

And I was just a country mouse (in this case, a city mouse) unaccustomed to uninhabited bedrooms and chirping crickets and settling foundations and bubbling hot water tanks and the dark-dark night. And the cold. So cold in the canyon. So cold in the house.

The anxieties of a city girl. That's all.

I think hung in the air, a cartoon arrow pointing at me, the woman God should strike dead. My left eye twitched so much that I closed them both. My heart—a mini-rhinoceros ramming at my chest wall—*boomboomboomed*, and as I struggled to breathe, my eyes filled with tears. One drop, and then another, and then countless drops slipped down my cheeks. "Holy crap." *Why the hell am I crying?*

Dr. Tremaine gasped and sat up in her chair: I was a premature ejaculator, and needed no foreplay to get worked up.

Embarrassed, I diverted my gaze to the walnut-size jade elephant near the psychiatrist's penholder. I swiped at my wet face, catching mucus and melting dignity in the palm of my hand. "May I have some tissue?" My stomach twisted, pissed that I had to *ask*, and also because I didn't see a box of tissue anywhere. Weren't all shrinks required to sit a box of tissue on their desks next to the Rorschach blots, the Rubik's cube, and the dish of peppermints?

"Umm . . ." Dr. Tremaine gaped at her desk as though it had transformed into a rotisserie. "Just . . . Hold on." She darted out of her office, and returned a moment later with a handful of paper towels.

Paper towels.

Not tissue.

I dabbed my face with the paper towels (industrial brand, and so it felt like bark scraping against my face) and pretended to pull myself together. I'd never talk to this woman about my life now. Not ever.

Over those remaining forty-five minutes, I didn't mention my haunted house again. I didn't talk about growing up with ten cats and Dracula at my window. Instead, I told the psychiatrist a fable about my mother Claire and my father Clifford. Before their deaths, Mom had practiced law, and Dad had delivered babies. Mom had favored rayon pantsuits. Dad had enjoyed chocolate pudding pops. They had competed in ballroom dance competitions to keep their love alive. While they were out fox-trotting, I stayed with the Evans family, our warmhearted next-door neighbors.

Four minutes to three o'clock, Dr. Tremaine plucked a prescription pad from her desk drawer. "I'm glad to have context for our appointment next week. Did Dr. Clark give you some kind of activity to do between your chats?"

Chats?

I said, "I kept a journal." And I had stopped writing in it after entry four. "She never read it. It was just to, you know . . . Get all my feelings out, I guess."

Dr. Tremaine said, "Paxil and Valium, right?" She offered me two prescription slips and said, "I write in a journal, too. It's a safe place to admit my fears, to open up and be honest with myself. I can write about things I could never say to anyone else. Not even my closest friends."

I nodded, and slipped the prescriptions into my purse. *Whatever, lady.*

Dr. Tremaine stood from her desk. "So, same time next Wednesday?"

I smiled, and said, "Of course."

CHAPTER 2

I am not a science writer by training—I earned my degree in English and American literature. After college, though, poems and novels could no longer answer my questions about life and love. Back then, I had applied for the assistant writer position at CelluTech, fifty miles north of Los Angeles because science never lied and never wavered. A molecule did this, and genes (even defective ones) did that. Sure: Science often reinvented itself. For instance, quantum physics contradicts traditional physics, and some researchers believe that cancer stem cells exist while other researchers believe that there are no such things. But even in this chaos, science still followed hard-and-fast rules.

I had stayed with CelluTech since then because science always anticipated the discovery of a better life and a better cure. And psychically, I needed to belong to any effort that offered that much hope to the world.

As I left Dr. Tremaine's office, though, I didn't drive back to work, and I didn't care about stem cells or quantum physics or belonging.

I had purchased tickets (third row, center) for Truman and me to see *Wicked* at the Pantages. I had made reservations at Providence for dinner afterward, and over lobster risotto for me and a rib eye for him, we would *talk* to one another instead of throw words in the air in hopes that the other person captured them in their intended order and spirit. Because sentences like, "Will you pull in the trash cans after the trash man empties them?" were becoming interpreted as, "You don't pull in the trash cans after the trash man empties them."

In honor of tonight's "date night" (Truman and I hadn't been out together in months), my husband sent me a bouquet of white Casablanca lilies. The tiny card nestled in the fragrant bundle read, *Can't wait to get wicked with you after* Wicked. *I love you, babe! Tru.* "I love you, too," I said with a smile, then placed the vase on the dining room table.

In the soft golden candlelight of a restaurant, Truman would remember falling in love with me thirteen years ago. He would realize that he was damn lucky to still be married to me, even though we no longer went out dancing or gave each other backrubs; or ate barbecued ribs like we used to every Monday night, even though the showers we used to take together had become solo endeavors. He used to tuck me in bed. We used to make love before he left the room. I used to fall asleep afterward, not waking until the morning.

If anything was haunting our house, it was the Ghost of Used To.

We couldn't blame ear infections, or PTA meetings, or soccer practices for our inability to communicate. We didn't have children. We didn't own a dog. Our recent bouts of bickering resulted from our failures to talk and listen to each other, husband to wife.

Now, instead of taking walks to the reservoir, cooking tacos together, or battling each other in rounds of *Guitar Hero*, I retreated alone to the upstairs den to watch *The Simpsons*. I'd sit there, pissed and uncomfortable about being pissed, waiting to hear the security panel ping and Truman shout, "Hey, babe! It's me." On many nights, *The Simpsons* melted into *Jeopardy!* Since his promotion to executive vice president, *Jeopardy!* melted into *Lost* or *C.S.I.* and then, the ten o'clock rerun of *Seinfeld*.

And it wasn't as though I had nothing else to do in my life other than wait for him to come home. I had been active in my sorority. I had attended author readings at bookstores. I had worked late at my office on many nights. But I didn't want to relax with my sorors. I didn't aim to share a life with bestselling novelists and their fans. I had married for a reason.

Truman and I had argued about his insane schedule, and he had apologized, and he would come home at a reasonable hour to eat tacos and watch *American Idol*; or see a movie at The Grove; or hike up to the reservoir.

Until the next week.

But on this night, he had promised—*promised*—to show up.

I slipped a Jill Scott CD into the player, and sang as I showered, dressed, and primped. I ignored the pipe's strange rumblings as I pulled on a crimson silk dress that clung to my hips, caressed my thighs and boosted my cleavage. I looked hot. Smoking hot.

I sat at the dining room table, still and stiff to avoid shiny face, flat hair, and sweaty underarms. I wanted to pop a Paxil, but I couldn't. Not anymore. The positive Clearblue Easy pregnancy tests had nixed my pill popping. So, I stared at the vase of lilies in the table's center, fantasized about standing in the lobby of the Pantages with Truman on my arm, and afterward, eating lobster risotto and chocolate ganache cake.

I glanced at the clock in the telephone's display: 7:33. The theater's curtain rose at eight o'clock.

Where is he?

He hadn't called, hadn't emailed, hadn't text messaged.

I dialed his cell phone number.

No answer.

I stomped to the living room and jabbed the stereo's power button—Jill, then no Jill. I dialed his number again.

No answer.

I retreated to the kitchen and peered out the window to the driveway.

Just my Volvo.

Where was he? What was he doing? *Are those his headlights zooming around the bend?*

At 7:40, I stopped keeping watch at the window, and started pacing. *Did he get in an accident? Did he get pulled over by the police?*

The telephone chirped and caller ID droned *Baxter, Truman, Baxter, Truman.* I grabbed the receiver, and shouted, "Where are you?"

"I'm still at the pool," Truman said. "Trying to get in some extra dive time. I didn't realize how late it was."

I rubbed my temples—anger headache. "The show starts at eight."

"I know, babe. I should've called earlier—"

"Yes, you should've." I lurched to the living room. A tear rolled down my cheek, and my fingers picked at my lips, drying beneath coats of lipstick.

"I didn't realize how late it was. When I got off work, we rushed down to the pool—"

"*We?*"

"Penelope and me," he said.

Penelope Villagrana worked with Truman at FOX Sports Network. She partnered with him on climbs, dives, and jumps. She was also single, had the body of an Amazon, and was rumored to be as adventurous in the bedroom as she was on the mountaintop.

"We got here late," Truman was saying. "And Flex was pissed. You know how he is. He doesn't care about anything else, and he doesn't want his students to care about anything else, either. When you dive, you're supposed to focus on being under.

"Plus, my allergies were bothering me, and my eyes were a little scratchy, and I couldn't take a Sudafed, and so my mind was just . . . This was the first time I glanced at a clock. You won't believe—"

"Are you coming or not?"

Truman paused, then said, "I can't, Nic. I'm sorry. I just . . . I don't want anything to go wrong when I'm a hundred feet under next week. And I know you don't want that, either, right?"

I didn't speak, angry that he had exploited my fears to justify his selfishness.

"I'll make it up to you," he said. "I promise."

"I'll add it to the list," I said, hoping that he sensed my dissatisfaction.

He laughed, not sensing anything. "I'll call when I'm on my way home. Love you."

A dial tone told me that he had hung up.

I threw the telephone at the fireplace, but it didn't shatter into billions of tiny pieces like I had wanted. Instead, the phone hit the brick with a thud, and landed on the floor with a crack. Anger unquenched, I buzzed around the room. My heart pounded so hard, I thought it would explode. My ears rang, and then, I couldn't hear my heart anymore. It worked, though—knife blades were stabbing at it like freshly sharpened Henckels in a rump roast. I grabbed my left arm and sipped air. Couldn't breathe . . . Pain in my chest . . . I was suffocating and having a heart attack at the same time.

I squeezed my eyes shut, and took deep breaths. *One . . . Two . . . Three . . .*

Penelope Villagrana.

I kicked the coffee table, and yelped. Tears burned in my eyes as fire blazed from my toes up my calf.

The house laughed—I swear it laughed. Not the low groans of a settling foundation, but high-pitched pings. *Hee. Hee. Hee.*

If I didn't leave, I would hurt myself again and destroy items more precious than magazines and telephones. Like the porcelain bowl from Paris. Or the delicate crystal picture frames from Tiffany. Or the black clay vase from Mazatlán. Exquisite, throwable things.

I limped to the breakfast bar and grabbed for my keys beneath the fruit bowl. Grabbed my purse from the pantry and stomped to the car.

Dark sky and distant stars hid behind thin, wispy clouds. Misty rain had thickened the musty smell of burned chaparral, and in seconds, my hair lost all curl and lay flat against my head. My eyelashes clumped, the mascara liquefying into a thick, gooey paste. *Melting. I'm melting. What a world, what a world.*

I climbed into the car, and at the base of the hill, I grabbed my cell phone and called Leilani. "What are you doing right now?"

Leilani chuckled. "You mean, *who* am I doing right now."

In the background, a man laughed.

Leilani and I had shared a dorm room during our freshman year at UC Santa Cruz. Her working-class Pentecostal family lived in Cerritos, California. Her father, Douglas Baxter, worked in construction on the week days and as a head deacon on Sundays, and her mother Cassandra made casseroles and frittatas between prayer meetings, choir practices, and world mission ministries. Leilani's big brother, Truman, had forsaken the church and Cerritos to earn a math degree at MIT.

I frowned. "Okay. TMI I'll call you later."

"It's cool," she said. "I'm done. He's leaving. What's up?"

"I need to talk or . . . or . . ."

She sighed. "What did Truman do this time?"

I bit my lip, not wanting to cry. "One guess."

"Did you eat?"

"No."

"And I sure as hell didn't cook," she said. "Let's meet at Dan Tana's. I'll call Mo."

Truman was climbing out of his car as I pulled back into the driveway. We didn't speak as we entered the kitchen. We didn't touch. Didn't kiss. Just strangers sharing the mortgage payment.

The house was quiet and cold. The living room smelled of my perfume and the lilies sitting on the dining room table.

I retreated upstairs to the bedroom as Truman checked the locks and armed the security panel. I kicked off my heels, pulled off my dress, then grabbed shorts and a tank top from the drawer. In the bathroom, I scrubbed my face free of makeup, then wrapped my hair in a scarf—a nonverbal cue that I had no interest in "making up."

Truman sat at the foot of the bed, staring at the hardwood floor. He looked pale sitting there, gazing at his blue Vans.

I hesitated in the bathroom doorway. "You okay?"

He didn't answer at first, and continued to stare at the floor. "Tired," he finally mumbled. "Been a long day." He glanced at me, his brown eyes dark and troubled. Then, he stood, an abrupt and noisy motion in the quiet. "I have some work to do. You shouldn't wait up."

Alone again, I stood at the window and pushed aside the crimson curtains. I rested my forehead against the cold pane. Darkness and fog kept me from seeing much, and I glimpsed the meaty, red petals of my peonies on the edges of our stamp-size backyard. Somewhere in the neighborhood, a German shepherd howled, ruining the quiet. I hated that dog, but his barks kept my mind from sifting through the tatters of the day.

"Hey."

I glanced over my shoulder.

Truman stood in the doorway.

I crossed my arms. "Yes?"

"Where were you? Before you drove back home, I mean."

I smirked, then said, "Out."

His shoulders hunched at his ears and his nostrils flared. "Who were you out *with*?"

"Why does it matter? I wasn't out with *you* like I was supposed to be."

Truman glared at me, and said nothing.

"You haven't even apologized for flaking on me . . . *again*," I said. "Who the hell do you think you are, standing there, looking at me like that, being pissed?" I turned to glare out the window. "*I'm* the one who gets to be angry. Not you."

"But I called—"

"Twenty minutes before the show started!"

Outside, the German shepherd's barks turned shrill—at war with a raccoon.

"Who were you with?" he asked again.

I snorted, then placed my hands on my hips. "I had dinner with your sister and Mo. Is that okay with you? Wanna call them to confirm?"

Truman shook his head. "I apologize for my reaction. And I'm sorry for not showing up tonight, okay?"

Still angry, I muttered, "Yeah."

"Great. See you in the morning." Then, he retreated back down the hallway.

On the next morning, sunbeams pushed through the usual June gloom, and my bedroom blazed bright with light. I glanced at the clock on the nightstand—a little past eight o'clock. I should've been zooming off my freeway exit by now, but sandbags weighed down my arms and legs, and I struggled to leave the bed. Couldn't tell whether Truman had slept beside me or not—the sheets were twisted around my hips, and the comforter had been kicked to the floor.

Morning sunshine filled the kitchen. Weird: In June, Los Angeles never saw the sun until late afternoons.

Truman had cooked himself breakfast, the stink of eggs and burned butter the only clues of his presence.

As I reached to open the refrigerator, I noticed that he had used words from my magnetic poetry journal to leave a message on the door.

Diamond goddess soars
Frantic turtle dreams
I worship magic
You twirl in purple
Use my sausage

Silliness as a peace offering.

CHAPTER 3

On my way home from work, I stopped at the village market for a bag of barbecue potato chips, five Slim Jims, and a six-pack of Diet Cherry Coke. And a pregnancy test. I scooted toward the checkout counter, resisting the urge to take the test in the market's bathroom.

"Hey, Nic."

I glanced over my shoulder.

My neighbor Jake Huston towered over me.

"Hey." I threw a *National Enquirer* over the pregnancy test, and smiled. "You're home early."

Jake's whiskey-brown eyes flicked to my shopping cart. "Have time to go next door for coffee?"

I shook my head and inched closer to the checkout counter. "Can't. We're supposed to be going to dinner tonight." A lie.

Jake grinned, and the corners of his eyes crinkled. "Who? You and Truman? Really?"

My cheeks burned. "Don't sound so surprised. We're going to a new place down by the studio."

"And he'll show up tonight?"

"Be nice, Jacob."

"You and I have had more meals together than you and your husband."

"Lucky, lucky you," I said. "Unless you're complaining now."

He held my gaze, and said nothing.

"I should go," I said as I tried to ignore that flutter in my heart. "Have to gussy up."

He bowed and stepped aside. "Please. Gussy away. Call you tomorrow?"

"Yep." I placed my basket on the conveyor belt, but didn't empty it until he had wandered toward DAIRY.

A pudgy clerk with spiky gelled hair and skin as pale as rice paper rang up my items. "Arnib" lifted an eyebrow and smirked as he scanned the pregnancy test. *Another Black girl in trouble after having wild, drunken sex with a rapper.* Sex with Truman after he'd returned from his Nepal-Everest trip weeks ago had been wild and sometimes drunken, but he was far from a rapper. He folded his socks, brushed and flossed his teeth with disturbing zeal, and had never fired a gun. I didn't tell Arnib this. Maybe he disapproved of my other purchases. Five Slim Jims combined with that much Coca-Cola couldn't be good for anyone.

Truman's crazy work schedule meant that he had started to flake on me. But this meant more than me going to the mall alone. It meant that he also kept postponing our plans to have a baby. Let's wait until my schedule normalizes, he'd say. Problem was he didn't budge from this even as his schedule refused to cooperate.

After five months of late-night gropings and early-morning quickies, and close to $600 spent on pregnancy tests, ovulation prediction kits, incense, and lingerie, I couldn't get pregnant. Not that five months of trying and nothing happening was a great span of time. Not that Truman knew I was trying in the first place.

I thought it was best this way—getting pregnant on the sly—and yeah, it was a selfish thing to do, but I knew that he'd be thrilled once the idea of having a baby became a reality. He'd get to be the father Douglas Baxter had failed to be for him: open-minded and kind, a lover of adventure, mud, and snow. For this initiative, I had to act as summit leader since I'd literally be bearing the burden of a baby at *thirty-seven-freakin' years old.*

On month five, day twenty-three of my conception adventure, Monica said, "You're insane."

"I'm not insane," I said. "I'm as barren as the Arctic."

Monica shot me a frustrated glance, then rolled her eyes. "You must not be doing it right, then."

"What do you know?"

"My momma had five kids. And she didn't consult no calendar, or scrutinize her cervical mucus, or none of that yuppie nonsense. Idiots have babies every day."

Monica had also attended UC Santa Cruz, and had lived in the dorm room next to Leilani and me. Back then, Monica, who grew up in Watts, wore long, golden weaves and giant door knocker earrings. She wore matching tennis shoes and tracksuits, and drove her boyfriend's purple Z28 until the repo man came for it during spring semester. She's been my best friend since.

"Something's wrong," I said. "Either I have bad eggs, or Truman has lazy sperm. I bet it's because of all his extreme sporting. He probably sprained his testes or something. Maybe if he went to see the doctor, and squooshed a little puddle of himself in a cup——"

"But then you'd have to confess that you've been trying to get pregnant on the down-low," Monica said. "You're freaking out, Nic. You read too much, that's your problem. You always think that something's wrong with you."

I dipped my toes in the pools of Hypochondria more than the average American. But I also grew up in a health store with an aunt who constantly shoved vitamins and minerals down my throat. There, I learned that you could always fix yourself by popping something. Psyllium for better bowel movements. Cod liver oil pills for shinier hair. Cinnamon bark tablets to freshen breath. At one point, I could swallow five horse-size pills at once, *without water.*

As an adult living in the age of the internet, I have self-diagnosed scabies, Legionnaires' disease, and a hernia. Went to the doctor each time in search of a pill to cure me; but there were no pills for the heat rash, wicked virus, and pinched nerve—maladies that I actually had.

I had been getting better about distinguishing true health problems from imagined ones, and had banned myself from surfing the pages of WebMD. Before my pregnancy attempts, two months had passed since my last search. And then my ovaries broke . . .

The baby dance reminded me of seventh-grade PE, with the cool kids choosing teams for dodgeball. I never got to be captain. Hell, I never got to throw. As bait, I stood in the middle of the court with knobby, ashy knees, wearing too-small gym shorts, ducking a rubber ball rocketing through the air at fifty-five miles per hour. Most times, the ball would hit me in my face, occasionally breaking my glasses. The other kids would laugh at me, and I would retreat to the bench in tears.

My ovaries represented the seventh-grade me I had longed to be. Except that sperm had replaced rubber balls. My stupid eggs dodged *those* throws. They needed to get hit to win.

"It's not like I'm twenty-five anymore," I had explained to Truman. "All eggs have expiration dates. Keep something for ten years, it comes back in style. Keep it for twenty, it's a classic. Keep it for twenty-nine? Antique."

"Honestly?" he said. "I'd be okay if it was just you and me for the rest of our lives. But kids would be great. I just want us to do everything we've dreamed of before they come."

By "us" he meant "him." By "we" he meant "him." And then he drove to Beverly Hills BMW and traded his Audi sedan for a Z3. Babies couldn't ride in two-seat sports cars. They rode in Volvos, Subarus, and Fords. Didn't matter. Who needed a kid when you had a BMW and a great career with a crazy salary?

Still, I respected his decision to wait because I enjoyed our last-minute trips to Santa Barbara and Las Vegas. We'd talk, laugh, and hold hands all the way. I'd gaze at him, and think, *I could do this forever. Drive around the country with the car's top down, listening to Earth, Wind & Fire, eating meals cooked in a kitchen by a chef and not by a teenager with a deep fryer and ketchup packets.* And I liked my quiet, clean apartment, and I enjoyed buying designer handbags and twenty-dollar rib eye steaks instead of diapers and Juicy Juice.

Because the alternative sucked. My friends and coworkers with children were miserable people. Madison always had an ear infection or diarrhea. Connor's teeth were always coming in or falling out. They couldn't see a movie. They couldn't go out for dinner. They were too tired. Too poor. Too everything.

Truman and I—we had each other . . . Until he found other people to hang out with.

The more he climbed, jumped, and explored, the stronger my desire to buy teddy bears and paint the guest room pink and yellow. I envied my neighbors as they walked with their kids up to the reservoir. Would they go out for spaghetti and meatballs later? Or would they drive to Target for toilet cleaner and paper towels, leaving the store sharing an ICEE and a bag of popcorn? My gaze lingered after them, and I coveted the intimacy I had experienced with my parents for only three short years, the intimacy I longed to share with Truman.

So, one morning, I "forgot" to take the Pill.

I "forgot" that next morning, too. And the next.

When Truman returned to the States from Nepal, we pounded each other as though two years had passed. I had lacked an agenda during those moments in bed (and in the shower and on the patio). I just wanted to be with the man I loved more than anyone in the world. I wanted to hear his laugh again. Listen to him breathe. Lay beside him, tucked beneath his arm.

And then it happened.

. . . Or didn't happen.

No period.

◆　◆　◆

At home, I dashed up the stairs to the master bathroom. I pried open the box, and read the pregnancy test's instructions:

1. Aim stick under urine flow.
2. Hold stick in steady stream for three seconds.
3. Place stick on flat surface for two minutes.

Two minutes later . . . A blue plus sign!

I drank another Diet Cherry Coke and four glasses of water. Sat at the kitchen counter, gnawed on Slim Jims, and pretended to watch *Judge Judy* on the television bolted above the sink.

How about Jack for a boy and Zoë for a girl? Or maybe Zora?

What's CelluTech's Family Leave policy?

Should Mo be the godmother, or Leilani?

My bladder filled again, and I raced to the bathroom to pee on the bonus stick.

Another blue plus sign. Light-light blue this time, but still blue.

Smiling, I slipped both positive pregnancy tests back into the box and stashed the box in the back of my lingerie drawer.

Lei should be the godmother.

And Zoë. Definitely Zoë.

CHAPTER 4

I placed my plastic cup of urine in the patient bathroom's two-way cubby. Then, I followed Nurse Charmaine to Room 9. I undressed, pulled on the paper gown, and perched at the edge of the examination table. A moment later, Dr. Corrine Silas breezed into the room with a bright smile. After updating my chart, she asked me to recline on the table.

The moment of truth had arrived. I'd get a glimpse of Zoë or Jack for the first time!

She clicked off the room's lights, then squirted ultrasound gel onto my bare belly.

I giggled, and said, "That stuff is cold."

Dr. Silas smiled, then moved the wand around my abdomen. She grunted and squinted at the monitor, but said nothing. And she said nothing for two minutes. Finally, she swiped tissue across my belly. With thirty-six years of experience as an obstetrician-gynecologist, Dr. Silas knew a pregnant womb when she saw one.

And my womb wasn't.

"I'm sorry, sweetheart," she said. "You're not pregnant."

I slowly sat up and opened my mouth to speak. But my mind offered nothing.

She offered a small, apologetic smile. "I wish I had better news."

"Are you sure?" My voice sounded small. Whoville small.

"The urine sample you gave came back with very low HCG levels. Almost nonexistent. But I wanted an ultrasound to confirm that."

I shook my head, unable to process her diagnosis. "But the pregnancy tests I took on Tuesday were positive. And my breasts are sore, and I'm more tired than usual, and . . ." My mind raced, grabbing other symptoms off the shelf before they vanished into the past.

Dr. Silas took my hand, and said, "It's unfortunate, but half of all pregnancies end in miscarriage."

"Miscarriage?"

She nodded. "Most times, women don't even know that they're pregnant. Since you've been trying, you're hyperaware of your body's changes. I think you may have had a chemical pregnancy. Which is, basically, an early miscarriage."

With tears in my eyes, I nodded, and said, "Okay."

"You may have a little cramping, but nothing serious," she said. "I didn't see any cysts or tumors during the ultrasound. It just . . . happened. But that shouldn't keep you from trying again."

After more talk about exercise and nutrition, she squeezed my arm, and said, "Come back in November for your annual. Or maybe I'll see you earlier. When you're pregnant." She closed my file, and sighed. "I'm sorry, Nicole. It wasn't the right time."

I thanked her, pulled on my clothes, and trudged to the parking lot. I sat in the car—*a chemical pregnancy*—and tried to think positive. *You have time, Nic. There was probably a defect or . . .* I lay my head against the steering wheel as sobs broke from my chest. Each time I gained control, another wave of sorrow crashed over me.

All cried out, I started the car and pulled back into the world with the resolve to eat better. To exercise more. To pop prenatal vitamins and tell Truman straight-out that it was time to have a baby. Busy schedules could kiss my ass . . . He wouldn't mind that last part.

The driveway was empty. Truman wasn't home.

Of course he wasn't home.

He had left a voicemail message. *Hey, babe. I'm gonna be late tonight. Conference call with China in an hour. I'll check in later.*

After popping two Tylenol to combat a tension headache spreading between my shoulders, I wandered to the foyer to sort through the day's mail. I spotted Jake ambling down the hill and opened the door. "Hey," I shouted. "Heading down for coffee?"

He nodded. "You comin'?"

"Only if you're buying." I grabbed my keys, and ran out to meet him.

On the first day of our move to Rockcliff Drive, Truman and the movers had disappeared into the house to place the couch in the living room. I had stood out front, guarding my immense library and my Le Creuset stoneware collection from thieves who sought a first edition *Treasure Island* and a blue French oven. Footfalls had pounded against the asphalt, and I turned to see a jogger nearing my house. He was tall and broad, tanned and dark haired. Spanish or Italian roots, I couldn't tell, but wow, he was beautiful.

On most days, my skin would be flawless and radiant. On most days, my shoulder-length hair would be combed, and my big, brown eyes would sparkle. Alas, this was moving day. A pimple had commandeered my oily chin. My hair hid beneath a dusty FSN baseball cap, and my eyes were bloodshot from packing until three that morning.

The jogger smiled, and stopped a few feet away from me. "Welcome to the neighborhood."

"Thanks." I grinned—at least my teeth were clean—and held out my hand. "Nicole Baxter."

He shook my hand and squeezed it. "Jake Huston." He nodded toward the modern white tri-level farther up the hill. "I'm right there if you need anything."

"Nic—" Truman returned to the porch and threw a surprised glance at Jake. "Oh. You're not alone." The two men shook hands and exchanged names.

Jake pointed to his house. "I'm right there. I just met . . ." He peered at me, then said, "Sorry. I don't remember . . ."

"Nicole," I said, disappointed that I hadn't made much of an impression.

Truman turned toward our neighbor's house. "She's a beauty."

But Jake kept his eyes on me. "Gotta agree with you on that."

I swayed as I held his gaze.

Then, the three of us chatted about the housing market, about rising crime, abandoned cars, and the dying economy. Jake was a partner at Tighe & Johns, criminal defense attorneys famous for defending shoplifting actresses and rich husbands with disappeared wives. Divorced, he had no children and lived alone in his big, white house.

The movers caught our attention, and Truman said, "Oh, yeah. Why I came out here." He turned to me. "The guys wanna know where you want the bed frame."

I nodded, then smiled at Jake. "Nice meeting you."

Jake smiled, then he and Truman continued their conversation about septic tanks.

After that, I had bumped into Jake at least twice a week. We passed each other driving up and down the hill. We saw each other at the village market and talked about movies in the bread aisle. We sat together at the coffee shop to drink our lattes and talk politics.

The sun would drop behind the hills, and the coffee crowd would thin. Jake and I would toss our empty cups into the trash can and make our way back home. Sometimes as we walked, we wouldn't talk, and the backs of our hands would brush.

He'd escort me to my front door.

I'd grin at him like a goofy teenager and thank him for his company and the coffee.

He'd nod, then retreat across the flagstone pathway, and start up the hill.

Weak-kneed and lightheaded, I'd wobble into the house.

Bad girl. Bad Nicole.

Why? I hadn't *done* anything. Racing pulse and tingling skin? Felt that way before, after a bout of food poisoning. And if Truman caught Jake and me together—not "caught" since I'd done nothing wrong—I would offer my husband an explanation. *Jake walked with me because a few homes were burglarized* (true) *and last week, a woman down the hill was raped in her garage* (also true), *and since you don't come home until late now and I'm alone, I'm a little jumpy* (very true).

And Jake and I were friends. Just friends.

As the house slipped into shadow, I filled the bathtub with hot water and eucalyptus oil. I slipped beneath the water, closed my eyes and slowly exhaled . . .

My eyes snapped open.

The bath water had chilled, and my fingers had shriveled into brown and pink sticks.

"Hey, babe! It's me!" Truman.

After drying off and slipping on a camisole, I peeked through Truman's office door. He sat at his desk with a Red Vine between his teeth as he played *World of Warcraft* on the computer. I turned away, deciding not to disturb him.

He called out, "Nic?"

"You're adventuring. I'll leave you alone."

"Come back," he said, eyes on the screen. "It's just a stupid quest to find some stupid key. What's going on?"

"Not much." I stood behind him, and wrapped my arms around his neck. "I went to the doctor today. Haven't been feeling well lately."

He nodded. "A virus is going around the office. We both need rest."

"Yeah," I said, knowing that my malady hadn't been a virus.

"Let's go away next weekend. Drive up to Santa Barbara and stay at the Four Seasons."

I smiled. "Can I get one of those massages where they slather you in lotion and wrap hot towels around your body?"

"My treat." Truman swiveled in his chair. "And I promise—*promise*—not to flake on you." His gaze swept over me, lingering at my breasts hidden beneath the pink silk camisole. He pulled me closer to him, and his hands ran up my thighs to my hips. Even through the lingerie, his touch warmed my skin.

I kissed him, and whispered, "I'm glad you're home."

"I'm glad I'm home, too. I miss you." He pulled my right leg up and wrapped it around his waist. I lifted my left leg, and slipped it beneath the arm of the chair.

We sat face to face, and kissed again.

"You taste like licorice," I said as I unbuttoned the strained fly of his Levi's.

"And you taste like . . ." His lips brushed across my neck and across my shoulders. He swiveled the chair again and lifted me onto the desk.

My skin tingled as that silky camisole slipped off my shoulders and past my hips . . .

Before climbing in bed, I grabbed the laptop and settled on the chaise lounge near the bedroom window. The Four Seasons had suites available June 29 through July 1. I typed in my credit card number, then clicked, "Confirm." I closed the computer, then slipped into bed. Fell asleep as I imagined splashing in the turquoise waters of the Pacific with Truman beside me.

CHAPTER 5

I rolled over in bed and glanced at the clock—almost ten thirty. Crap. Didn't plan to sleep late—I had a hundred tasks to complete before Truman's fortieth birthday party that night. But my body didn't care about tasks or parties. It needed rest as it recovered from its "chemical pregnancy."

Truman had already left the bedroom.

Probably fixing the broken latch on the back gate, I thought. Or unpacking one of the fifty boxes we had consigned to the guest room.

I sat up in bed, and called, "Truman?"

No answer.

I slipped over to the window and looked down to the yard. Didn't see Truman. I cocked my head and listened for music playing from the downstairs den, or animated gunshots from a video game. Silence.

Hunh.

The empty kitchen smelled of warm sugar. A plate filled with fresh-baked cinnamon rolls sat on the breakfast bar. Truman had also left a fresh-cut peony in a crystal bud vase. I smiled *(he's so sweet)* and read the Post-it note he had left near the plate.

Know U got a lot 2 do. Went 2 the pool w/Penny 2 get in some dive time. Enjoy the sweets, Sweets.

I crumpled the note and threw it across the room.

Freakin' Penelope.

I leaned against the counter, and gobbled three cinnamon rolls . . . Because gaining weight always keeps a man at home.

Nauseous, I tossed the last two rolls into the trash can, then pulled the French oven from the pantry. Truman had requested a French meal, but I didn't like duck, and he hated fish, and chicken had been fried, baked, and roasted to death. A few days ago, though, I saw a picture of The Birthday Meal on epicurious.com: chunks of beef chuck pot roast covered with caramelized onions, steamed parsley potatoes on the side.

A perfect meal for a perfect night.

When we were first married, Truman awakened out of sleep with a smile, often begging me to climb back into bed with him. Since our eleventh anniversary, though, he muttered and whimpered as he slept, scowled as he opened his eyes.

"What's bothering you?" I had asked once.

He had stared at me before saying, "What are you talking about?"

"You were thrashing around and moaning."

"I don't know what you're talking about."

I had tried to chuckle. "I'm not blaming you for anything. I just . . . Never mind."

I never mentioned his nightmares again.

Truman was muttering now, just an hour before the start of our perfect night, and he lurched out of sleep with that scowl in place.

I sat at my vanity, dressed in a silk robe, contemplating my malfunctioning womb and whirling the blush brush across my cheeks.

"It's past six," he grumbled. "Were you gonna wake me up?"

I didn't answer him—didn't like his tone—and shifted my eyes to the vanity's surface. Nail polishes there, powders and pill vials here, remote controls to the television and ceiling fan lined up like matchsticks. Organized, just like my life.

"Hello?" Truman said. "You there?"

Who was he talking to like that? Snippy. Expectant. Like my name was Jeeves. "Wake up, Truman," I said. "People will be here soon."

He climbed out of bed, kicking the scarlet comforter to the floor. "I've been knocked out since 4:30. Did I somehow manage to piss you off in my sleep?"

I grabbed the vial of Paxil, and popped off the top. No prohibitions now.

"It's a party," he said. "You don't have to dope up."

"When you were away on your Big Adventure, I doped up a lot." *To deal with the stress. And that's why I was pregnant on one day, and not pregnant on the next. My body can't function cuz of my stress levels and your sperm that's messed up from climbing icy mountains and breathing air that doesn't have oxygen.*

"Technically," I said, "I'm not doping up. I'm supposed to take one a day, and I forgot this morning cuz I was getting the house ready for tonight." I cocked an eyebrow. "I've had this same prescription for over a year. You haven't noticed until now?"

"Let's not argue today," he said as he stretched. "Let's talk about something else."

"Like how you should've told me you were planning to be at the pool with Penelope all day?" I swiveled on my stool to face him. "We didn't talk about that, you know, since you've been asleep for two hours. And honestly? I wasn't even sure you'd show up tonight. I thought you'd flake out on me again."

Truman cocked an eyebrow, then offered a lazy grin. "I'm selfish and inconsiderate. I got the better deal when you said, 'I do' and I'm sorry about that, all right? But the dive is next week, and . . . I had a little accident at the pool this morning. Something with the tank—"

I slapped my knee, and shouted, "I *knew* something was . . . You shouldn't have been out there—"

"But it's fine now. Flex fixed everything. And he showed me what I'd done wrong, and it was a stupid mistake. Won't happen again."

I narrowed my eyes. "What kind of stupid mistake? You forget a step? You read the gauge wrong? What happened?"

"Nothing big. Don't freak out, okay?"

"That's like telling a bear not to . . ."

He crossed the room, and stood behind me now, bare chested, wearing blue-striped boxers.

I blushed, and forgot words at the sight of my nearly naked husband. I loved his smile. His cognac-colored eyes. He had lost weight and had gained muscle because of his adventuring. I did benefit from *that*. "You have to be careful," I said, coming out of that spell. "You're stuck in this marriage for another fifty years, and I don't want you shortchanging me. And stop flaking on me. It hurts my feelings."

"You forgive me?"

"Don't I always?"

"You promise to have fun tonight?"

I let my robe slip off to show off black lace lingerie. His favorites. Then, we fell into bed together to get the party started.

Even though I had planned dinner for *close* friends, Penelope Villagrana had arrived early with a bouquet of sunflowers for the birthday boy, with her boobs and ass spilling out of a fake Hervé Léger bandage dress. Muscle-bound and bulky, she resembled Rambo in drag. I had curves and softness, and Truman liked curves and softness. He told me that just an hour before.

During dinner, Penelope complimented my cooking. "I'm all thumbs in the kitchen," she confessed. "I can't even make tuna salad. Not that I have time to cook."

As I passed around dessert plates for the apple tarts I had baked, Penelope cooed about the color of my dress. "I can never find shades that flatter me," she said. "And I'd never choose anything as bold as that pink. Not that I'm into clothes."

As we enjoyed a final cup of coffee before the other guests arrived, Penelope suggested that I join her and Truman on their next adventure. "You do swim, don't you? Oh, you can't? You really should learn."

Taught to be polite even in the most difficult situations, I offered benign responses to Penelope's flatteries:

I don't cook much, but I can whip something up if I have to.

I never wore this pink until Monica bought me a sweater in this shade.

Swim? No, I never learned. Don't care to try now.

After dinner, as we all wandered out of the dining room, Truman took my hand and whispered, "Thank you for being nice."

"Your friend's just as sweet as cod liver oil, isn't she?" I whispered back.

He smiled. "And you're going above and beyond."

"Only for you."

He pinched my ass. "I know."

Penelope gasped as she entered the den. "Nicole, I just *love* this room. I am totally clueless when it comes to decorating and paint and all of that. I'm missing that gene. And really, I just don't have the time."

The downstairs den *was* pretty swanky. We had painted the walls cranberry, and in an inspired moment, I had purchased saddle brown curtains and chocolate-colored couches and armchairs. Truman had installed a drop-down seventy-inch monitor, and an audio system that cost more than a decent Japanese sedan. So, yeah: nice. But Penelope's reaction, combined with all of her other remarks? Bugged the hell out of me. Was she being passive-aggressive, making me more girly-girly and superficial than I was? A weak woman who didn't swim, but only sought to cook the perfect roast for her husband's birthday dinner, to find colors that favored her, and discover a paint chip and fabric swatch that would make her neighbors envious? Was she casting me as Lucy Ricardo instead of Clair Huxtable?

Exhausted from cooking all day, I poured myself a glass of wine and collapsed on the sofa next to Truman.

Penelope, water glass in hand (*I don't drink alcohol,* she had sniffed), plopped in the space on his right.

"Dinner was good, babe," Truman said, then kissed my forehead. "Everybody ready to see what we didn't show a few weeks ago?"

Monica's husband Gary and Jonathan, who was Leilani's . . . whatever, sat in the room's rear. Leilani and Monica sat near the windows, whispering to each other and casting glances at Penelope and the dress that crept up her bulky thighs.

My husband, clueless, grinned as his bravura shone on screen in HD.

I jiggled my leg and nibbled on my bottom lip as I watched Behind-the-Scenes Truman talk about dying on a faraway mountain named Everest. "You have to trust your partner," he was saying. "There may be a time when that person holds your life in her hands. But Penny's strong. She's done this before. Right, Pen?" The camera panned to Penelope, her skin rosy and her lips chapped from the killing cold.

She had more courage than I could ever buy—she'd reached Everest's top twice now. I freaked if temperatures dropped below fifty.

"You okay?"

Truman was studying me, his eyebrows crumpled in concern.

I nodded. Even though I knew the story's ending—*Truman makes it up the mountain and comes home alive*—seeing it happen in high definition still made me cuckoo.

Video Truman shouted, "I can't believe I'm here. This is *awesome.*"

The camera zoomed out: Truman stood atop a snowy summit. Several miniature flags representing the world below fluttered at his feet. Lesser peaks and a bleached blue sky splayed behind him. Video Truman, his brown face hidden by frost and reflective sunglasses, raised his arms and shouted, "The top of the world. Everest, man. Hell yeah!"

Our friends clapped. I squeezed Truman's hand. *My* husband had climbed Mount Everest. It wasn't everyday for a Black man to climb the tallest mountain in the world. Symbolically, yeah, but literally?

Video Truman said, "Now, Nic can stop worrying," and everyone in the den laughed.

Funny cuz it was true.

"Nothing matters," the smiling man on camera was saying. "The cold, the frostbite, losing brain cells. Hell, knowing that I can die at any moment. This is better than sex."

I glanced at Truman, and playfully cocked an eyebrow. "Oh?"

Truman took my hand and kissed it. "Not really, babe."

His first lie of the night. That was fine. Climbing Everest was something you didn't do spur of the moment. Getting laid, however, could happen while you're picking up a chicken and laundry detergent from the grocery store.

Video Truman shouted, "I did it. We did it, Nic! I couldn't have made it up here without you."

"Aren't you forgetting someone?" a woman asked off-screen.

Video Truman laughed. "Penny-hon, I *really* couldn't have made it up here without you."

Not a lie.

Then, Truman took Penelope's hand, like he had just taken mine, and kissed it.

Monica, Leilani, and I retreated to the patio's perimeter to escape the fifty additional guests invited to Truman's birthday party. People spilled out of the house like batting from a stuffed bear, and music and laughter echoed across the canyon's face. Truman kept company with Elene Givhan, one of the network's finance managers. Elene's long, black hair tumbled in waves past her shoulders, and her mint green eyes sparkled as she talked. She clasped her hands in front of her breasts (barely hidden in *that* dress) as she laughed at the whatever-couldn't-be-that-damn-funny anecdote Truman was sharing.

I preferred Penelope over *this* siren. Penelope with her man-thighs and butchy haircut and . . . Where was she when I needed her?

I had tried to join in Truman and Elene's conversation, but her nasally voice and grating accent made my eyes cross. The woman never left Truman's side. Not to refresh her drink. Not for a smoke. Not to pee. For a moment, I was cool with that—we all like hovering around handsome, powerful men. And like Elene, we all like to giggle, blush, and touch when we're around them. But Elene's giggling and touching of this *married man* continued, and she started plucking pot stickers and shish kebabs from his plate.

Is this bitch hitting on my husband in front of me?

Monica and Leilani didn't say anything about Elene, but each time they glanced in Truman's direction, their eyebrows raised and furrowed. Then, they nodded to each other—*you see that?*—before turning back to me and to the conversation we were pretending to have.

"If I hear him laugh one more time," I said. "If she touches his arm . . ."

He laughed, she touched, and I growled.

"You should see your face," Monica said, trying not to giggle.

"This ain't funny, Mo," Leilani said, hands on her hips. "Nic, you need to go over there. Right now."

"Be chill about it, though," Monica advised.

After taking several deep breaths, I forced a smile to my lips, then sashayed over to my husband and his colleague.

"Hey, Nic," Truman said.

Elene sighed, then ran her fingers through her hair.

"We were talking about the X-Games," he said. "Elene's brother is in the BMX—"

"That's great. Dance with me." I grabbed Truman's hand.

"Nic," he said, "I'm talking."

"Talk later," I said. "I'm sure Elene will be here when you get back. Won't you, Elene?"

Elene smirked at me like the Mean Girl she had been since the fifth grade.

Meanwhile, the eyes of Leilani and Monica burned holes in my back.

"Come on," I said, tugging Truman's arm. "I love this song." I didn't know what song was playing—I could only hear the sound of blood boiling in my head. Really: Neil Diamond could've been singing "Sweet Caroline" and I would've danced to it as though he was MC Hammer.

"Later, okay?" Truman snapped. "And you know I can't dance."

He couldn't catch a beat if it was chained to a cup.

Truman offered an apologetic smile. "Later. I promise."

I stomped back to my friends, and shrugged, "He doesn't want to dance right now. It's his birthday. He doesn't have to if he doesn't want to."

Minutes later, though, Elene had pulled Truman to the dance floor. There, he found his inner Travolta as "Erotic City" blasted from the speakers.

Monica gawked as she watched the couple dance. "Hell. No."

Leilani said, "Nicole Porter Baxter, if you—"

Elene turned to grind her ass against Truman's crotch.

"What the *hell?*" I said, slapping my hand against my thigh.

"Maybe you should ignore them," Monica said, wide-eyed, unable to follow her own advice. "Maybe you're just hormonal. You know, from being pregnant? You're just extra-sensitive, or—"

"Nuh uh, Nicole," Leilani said. "Go over there right now, and tell her to step the hell off. This ain't no strip club up in here. You want me to do it? Cuz I—"

I stomped across the dance floor and pulled Truman to a tiny nook on the patio. I poked his chest with my finger and snarled, "I'm not gonna stand here and watch you two stumble against each other like drunk college kids."

"What the hell are you talking about?" he slurred, rum and Coke fumes hot on my face. "You need to relax, Nic. It's a party. *My* party."

"Fine," I said. "Have at it. Go on with your grind-fest, Birthday Boy." Then, I turned on my heel and stomped into the house.

Monica followed. "What are you about to do?"

Leilani, trailing after her, shouted, "Go out there and kick her ass!"

I raced to the kitchen and grabbed my purse from the pantry and the keys from beneath the fruit bowl on the breakfast bar.

"Where are you going?" Monica asked as she followed me out to the driveway.

"If I don't leave," I said, opening the Volvo's door, "I'm gonna freakin' . . . spontaneously combust, and kill every living thing around me. I just need to calm the hell down. Get some distance. I'll be back."

I usually don't do this: desert a party that I'm hosting. But desperate times, desperate measures, and so on. I screeched out of the driveway and zoomed down the hill to Beachwood Drive. At Sunset, I headed toward Downtown.

Were Truman and Elene still dirty dancing?

Were they now sharing one skewer of meat?

Had he even noticed that I had stormed out of the house?

I pulled into an empty grocery store parking lot. Pearly fog softened the orange glow of the lot's safety lights. A pack of stray dogs ripped apart a discarded bag of food. A dark homeless man pushing a shopping cart filled with cans shooed the dogs away and claimed the bag for himself.

Truman's ringtone played on my cell phone inside my purse. "Yes?"

"Where are you?"

"Driving."

"I can't believe . . ." He sighed, then shouted, "What's wrong now?"

I shook my head, too angry to talk.

"Are you upset because I wouldn't dance? I'm sorry, Nic. I—"

I hung up and turned off the phone before he could promise me a better life. What about *this* life? And when had he found the time to take scuba lessons? Three-hour meetings and business lunches filled his days. That's why we didn't go to the movies or out to dinner. That's why

I never saw him before bedtime. That's why our marriage was dying. He had been incredibly busy being an Executive.

But he had somehow found the time to browse pamphlets and brochures for climbs and jumps. He had found the time to study specs and option packages, and had filled out paperwork, reams of paperwork, that needed his signature. Each day, he had talked to Greg the climb guy, and Flex the scuba guy, and all the other guys who supported his habit. He had sat at his desk in his home office, gnawing licorice whips and studying catalogs of new adventures.

And tonight, he had found the time to dance with someone else.

How long did I have to grit my teeth and say nothing? How much more was I supposed to take?

The party had ended. Plastic cups and party hats were strewn across the deck and my tiny backyard. Nikes and Kenneth Coles had trampled the grass; Manolo Blahniks and Jimmy Choos had punctured the earth.

I shivered in the cool, moist air.

So quiet.

I gazed at the glowing light in my bedroom. The quiet wouldn't last long.

"I didn't *sleep* with her," Truman said as he fell back onto our bed. "We were talking. Joking around."

"Ha, ha, *hee*." I paced the room, not caring if he had or hadn't slept with Elene. He could've given the woman a Bible study, and I would've said "so what." I was hot with righteous indignation, terrified of the possible, smarting from pure embarrassment. Rational thinking had been banished to the cramped attic of my mind. "And then you foist

Penelope on me. Kissing her hands and saying how she fucking saved your life."

"Will you calm down and think for a moment?" Truman shouted.

"Did you *see* yourself tonight?" I screamed. "Cuz everyone else did."

"I don't care what everyone—" His hands flew to his head. "Can we not scream?" He glared at me, frustrated and exasperated—the look a mother gives her two-year-old who purposely pees on the carpet. "It was a party, Nicole. Why are you acting like this? She's our friend. I'm not stupid enough to have an affair with a *friend*."

"First of all," I said, "she's not *my* friend. Second: Does that mean that you'd have an affair with an acquaintance? An associate? A colleague? *Penelope?*"

He chuckled and shook his head. "You know the answer to that question."

"No, I don't," I said. "Because I don't understand *you* anymore." With that, my throat thickened with pre-crying goo, and I stomped over to the window. The peonies' petals, violated by our guests' rear ends, lay scattered across the grass. "I don't know, Truman. You're . . ."

"Happy?" he asked. "Content? Satisfied for a change? I worked my ass off getting where I am, Nicole. It's my birthday, and I wanted to celebrate and not think about anything stupid or petty tonight. But where's my wife? She drives off somewhere because she's being an insecure . . ." He didn't finish his sentence because I had turned to face him. Even after eleven years of marriage, Truman would not call me a "bitch" to my face.

I shook my head. "You haven't spent more than two hours with me—"

"I take you to musicals and plays and expensive restaurants that suck," he shouted. "I *hate* that crap, but I do it because I want *you* to have everything you've ever wanted. But you're pissed because I didn't dance with you tonight? Are you kidding me?"

So, he was saying this: *You, Nicole, have no right to complain because I went to see* Rent *that one time even though I fell asleep, but still, I was there, and that should count for something.* Was he *high?* Did he not remember me shaking him awake at the Ahmanson that night because he was snoring so frickin' loud that people looked over their shoulders to glare at us? How was that a fabulous time?

It wasn't a fabulous time.

And what about those occasions when he stood me up, or didn't plan me into his calendar? Was I supposed to thrive on good intentions? I, too, had busted my behind so that *we* could have everything *we* wanted.

Truman unbuttoned his shirt. "Sometimes, this marriage feels like I'm in lockup."

I winced—this was something new, something ugly. "Wow. I'm a *prison* warden now?" A tear slipped down my cheek, and I swiped it away. "Are you having an affair or not? Yes or no? It's a simple question."

Truman, his bare chest heaving in anger, gawked at me.

I stood there, arms crossed (*warden-like?*), waiting for his answer. "Hello? You deaf now?"

He shook his head. "I'm taking a shower." Then, he brushed past me without another word.

CHAPTER 6

Why didn't Truman say, *No, Nicole, I'm not having an affair. Can we bitch about something else now?* And as I sat across from Jake, that question—*Why didn't he say no?*—made my head ache.

Jake reached across the table and placed his hand atop mine. He smiled, and his brown eyes crinkled at the corners. "I could've saved a hundred dollars if you're just gonna stare at the breadbasket. What's going on today?"

"Still thinking about the fight." I draped the cloth napkin across my lap for the fifth time. "I asked him if he was having an affair."

"And what did he say?"

I grabbed my fork and stabbed at my salad as though it was Elene's face. "He didn't say anything."

"Ah."

"He basically called me a warden. Said that sometimes, he feels like he's in lockup. Like I'm keeping him somewhere he doesn't wanna be."

The argument about the party and Elene had not brought any immediate apologies or surrenders from Truman or me. That Saturday night, several minutes had passed as he took a shower and I pouted in bed. After his shower, he had stood over me, and I had rolled over, turning my back to him. He had stomped to his office, and I had cried into my pillow.

Sunday came without us talking to each other or passing each other in the hallway. I washed dishes, did a few loads of laundry, and read a few pages of *No Country for Old Men*. At one point, I heard his footsteps tap up and down the hallway, and his cell phone ring. Heard the BMW roar down the canyon.

"Eleven years is a long time," Jake said with a shrug. "I only made it with Dana for three. Isn't it seven for the itch?"

"So?"

"He's a man," Jake said, his tone reasonable and matter-of-fact.

"And last time I checked, I was a woman."

"True."

"I'm not a priority to him."

"You haven't been for a while."

"He practically ignores me when he's at home."

"Some men require a lot to keep their attention."

"Aren't I interesting?"

"The most interesting woman I know. The only person who can tell me how a NanoDrop spectrophotometer will rid the world of diabetes."

"Not just the world, but the universe," I said, brightening. "And I'm attractive, right?"

"You're beautiful."

I cocked an eyebrow. "And I can have any man I want, right?"

Jake smiled. "You certainly can."

I reached across the table and squeezed his hand. "You do wonders for a woman's bruised ego."

"You think that's what this is? That you're being overly sensitive? That he's not cheating?"

I sighed, shrugged. "The more we ignore each other, the angrier I become. The angrier I become, the more I believe."

Jake shook his head, then sipped from his glass of scotch. "Well, if he does leave, I doubt you'll have any trouble finding someone to replace him. You know I'm not going away. I'll just bide my time, hoping he keeps screwing up, or until you decide to end it."

I didn't say anything, preferring to stare at the lime slice floating in my glass of Pellegrino.

"Do you think he knows about us?" Jake asked.

I chuckled. "There is no 'us.' We're friends. That's it."

"Why did you call me today instead of Monica?" he asked. "Why are we here right now, way the hell in Woodland Hills, even though I work way the hell in Century City? Do you think I'd do that for anybody? Would you ask 'just a friend' to drive fifty miles to eat lunch with you? Has Truman ever come over the hill to have lunch?" He chuckled—he knew the answer to that question. "We're *something*, Nicole."

I clenched my jaw, then relaxed it.

He held up his hand and considered me with that lazy smile. "Okay. Whatever you say. I'm in no rush." Jake was eight years older than me, and his age showed in his patience. He was so relaxed, so *convinced*.

My cheeks flushed, and my gaze dropped back to the breadbasket. "There is no 'us,' Jake."

He placed his hand back over mine. "Forgive me if I refuse to believe that."

My breathing remained constant as the dining room faded around me. "I'm married."

"Obviously," he said, lifting my left hand. "That diamond's damn big."

I considered my engagement ring as though I had never seen it before.

Beneath the table, Jake shifted his foot until it settled against my pump. And we sat like that, shoe against shoe, for several moments. I glanced around the dining room—Jake and I stood out. If a private investigator asked, everyone in the restaurant would remember seeing us together. *Oh, you mean the gorgeous white guy and that Black chick?*

"If you ever said 'yes,'" he said, "you'd never be alone again." Then, he kissed my hand.

I nodded, then opened my mouth to say something noble, something virtuous. Instead, I said, "So a cocker spaniel goes into a bar . . ."

He laughed, and I reclaimed my hand. Not as a declaration of my marital commitment, but to glance at my watch. "It's after one."

He pushed the tumbler of scotch toward me. "Somewhere to go?"

I stared at the glass near my hands, then picked it up and drank.

We wandered back to the parking garage, and the cool air cleared my head. The food, the scotch, Jake Huston—all of it made my knees goopy, made my heart beat too fast.

I unlocked the Volvo, and smiled at him. "Thanks for lunch."

"Nic," he said, "we really need to talk about this. About us."

Footsteps clicked down the garage's metal staircase, and a door slammed against the wall.

Jake startled and looked over his shoulder.

An old man in a rumpled suit shuffled into the lot. He was not a suspicious husband, gun in hand, stalking his wife and her not-lover.

I hugged Jake before he could speak again, before he tried to kiss me. I didn't know what I would do if he kissed me . . . Yeah, I did know, and that scared (and thrilled) me.

Jake said, "You're avoiding this."

I opened the car door. "Yes, I am. Jogging tonight?"

He shook his head. "Got some reading to do before court tomorrow." He paused, then said, "You should come over. I can grill steaks, and you can tell me about the cytomegalovirus or finish that joke about the cocker spaniel."

I shook my head.

"Some other time?"

"I should get back to work. I need to finish a report." I climbed behind the steering wheel and closed the door. *Safe.* My shoulders relaxed as I leaned back into the soft leather seat.

Jake backed away from the car and shoved his hands deep into his pockets. The harsh fluorescents cast his face in shadows, and made his brown hair silver.

I started the car, then rolled down the window. "Thanks again."

"If you change your mind," he said, "you know where I am."

Really: What did I know about Jacob Huston?

He practiced law—an easy one.

He liked his coffee with cream-no-sugar, and preferred butter croissants over muffins, but the redheaded barista at the village coffee shop knew that.

He opposed the war and the death penalty. He supported a woman's right to choose. He donated to homeless shelters around the city.

But why had he divorced?

What annoying habits did he have?

What views did he hold that I'd find reprehensible?

And what kind of man goes after a married woman? And how many wives had he slept with?

Didn't want to know the answer to those last questions. I wanted to believe that I was special to him, his one-time lapse in judgment. Because he was special to me. The only man that made me even *consider* . . .

I stood on Jake's porch for an eternity, casting anxious glances toward my house, not believing that Truman would work late, even though he worked late every night. My skin crawled as I stood there, beneath the disapproving gaze of my guardian angel.

What was that?

I glanced back at my house again and stared at the light shining in my downstairs den.

Was that on before?

Couldn't remember. *You don't have to ring the doorbell. You can step back and go home and . . .*

But I remembered the way Jake had looked at me. Remembered the touch of his hand against mine. How my foot ached against his . . .

My finger jabbed the doorbell, possessed by the need to touch him again.

You can still go home.

Jake opened the door, his eyes wide with shock. He closed the thick law book in his hand.

"So the second cocker spaniel says, 'You think that's bad, I couldn't even get up on the bed.'" I paused, then added, "The end."

"Didn't think I'd see you again today," he said.

"Oh, I'm just full of surprises." I stepped into a foyer three stories high, and gazed at the skylight, then down to a floor made with glazed pieces of jewel-colored glass. "This place is incredible. Like a mini Hearst Castle."

Jake smiled. "Is this your first time inside?"

I nodded. "You've invited me over several times, but I've resisted until now. Are you baking something? I smell bread and lemons."

"Nope," he said. "The house just smells like that."

I wandered into the living room. Edward Ruscha paintings hung on every wall. A shiny baby grand sat in a corner. Floor-to-ceiling windows let in sepia-colored light, and outside, sunset colored the canyon gold while Downtown shimmered like a dusty mirage.

"Let me know if it's too warm in here," he said.

"It's perfect," I said, unable to force my eyes from those diamond-like skyscrapers. "How is it that we have the same view, but here . . . ? Does it look like this every night? Because it's so . . ." Not beautiful. More than beautiful.

He stood in front of me. "Guess it depends on your perspective." He tilted my face toward his and kissed me.

I caressed his face as we kissed, as his lips trailed down my neck to the cleft between my breasts. His hands cupped my ass, then clenched my waist. My hands wandered across his back as I pushed harder against him.

He urged me backward until we found the couch. He sat, and I straddled his waist and tugged at his track pants. His fingers dipped into my panties, then slipped them off. My hands eased down his tight abdomen and into his boxers. He tensed for a moment, then relaxed. Our eyes locked as I pushed his pants past his hips . . .

Lightheaded, I lay on top of Jake with my skirt bunched around my waist. "That wasn't supposed to happen."

He said, "I know . . . But I'm glad it did."

His finger traced my face and lips, and I clenched it between my teeth and pulled it into my mouth. And as the canyon darkened beyond those tall windows, as fog drifted in from the Pacific Ocean, we found each other a second time.

I opened my eyes—I lay stretched beside Jake on the couch.

"You awake?" he asked.

"Um hmm."

He played with my hair as I stared at the smudges in the piano's slick varnish. The air conditioner clicked, and a breeze moved across the room, cooling my feet, and creeping up my shins until I shivered. Shadows draped across the cream-colored sofas. Po-Mo stuff. Stiff. Impersonal. Cold, like this room. "I should go," I said.

He hesitated, then said, "Okay."

We stood on his porch, unsure of what to say. Jake offered to walk me home, but I asked him not to.

"Get some work done," I said.

He said, "I will."

I headed down the hill, my skin clammy, my legs weak. So quiet out on Rockcliff Drive. No one jogged or walked their dogs. I glanced over my shoulder: Jake hadn't moved from beneath the yellow glow of his porch light. He waved to me.

I waved back and continued down the hill.

Why did I do that?

Didn't I love Truman?

How could I love him and betray him like that?

Would Jake and I pretend that nothing happened?

Would we do this again?

Did I *want* to do this again?

What would Jake do, what would he say if I told him that tonight was it?

I couldn't fit the key into the door lock—my hand couldn't stop shaking. My mind raced. Couldn't stop thinking about Jake's body against mine, about the way he said my name, how he kissed me, how my skin tingled . . .

In the shower, I scrubbed until my brown skin reddened. Dried off with a towel, slathered on scented lotion, and pulled on sweatpants.

I retreated to the living room couch and gazed out the large picture window. The sun had disappeared, and the moon blinked in nickel-colored fog. In the distance, cars and trucks sped toward their destinations. Red lights headed east to Downtown. White lights headed west to Hollywood and beyond. Picture frames, books, everything in the room had disappeared into the dark. I stretched back to turn on the lamp, but changed my mind.

The telephone rang on seven different occasions. Caller ID droned, *Baxter, Truman, Baxter, Truman.* I closed my eyes as my husband's name echoed throughout the house.

If I confessed to him, what would happen?

Would we divorce? Or would he give me credit for remaining faithful 99.9 percent of our time together. If I were him, would I forgive me?

Being with Jake had been a moment of weakness, a perfect storm of physical attraction, anger, opportunity, and the need for petty revenge. This was no *Bridges of Madison County* love affair.

What would happen if I pretended nothing happened?

We could sell the house, move to Tennessee, and I'd never see Jacob Huston again.

As the earth moistened, the house creaked and settled deeper onto its foundation. A night breeze rattled a window screen in one of the rooms . . .

The house's phantoms had come home.

CHAPTER 7

All night, I dreamed.

Truman picks up the ringing telephone. A muffled voice—Jake?—says, Do you know what Nicole did last night? *Truman says,* No. What? *Then, he screams.*

I lay in a hospital bed, in a room filled with flowers and balloons. Truman stands at the window, gazing out at the Santa Monica Bay. A nurse enters the room. She holds a baby wrapped in a blanket. Here's your little boy, *she says, then hands me the bundle. The nurse removes the blanket from my boy. He has skin the color of café au lait, and Jake's whiskey-brown eyes. Truman looks at us over his shoulder, then opens the window, climbs up to the ledge, and jumps out.*

After each nightmare, I lurched out of sleep, panting and tugging at my sticky tank top. Wide-eyed, I'd throw a startled glance across the room—no bassinet, no biracial baby, and Truman, not talking on the telephone, but asleep and snoring beside me.

My heart raced as I lay there, but the rhythm of Truman's heavy breathing and the soft *whoomp* of the ceiling fan urged me back to sleep.

Sunlight splashed across the kitchen, and colored the silver appliances copper. *Another strange-weather day in Los Angeles.* I sat at the breakfast bar, coffee cup to my lips, eyes on the television. On *Good Day LA,* the host announced that temperatures in Los Angeles had already reached a humid eighty-eight degrees. I glanced at the refrigerator for the fifth time that morning, but nothing about it had changed. Truman had left the house before I had awakened and hadn't left a message on the door.

I poured my coffee into the sink, then turned back to the refrigerator. I studied the magnetic words there until a message formed in my mind.

Light crackles blue when I dream of you
Love rockets fly twirl soar
You light my sky with languid magic

As I stood in the driveway, I heard the *thump-thump* of Jake's running shoes. Usually, my heart soared knowing that at any moment, I would see him sprint past. On this morning, though, I held my breath as I listened, and hoped that the runner would be another man in size 12 Nike Airs.

No luck.

Jake jogged around the bend, and slowed as he neared my house. "Mornin'."

"Hey." That one word sounded strained, and I cleared my throat, then jangled my keys.

"Guess you're not used to awkward morning-afters." He stepped closer to me. Heat rolled off his body. He smelled like the canyon—smoky, green, and wild.

"Guess not." I shivered even though it was eighty-eight degrees.

"What happened between us last night . . . It wasn't some random thing to me. I really care about you, Nicole. I don't go around sleeping with people's wives for fun."

I bit my lip, unsure of what to say.

"Nic." He touched my chin.

I jerked away.

His eyes darkened, and he dropped his hand. "I couldn't sleep last night because I knew you'd freak out on me. We're not awful people. That's what you're thinking, right?"

I turned my head, and said, "I betrayed someone who loves me."

"A man who's neglected you and continues to fail in his commitment to you and—" He stooped so he could see my eyes. "I don't care about hurting Truman, to be honest with you. He deserves whatever heartbreak is coming to him. I care about you, though. I care that you hate this house. I care that your last therapy session with that Tremaine woman was a bust. Does he even know that you're seeing another shrink?"

Tears burned my eyes—I didn't know. "Still, Jake. All of this, even standing here with you right now, makes me nervous."

He said nothing.

I gawked at him. "You don't care what his reaction would be? What he'd do if he found out about us?"

He laughed, then leaned against my car. "I wish he'd say something to me, but he won't. He's not a stupid . . ." He paused, then narrowed his eyes. "Oh. Crap. Do you mean . . . ? You think he'd hurt you?"

I coughed—his question a punch to my gut. Through my choking fit, I said, "No. Truman? No. He'd never—" I grabbed my clammy neck and caught my breath. How could I lead anyone to think something so horrible? "Truman can be an insensitive jerk sometimes, but he'd never hurt me. He's not like that."

"Would you tell me if he was?"

I blinked at him. "Did you just say that?"

"Do you know how many pro bono clients I have who beg me to believe that their guy is all sweetness and light? He's an angel, they tell me, but I'm sitting there, looking at his anger on her busted lip."

"You're being an ass right now, Jacob, and it's pissing me the hell off."

He exhaled, then placed his hands on his head. "You're right. I believe you. Truman's not that guy. But you know I'd do anything for you, anything to protect you, Nicole. You know that, right?"

I covered my face with my hands, and said, "This is way too intense a conversation for seven thirty in the morning."

Jake thought about that, and his shoulders relaxed. "I'm sorry. It's the lawyer in me. I can become a little irrational in my defense sometimes."

In the distance, a weed whacker buzzed, and the *thwap* of blades against wild grass echoed throughout the canyon. A garbage truck rumbled down the street, and I realized that Truman hadn't rolled out the trash cans. I sure as hell wouldn't haul out a week's worth of garbage wearing a Calvin Klein linen pantsuit. Maybe on an Ann Taylor separates day, but not today.

Jake took my hand, and said, "Let's talk about this at a villa in Tuscany or Provence. You won't ever have to come back to this house again. I'll gladly give you everything he's not."

I withdrew my hand. "It wouldn't be fair."

He laughed. "It wouldn't be *fair*? Not, *Jake, I love him*, or *Jake, he loves me*. But *it wouldn't be fair*? Romantic."

I couldn't say any of those things—I love him, he loves me—because those things didn't matter right then. And it would be ridiculous to claim "love" after having slept with another man less than ten hours before. This *did* matter: Truman had put up with me for thirteen years. For ten of those years, he had been the best husband in the world. It wasn't fair of me to throw that away and travel the world with another man who hadn't done any of the heavy lifting.

"Think about my offer," Jake said. "Weigh your options. The pros and the cons. Think about how we feel about each other. How we feel when we're together. Then . . ." He grinned, certain that, in the end, he would win.

"Okay," I whispered.

"I'm starting to sound like a Prince song. Do you want him or do you want me?"

I smiled. "I love Prince."

He blushed, then tugged at his sweaty T-shirt. "So, I stink, and you're being polite about it."

I wrinkled my nose. "You're not too bad. Pungent but not offensive."

"We'll talk later?"

I nodded.

He kissed my cheek, and then, dashed up the hill.

It wasn't some random thing. Didn't matter if it was random or not. I knew I'd tell Jake "no." And I would say nothing to Truman about the affair, or Jake's offer to leave the States, or any of it. I would cook, clean, and swallow all dissatisfaction about Truman's work schedule and his hobbies without comment. I'd develop an ulcer from all of this repression, but I could afford bottles of Maalox. Maybe Truman and I could see Dr. Tremaine together for marriage counseling. She had been awful during our first "chat," but maybe she'd had a bad day.

If I deserved a second chance, Dr. Tremaine deserved one, too.

But for counseling to work, I would have to confess. Or could I talk *around* the affair, my secret attempts to conceive? Could I ball all of that up into one load of dirty laundry?

Because I *did* love my husband. I missed him when he wasn't with me. I enjoyed his company when we weren't fighting. I wanted to forsake my firm abs and thighs to have his baby. That had to count for *something*.

By ten o'clock, I had finished an endocrinology report and had started on a draft about recent advances in nanomedicine. Truman hadn't called to apologize, and I hadn't called him. This silence, this opportunity to breathe and to think clearly, left me torn. I had been relieved that no one (i.e., Jake) had called to threaten me with the truth; on the other hand, the quiet was *too* quiet. The kind of scary-movie quiet that always ended with screaming, chainsaws, and bloodshed.

Jake had sent me a vase of Casablanca lilies. The bouquet had been waiting for me on my desk, and now sat on my credenza. As I reread the card, I didn't know how to feel.

Babybabybaby, I'm crazy about U and I want 2 please U.

Someone knocked on the door.

I looked over my shoulder—Truman stood in the doorway. My pulse exploded, and I jammed Jake's card into my slacks pocket. "Hey."

"Thought I'd come over the hill and surprise you." He closed the door behind him, then said, "It's been pretty bad between us. Scary bad." He wore khaki-colored shorts, a Body Glove T-shirt, and his fading blue Vans. Ocean wear.

I grunted again, then plopped back into my chair.

He wandered to the credenza and touched the lilies' petals. "These are beautiful. You bought them?"

"Yeah."

Neither of us spoke. The muted roar of the copy machine down the hall filled the silence.

He squared his shoulders, and said, "Nicole, do you wanna keep doing this?"

"What is 'this'?" I asked. "You mean our *marriage*?"

He nodded, then sat in a chair on the other side of my desk.

"See, that's a problem," I said. "You talk about being married to me like it's a death sentence. Like our marriage is a wart on your ass that needs to be—"

"I'm sorry," he said. "What do you want me to do? Go to counseling with you? Go to church? Attend some workshop where we talk about our feelings and hit each other with pillows?"

I spun my chair to face a wall filled with pictures of Truman and me on our last Caribbean vacation. *Clear turquoise waters. Sea rays brushing against our calves. Rum cake.*

"And you've changed, too," he said. "You're always pissed at me. You barely let me touch you. You're not . . . interested in me anymore."

I muttered, "And it's still all about you."

He hadn't been around to talk to, to watch television with, to play *Guitar Hero*, even though he had promised. He never asked me about work, or about the book on my lap, or about my thoughts on anything. How could I have sex with him? Most times, I was too pissed off to orgasm.

"I'm so tired of this," he muttered. "Why come home when this is all you do?"

I considered him with narrowed eyes. "All *I* do? I *like* arguing nonstop with you? I wait until you decide to pop into our marriage so that I can pick a fight? I'm now some nagging hag bitch of a wife who doesn't understand?"

"You don't understand," he said, shaking his head. "And I'm tired of trying to make you understand."

"Make me?" My love for this man was melting like ice cream beneath a hot sun. It was still there, but if we kept going in this direction, kept having these types of arguments, that love would soon be a sticky used-to-be. And I didn't want that. "If you don't want to be with me—"

"I want to be with you, okay?" He rubbed his face, then released a long sigh. "I love you, Nicole. I'm stressed out. Can't you see that? I know I'm not spending time with you but you have to understand that I'm doing this for the both of us. I'm supposed to be at the pier right now, but I'm here with you because you matter to me."

I smirked. "What time's your dive?"

He hesitated, then said, "Two thirty."

I chuckled—*such a sacrifice*—then gazed at the lilies on the credenza. *Has Truman come over the hill for lunch?* No. Not once.

"I'm trying," Truman said, weaker. "Can I get ten points for trying?"

"Ten points for fitting me into your busy schedule?" I asked. "Sure. And thank you."

He either ignored my sarcasm or did not pick it up, and continued: "And I'm sorry about Saturday night." One side of his mouth lifted into a weak smile. "Most of those people who came to the party don't care about me. Not really. And I know that. Most of them only give me the time of day because of my job title. Including Elvia."

"Elene," I corrected.

"Elene?" He grimaced. "You sure?"

Truman wasn't being funny. He probably didn't remember the skank's name. As the Historian, Parliamentarian, and Secretary of our union, I remembered names, dates, directions, and the places we parked the car. As President, Treasurer, and Sergeant-at-Arms, Truman made the most money, checked the locks at night, and killed the bugs.

He walked over to me, and pulled me to my feet. He leaned forward until our foreheads touched. "You're the only person in this world who'd never intentionally hurt me. Who loved me when all I did was study ratings and statistics all day. I don't wanna do anything stupid enough to make you leave me. And I'm sorry, okay? I'm really, really sorry."

"And I'm sorry for the prisoner remark. I don't feel that way at all. You've never forced me to do anything, and I shouldn't have said that. And I do enjoy going to restaurants with you. I was just angry and I wanted to hurt you."

I dipped my head and clamped my mouth shut. I felt a confession coming. Felt like that tickle on the back of your throat before you cough.

"Let's do better, all right?" he said. "*I'll* do better. I promise, Nicole. Don't give up on me yet. We put too much into this to throw it all away, right?"

I nodded, relieved that he didn't want to leave me, relieved that I was relieved. Because I didn't want a new life in Provence, or in Tuscany, or on the moon with another man. I'd take Truman in a hut in the outback over Jake in a villa near the Versailles.

I had screwed up. Plain and simple. No excuses. I was attracted to Jake, and I wanted him and I had him—it didn't help that I had been pissed at Truman, but Truman didn't force me into another man's arms.

I'll tell him about the affair when he comes home from the dive tonight.

He'd be pissed at me. Beyond pissed. He'd shout, curse me out, all of that. He'd leave the house for a day or two, but he'd come back because he knew my heart. We cherished our marriage. Even more, we cherished our friendship.

Truman and I walked to the parking lot in silence. We didn't bump into my coworkers, and so we didn't have to pretend that we hadn't just ended two days of angry and uneasy silence.

Waves of heat shimmered above the car tops, and cindery dust scattered across windshields. Napkins, wrappers, and receipts raced across the asphalt. A dirt devil pulled all of the trash into its belly, then sent the mess circling toward the cloudy sky.

"You ever wish you could disappear sometimes?" he asked. "I don't mean dying. I mean leaving behind all your responsibilities, and finding a place where no one knows you, or expects anything from you."

I said, "Sometimes."

"You wake up, have breakfast, and just sit and stare at the ocean. You don't read the paper. You don't check your phone. You just . . ."

"Chill?" I asked. "I do. A lot."

He nodded, then dropped his head.

"You wanna talk about it?"

"There's nothing really to—" He rubbed his face, and said through his hands, "I'm just tired of trying and failing, that's all. Tired of disappointing people. Tired of being disappointed. Tired of being lied to. Tired of the drama. Maybe because I'm forty now and I just don't have the patience anymore." He dropped his hands and chuckled. "You're the only person I can say that to without feeling stupid. Without feeling weak. And I feel better just saying that."

I clutched his arm and squeezed. "What's going on?"

"You have to get back to work."

I smirked. "What are they gonna do? Fire me?"

"In this economy? Yes."

"Then who would write about the SIRT1 gene and its role in the genesis of cancer? Huh? Who?"

He tried to smile. "It's just . . ." He shook his head and shrugged. "Nothing new. Dealing with the Black tax at work. That's one thing."

The Black tax: having to work and perform twice as well as your white peers.

"You think I'd be used to it by now, but . . ." He took a deep breath and slowly exhaled. "I came up with the Everest program, right? It's beyond great. One of our most-watched shows of all time. But we didn't get an Emmy for it, even though we were nominated. Our ratings are up ten percent, and I'm expanding our programming in China, but my bosses are saying, 'Awesome, but what about Australia? And why are you working sixty hours a week and not seventy?'

"And I feel like saying, 'Kiss my ass, take your job and go to hell,' but I won't because then they'd say that they were right, that I was too young and too colored to be executive vice president of a major network."

I nodded, wondered what to say.

"Everything I do nowadays just isn't good enough," he said, staring past me. "And I find myself wondering: When will it ever be? When will I be able to just . . . live and not have to prove myself every damned day?"

I touched his cheek. "We can sell the house. Retire early. Move to the Maldives. Eat off the land. Coconut cream pie every day, just like on *Gilligan's Island*."

He kissed my hand and chuckled. "You're allergic to coconut."

"I'll bring a crate of Benadryl, then. And I'll buy a red wig so I can pretend to be Ginger."

"You're more of a platinum blonde."

I playfully shoved him. "You'd be free, though, and that's the point."

He held up three fingers. "That's how long I have left on my contract. And I want to make sure that we'll be okay when we retire in twenty years."

I sighed, shrugged.

"I know," he said. "Shut up, then, and deal, right?"

"That's not what I meant," I said. "If you want to quit, do it. I'll support your decision. *You* matter to me, and I don't want you stressed out and unhappy because of a stupid job. We'll be fine. We both grew up without cable TV and cell phones and ten-dollar cheese."

"Yeah. You're right." Truman took my hand and kissed it. "We haven't talked in two days, but here we are, quitting jobs and living on a deserted island together."

I smiled. "We know that we only have each other."

"I hate it when we argue."

"I do, too." I closed my eyes as he kissed my forehead.

"Let's go hiking and fishing like we used to," he said. "Safe stuff that you like doing. Except I already booked a hot air balloon ride for our anniversary next month. Wine, sunset, a diamond maybe." He kissed my cheek. "I should get going."

I glanced inside his BMW. A wet suit, two oxygen tanks, and a scuba mask sat in the car's front seat. Seeing all that made my heart ache. *Tell him. Tell him* now. I closed my eyes. "Truman, I need to—"

He pulled me into his arms. "Remember last Christmas when you told me you wanted to have a baby?"

I nodded. "You said after everything settled."

He smiled. "After the dive today, I would've gone on half the adventures on my list. And I hear being a dad's the greatest adventure of all. I want us to have a family."

Tears stung my eyes. "Are you sure?"

Truman hugged me, and said, "Positive."

I held him tight and inhaled his scent. Sunscreen and citrus.

"You have no idea how much I love you, Nicole Porter Baxter," he said. "Even if you get tired of me and kick me out of the house, I'll still sneak back home and climb up on the roof just to watch you read."

I swiped at my wet eyes and tried to smile. "A stalker now?"

He laughed, kissed my nose, forehead, and lips. "Best friends forever, babe."

I glanced at the flat and cranky clouds above us. Maybe it would rain, and the dive would be canceled. I could pray for a storm, but with my recent behavior, that would be the one prayer to go unanswered. "The weather's right for this?" I asked. "It's hot, humid. I'm thinking thunderstorms."

"The skies are clearer over on Catalina," he said. "I checked the weather before leaving the house this morning." He pulled me close again. "Leave work early and come down to San Pedro for dinner. We should be back at the dock by five."

"You sure you're ready for the open ocean?" I asked, not ready to talk about dinner plans as those clouds hunkered over us. "I've read how nitrogen bubbles can fill blood vessels—"

"The bends. Don't worry. I'm in good hands. Flex is the best dive instructor in Southern California, and I've logged in more than enough training hours."

I shook my head, not accepting Truman's or Flex's bona fides. "It's life-threatening. Heart attacks, stroke—"

"I won't be a hotshot in a hundred feet of water," he said. "Almost drowned last week. Don't plan on doing it again."

"Where, *exactly*, near Catalina?"

"The backside. Farnsworth Banks."

A warm wind blew through the parking lot and brought goose pimples to my skin. "Is there somewhere shallower you can dive?"

"Like the bathtub?"

I smirked. "You've only splashed in swimming pools, Mr. Baxter. *Variables* live in the open ocean. Sea lions, jellyfish—"

"Jaws, mermaids, and Nessie." He pulled me into his arms. "I miss hugging you. You must get tired of me touching you all the time."

"I don't." His eyes looked too red. Could he see clearly? Were his allergies acting up? Had he taken an antihistamine? And if he had, how would that affect his diving? I took a deep breath, pushed those thoughts out of my mind, and forced a smile to my face. "Dinner sounds good. I'll probably get out of here by noon—I'm not feeling the writing thing today. I'll get to San Pedro for six."

Truman climbed behind the BMW's steering wheel. "We'll go to Barbados," he was saying. "I can dive, you can worry. Then, we'll get drunk and make a baby. How does that sound?"

I laughed. "Terrifying."

"Are you stopping at the store before going home?"

The simple joys of marriage. Lingering small talk. Requests for Oreos and grape juice, razor blades and potato chips. "I can. What do you need?"

"Ice cream." He started the car, then turned to me. "I love you, Nicole. I mean that."

"I love you, too," I said. "And I mean that. Be careful, okay? Do you hear me? Don't be Jacques Cousteau."

He shifted the car into reverse. "Yes, dear."

"I'm serious."

"Relax, babe."

"And don't drive too fast."

"Fifty-five to stay alive." He slowly backed out of the space, then honked the horn twice as he pulled out of CelluTech's parking lot.

CHAPTER 8

I stood before the ice cream cases in the village market, unable to remember which flavor my husband Truman had requested. He loved ice cream, but he never overindulged—his mother had died from type 2 diabetes complications, and his father had died six months later from a heart attack. Truman, aware of his sketchy genetics, allotted himself one pint of Ben & Jerry's a month.

And because he only ate a pint, I didn't want to select the wrong flavor. "Wind Beneath My Wings" blasted on the store's Muzak system, making it harder for me to focus. So, I plucked my phone from my handbag and called his cell.

No answer.

He's probably one hundred feet below right now. I pictured him exploring the Pacific Ocean, silver bubbles burbling from his scuba regulator as he glided past red coral and sea fans.

After five rings, the phone rolled over to voicemail. *This is Truman. Leave a message.*

"Honey," I said, shouting over Bette Midler, "I'm at the store. Did you want Brownie Batter, Cake Batter, or Cherry Garcia? Call me sooner rather than later."

I closed my phone and opened the freezer door.

Truman's ringtone—"Tonite," DJ Quik—played from my purse. He always returned calls for ice cream selection. And even though he was now in the middle of his first open-ocean dive, he would not let me leave the store with a pint of Chunky Monkey. Happened once. He couldn't let it happen again.

"Hey," I said. "I literally have my hand in the freezer. Which flavor do you want?"

". . . Hello?" A man. Not Truman.

"Who's this?" I leaned against my shopping cart, already filled with ground turkey, bell peppers, and several kinds of cheeses.

"Nicole? This is Flex D'Onofrio. Truman's dive instructor." He sounded far-off, as though he was calling from Mars.

"Oh," I said. "Let me guess: He's running late." With Flex's call, I exhaled, relieved that six o'clock would come and go, relieved that Truman would flake on me and not come home until after I had gone to bed, relieved that I'd have one more day . . .

"Where are you?" Flex asked as thousands of people shouted behind him.

"At the grocery store."

"I've been trying to reach—" A burst of static.

"Reception's in and out in the hills," I shouted into the phone. "What's up?"

Another burst of static, and then, ". . . been an accident."

I kept the phone to my ear, unable to hear all that Flex said. What I did hear made my bladder release. A moment later, I raced out of the market, leaving my shopping cart in the frozen food aisle.

I don't remember sticking the key into the Volvo's ignition, or backing out of that space in the market's parking lot. I do remember careening down Beachwood Drive as buildings flew into the past, and neon signs melted into one colorless blur. I struggled to breathe—it hurt to breathe. I trembled so violently that my ribs threatened to snap under the stress of the seat belt. If that happened, I'd never reach the harbor, and I'd never reach Truman . . .

I raced onto the freeway, then auto-dialed a number on my cell—didn't know who I was calling.

"What's up, girlfriend?" Monica.

"Truman's hurt," I shouted. "Can you come to the marina? San Pedro. Where all the fishing boats dock."

Monica said, "I'll call Lei. I'm on my way."

By the time I reached San Pedro, the weather had deteriorated, and now, high winds made the dark Pacific spike with whitecaps. I parked the car somewhere in front of something, I don't know, and heard a parking guard or someone yell, "Hey, lady!" I had stopped obeying traffic laws, stopped paying attention, stopped being thoughtful. My husband was somewhere out on the ocean, or on a boat, or somewhere . . .

Bright red rescue vehicles had converged in the closest parking spaces, and their red emergency lights glowed bright beneath that gray sky. Paramedics dressed in blue glanced at the stormy sky as they wove past lookie-loos who had originally come to San Pedro for mariscos and Corona. A coast guard chopper hovered over the docks and the 65-foot SS *Deep-Cee*. The white yacht bobbed like a toy boat in a bathtub, a dinghy in this weather, beneath that zinc-colored sky. Even the red and white of the dive flag flying from its mast looked dull and flat.

I pushed through the crowds, but a police officer wielding a clipboard stopped my progress. He looked young, *High School Musical* young, too young to keep the peace and tell a grown-ass woman what to do. "Sorry, ma'am," he said to me, "but you can't—"

"My husband's on that boat," I shouted. "Truman Baxter. He needs me. They take him to the hospital yet?"

"Umm . . ." He consulted a scrap of paper clipped to his board.

I wanted to shake that kid. Shake him until information dropped off his body like fleas. Yeah, he had a job to do, but so did I.

Back on the boat, a lanky paramedic was talking to a middle-aged white man with a grizzled face and toffee-tanned skin. Another paramedic, blond and red-faced, desperately performed chest compressions on someone who lay collapsed on the deck. "*One-two . . . one-two . . .*"

I pointed. "Who's that down there? Is that him?"

The helicopter continued to roar above us, and the boat rocked from choppy waves and violent air displaced by the aircraft's four blades. The tanned man covered his ears and shouted, "Not responsive. Search and rescue's still out there but . . ." To the paramedic performing CPR, he said, "Dude, we did that for ninety minutes. It ain't happening."

The standing paramedic signaled up to the pilots in the chopper. Soon, a stretcher lowered from the helicopter and onto the deck.

"Flex!" I slipped under the police officer's arm, and made it a few steps away from the boat before the boy grabbed my hand again. I must have growled at him because his eyes widened as he released his grasp and hopped away from me.

The tanned man—Flex—turned in my direction and watched as I rushed to the boat.

By then, the diver had been strapped in, and now, the stretcher rose above the deck and into the air.

Flex said, "I called in a Mayday as soon as I—"

"They can't take him away yet," I said, my voice strained. "I need to see him. He needs to know that I'm here—"

The boat pitched starboard, and Flex clutched my arm so I wouldn't fall overboard.

"They can't take him yet," I shouted.

"Nicole, listen," Flex said. "That ain't Truman up there."

Confused, I shook my head. "You said there was an accident."

The blond paramedic tapped Flex's shoulder. He held a small notepad and a pen. "What was her name?"

Flex said, "Penelope Villagrana."

Penelope?

I reeled around to gape at the rising chopper. "What happened?"

"Ten minutes past their dive time," Flex said, "I got worried cuz they were cutting into decomp time—"

"Where is he?" I turned to face him. "Where is my husband?"

"Penny got caught," Flex continued. "Her line had tangled on some coral, but Truman got her loose. But she freaked out, and bolted to the surface without decompressing.

"And that's the worst thing a diver can do. After a long dive, the body needs to come up slowly. Adapt to the pressure of the surrounding water." He was staring at the ocean as he talked. Talking to remain calm. Convincing himself that there were rules to the sport, that if you just followed the rules . . ."Dennis, another diver, saw his line all tangled up in Penny's line and in the coral, and that probably got Truman panicking and . . ."

"Did Dennis free him?" I asked, forcing calm into my question.

Flex shook his head. "Dennis is a good diver, but he's still learnin'. He couldn't get him loose."

"Did *you* go in?"

He nodded. "I got to the spot with the coral and Truman wasn't there. I swam around looking for him. Then, the search-and-rescue guys went in. They couldn't find him, either."

Couldn't find him? What the hell did that mean?

"He had two tanks," I said. "His lungs are strong. He just came back from climbing—"

"He's not down there," Flex said.

I shook my head again. *Bullshit.*

"Even if he shot himself to the top somewhere . . ." Tears glistened in the man's smog-colored eyes, and his hand returned to his mouth. "His blood would be foam, his insides . . . Nicole, I'm sorry. We're still searching but . . . I'm sorry."

Sorry?

Flex grabbed Truman's dive bag from the deck, and handed it to me. Through the mesh, I saw Truman's paperback edition of *Cell*, two cans of Red Bull, an open package of licorice, and his eye allergy medication. But *he* was still out there. That's what Flex was telling me. And no one knew where he was. My husband was just . . . gone.

CHAPTER 9

Monica found me standing on the pier—a miraculous discovery in the growing crowd of onlookers and rescue workers. She took my elbow and guided me to the parking lot. There, Truman's sister Leilani was leaning against her red Honda with her hands pressed against her face.

"Where's Tru? Is he okay?" Leilani asked, taking the dive bag from my hands.

Monica shook her head.

Leilani paused before asking, "Where is he?"

Monica shook her head again.

Leilani whispered, "They can't find him?"

"No."

"So what now?"

Monica shrugged. "Don't know." She pointed at the piece of paper in my left hand. "They gave her an accident report but I guess that's it."

There was no hospital to rush to. No morgue to visit. Truman was just . . . gone.

Leilani's eyes shimmered with tears, and she threw a worried glance toward the ocean, and then at her brother's dive bag. "So we go home?"

Monica took her hand. "You okay?"

Leilani considered Monica for a moment, then said, "No." She hugged the bag to her chest and dropped her head. "No."

The accident report crumpled in my clutch as I gazed past my friends, past the vast sea of Fords, Toyotas, and rescue trucks. I couldn't move—blood slogged through my veins like heavy, clotted cream. Thunder boomed from the approaching storm, and the explosion kicked me out of my daze. "I don't remember where I parked the car."

"Nic," Monica said, "you shouldn't drive. And Lei, you shouldn't drive, either."

Clear-eyed now, Leilani tugged at the red string around her wrist. "I'm fine. I'm okay."

"I'll drive Truman's car," Monica said. "Gary and I will come back later for Nic's."

Monica loaded me into the Honda, and the leather seats chilled my back. The cold made me remember. "I peed in my pants."

Leilani didn't speak as she pulled out of the parking lot.

"I'm sitting in your nice leather seats, and I peed in my pants."

Leilani glanced at me with eyes red from crying. "I don't care. Pee again if you have to."

I gazed at my engagement ring—an oval-cut diamond embraced by ruby and sapphire side stones. Truman and I had been sitting on the Hollywood Bowl lawn when he slipped the ring on my finger. *I want to spend the rest of my life with you, Nicole.* The philharmonic played "America the Beautiful" as red, white, and blue fireworks burst in the skies above the city . . .

The heavy rain didn't keep other cars from speeding past us. After all, refrigerators needed cleaning, clothes needed laundering, and floors needed mopping. Strong winds forced rain to fall sideways like drying bedsheets caught in a draft. A miniature river coursed down Rockcliff Drive, and clumps of pine needles, plastic grocery bags, and wads of paper blocked the sewer grates. With no available sewers, and no other methods of escape, the foamy sea of debris flooded onto the sidewalks.

Leilani parked in front of my house as Monica drove past to park Truman's car in the driveway. I climbed out of the car—the rain soaked my bare arms and hair within seconds. We plodded across the flagstone pathway toward the front door. A vase of white Casablanca lilies, almost fluorescent beneath that sky, sat on the porch.

Monica ran to join us. "This rain is crazy."

I stopped in my step and turned to her. "They made a mistake."

"Who made a mistake?" Leilani asked.

"Flex," I said. "The search team. The coast guard makes mistakes all the time." I lifted my face to the rain, and closed my eyes. "Remember those Mexican fishermen? Everyone said they were dead since they had been lost for months. But they were alive, remember?" I considered my friends and nodded. "And Truman's alive. He's smart and he's strong and he'll be found just like those Mexican fishermen."

Leilani's face darkened, and she turned away from me.

"Nic, hon," Monica said. "That's not . . . Truman wasn't on a fishing boat. He was . . ." She sighed, surrendering for now.

In the bedroom, Monica watched me undress. She leaned against the sink as I showered.

"I'm okay, Mo," I said, stepping out of the shower. "You don't have to hover."

She nodded, then handed me a towel and a T-shirt and boxers to wear. Without a word, she followed me back into the bedroom.

The vase of lilies now sat on my nightstand.

"Where's Lei?" I asked.

"On the couch in the downstairs den," Monica said. "She's not doing well. She's threatening to light up a joint, but she doesn't want you freaking out."

"Tell her that I don't care. She can do whatever she needs to do . . . Remember the last time you did this?"

"Acted like a fretful mother?" Monica shook her head.

"Senior year. The night we crossed and finally became sorority sisters. I drank too much tequila. Threw up in your Celica."

Monica pulled a vial from her pocket.

"What's that?" I asked.

"Valium," she said. "I found it over on the vanity. You should rest."

"I need to stay awake. So I can drive back to the dock as soon as they call."

"As soon as *who* calls?"

"The coast guard."

"You shouldn't do anything right now except sleep." Monica shook out a Valium, then offered it to me.

I took the pill, and stared at its rounded perfection in my palm.

"Here." She handed me a glass of water.

"Can you see if the phone works?"

Monica picked up the cordless from the nightstand and punched TALK: a dial tone.

"Wake me up when they call," I said.

Frustration flickered across Monica's face, then softened into sorrow.

I placed the pill beneath my tongue. Didn't need water because my mouth filled with tears and spit. "I don't care what he says. No more extreme sports. I can't take it anymore."

Monica nodded.

I reached into the bouquet of lilies and found a small card stuck in its plastic pitchfork.

Babe, you're better than a million Everests. I love you. Truman.

I lay back in the pillows, the card still clutched in my hand.

Monica clicked off the lamp, and the room fell into darkness. "I'll be down the hall," she said.

Better than a million Everests.

A sharp explosion blasted against the house, and the windowpanes shuddered. I sat up in bed, yanked from a deep, Valium-induced sleep. The card that came with the lilies was now pulp in my palm, and I placed its remains on the nightstand. Another explosion started low, gaining enough strength to force another blast across the sky. The bedroom brightened with lightning, and thick drops of rain pounded harder against the windowpanes and the patio.

Truman, hidden beneath the comforter, was sleeping right through the storm. Didn't he hear all this madness?

"Honey?" I whispered. "Wake up."

"What?" he grumbled. "It's late, babe. It's rain, not acid."

I clicked on the lamp, then turned back to him.

The bed was empty.

He had just spoken to me. Heard him as clear as I heard the storm.

Confused, I climbed out of bed, and tiptoed out of the bedroom. The hallway was empty, and the upstairs security panel glowed green in the darkness. He hadn't armed the alarm. I crept down the cold corridor, long and unfamiliar in this storm, at this hour. I glanced behind me—the cupola's windowpane was bright with rain. Another flash of icy lightning made me jump, and I waited until thunder rumbled past.

I crept to the guest bedroom on my right and peeked in. Stacks of boxes. Shadows. The damp stink of stale cigarettes.

I passed Truman's home office on my left. Empty.

I continued down the hallway, nearing the upstairs den.

"I knew that going up there . . ."

I stopped in my step and cocked my head.

Truman was talking.

"Almost two hundred people had bit it on this mountain."

Who is he talking to?

Maybe he had called Keith or Manny at the office to tell them about his strange, jacked-up day.

"I'm standing there anyway," Truman was saying, "looking at this wall of ice—"

I reached the den's doorway, and poked my head in. A blue blanket spilled off the arm of the couch to the floor. The lamp burned on the computer desk, and the television played video of Truman at Mount Everest's base camp. "And I kept thinking," Video Truman said, "will I be a trivia question? You know: How many climbers died on Everest this year?" He glanced at the snowy peak behind him and shook his head. "Seeing Nic again . . . That's what's driving me."

"Truman?" I whispered. "You in here?"

"Hey."

Monica popped up from the couch.

I shrieked, surprised at seeing her there.

"It's the DVD," Monica said, aiming the remote control at the television. "Sorry for scaring you."

"I forgot you were here," I said, catching my breath. "Where's Lei?"

"Sleeping downstairs in the living room. What's wrong?"

"I was just looking for Tru. The storm's making me a little jumpy."

Monica's eyes narrowed, and she whispered, "Truman isn't here, remember?"

"He *is* here. I saw him. He was in bed just a minute ago."

Monica stared at me, then said, "What you're experiencing is normal."

I saw something strange and sad in Monica's ashen face. "What am I experiencing?"

"Maybe you're seeing Truman because you need to believe that he made it out of the ocean. That he's still . . ."

"Still what?"

Monica swallowed, then bit her lip. "Nothing's changed, Nic. I'm so sorry."

"Why are you apologizing? Where is—"

Flex's phone call at the market.

The frantic drive to San Pedro.

The coast guard chopper racing north beneath a battleship gray sky.

Truman's dive bag . . .

"No," I said. "I just *saw* him. I woke him up and he complained, and . . . and . . ."

It's rain, not acid. That's what he had said.

I lurched out of the den, ran past his office and the guest room, and rushed into my bedroom.

Only my side of the bed was rumpled.

I had insisted on buying this bed. A California king with sixty yards of space for video gaming, reading, and lovemaking. It had appropriated two-thirds of our old bedroom.

"It's big," Truman had said.

"Huge," I said, smiling.

Truman grabbed me from behind, and threw me onto the mattress. "I'll miss you. You'll be on the other side of the world."

"China," I said.

"The east side of the South Pole."

Then, we wrestled and crawled to the head of the bed. I nestled in the crook of his arm like a kitten, and told him that he was being dramatic. That I planned to snuggle and cuddle and terrorize him with my chronically cold feet forever. It would be just as it was in our full-size bed but better. Nothing would change.

But in less than a year, everything had changed.

I clicked off the lamp and the bedroom fell back into darkness. I slipped beneath the comforter and pulled Truman's pillow to my chest. Gazed at that empty space, and waited for the magic of medicine to dull my pain, to send me back to those Sunday mornings with snuggling, video games, and sunshine. Still clutching his pillow, I rolled over and stared at the rain-soaked windowpanes, at silver raindrops zigzagging down the glass in unpredictable paths. Beyond those panes, only darkness existed. Past that darkness, nothing at all.

I slid out of bed again, grabbed my own pillow and the comforter. I couldn't sleep in a California king, not without my husband, so I settled on the chaise lounge.

Thunder rumbled, lightning flashed, and weird shadows—lagoon monsters and forest trolls—twisted on the walls.

I kicked away the comforter and slipped back to the nightstand. Groped in the darkness until I found the television's remote control. With one push of a button, *Roseanne* popped on. No longer alone. I sank back onto the chaise, remote in hand, the bedroom now bright with man-made light.

PART II

CHAPTER 1

I pulled open the church's heavy double doors. The vestibule bustled with children and old people, with women kissing cheeks, and men slapping backs. Organ music—"How Great Thou Art"—played over the PA system. As I weaved through the crowd, the smells from my childhood washed over me: White Shoulders perfume and Old Spice cologne, veggie meat in gravy and spearmint gum, lemon-scented furniture polish and fresh-cut flowers.

Not the Four Seasons vacation I had envisioned just a week ago. A three-day getaway I had canceled two hours before dressing for church. The hotel's customer service rep had asked, "Do you wish to reschedule?" I said, "Maybe later," then ended the call without saying goodbye.

Sister Cornelia Claypool and Sister Helen Easter gasped when they saw me navigating through the crowds. Other women joined them and waited their turn to pull me into long, tight hugs.

Don't you look pretty in yellow!

Child, we're so happy to see you.

I was just thinking about your aunt Beryl the other day.

Where's that fine husband of yours?

I sighed, and said, "Well . . ." And then, I told them about my fine husband.

On the day after the accident, Flex had called his friends at an ocean survey firm in San Diego. Engineers at Bayside Technologics, Inc. had used sonar and an underwater robot to scour and search the ocean floor near Catalina Island. They looked for three days, and despite all the software and hardware within their grasp, as well as the teams of oceanographers and divers on payroll, Bayside Technologies could not find my husband.

The sisters' smiles vanished as they listened to my story. Then, they offered encouragement.

God is in control.

The Lord has a plan.

He will make a way out of no way.

After more hugs and kisses, an usher in a smart black suit led me to a center pew. A church elder welcomed guests, and then we all sang the opening hymn.

Fairest Lord Jesus,

Ruler of all nature . . .

Offering came, and I slipped a check into the velvet bag. Not as a bribe . . . Yeah, as a bribe, but I had to do *something*, even though you can't influence the Lord with a $250 kickback.

As I slipped my checkbook back into my purse, I noticed a crumpled sheet of paper had fought its way to the surface. *Incident Report. Victim: Truman S. Baxter. Incident Type: Drowning . . .* That day at the pier, I had stuffed the document into my purse and had forgotten about it until now. Now, I studied it until tears smeared my vision, then I crammed it back into my purse's basement.

After a musical selection from the choir, another elder stood in the pulpit. "And He said, 'Come unto me all ye that labor and I will give you rest.' Let us come before the Lord in prayer."

I glanced at my watch: 12:37. In my former life, I was supposed to be lightheaded from sipping too many mimosas and Bloody Marys. I was supposed to be wrapped in a towel, sprawled across a padded table as a Four Seasons masseuse worked the kinks from my shoulders . . .

As the congregation clambered onto their knees, the organist played the first bar of "Have Thine Own Way, Lord." A bevy of older ladies surrounded me and soon began muttering, "Yes, Lord," and "Please,

Father." The elder thanked God for another blessed day, for putting food on the table, for giving us shelter and sanity. And after listing each thing we should all be thankful for, he asked the Lord to heal the wounded and brokenhearted, to protect the youth from gangs and drugs, to comfort the widows . . .

As he pled with God to return to this sinful Earth and deliver us all, I hid my face in my hands, and whispered my own prayer:

Please find him, Lord. Let him be alive. He has so much to do. I know I've haven't been the best wife, and forgive me of those sins, of those secrets. Nothing lasts forever, but I love him, Lord, and I ask that you give us one more chance to spend our lives together. Please.

The women did not leave my side after the elder said, "Amen." Sister Claypool sat on my right and held my hand. Sister Easter sat on my left and whispered that I must remain strong and faithful. Another woman (she owned the largest Bible I've ever seen) passed me a freshly starched handkerchief while others offered me sweets. I ate more peppermint candies on that Sabbath than I had my entire life.

Services ended a little past one o'clock, and I drove home, stronger than how I had come. At that moment, I *was* stronger, ready to handle the upcoming week. God would answer my prayer. As the sun dropped behind my house, and as the Sabbath ended, that strength vanished. My realization that God could say "no" sharpened in the darkness.

As a child, people told me all the time that I would move past my parents' death. That if I prayed hard enough, the pain would ease and would eventually go away. "You didn't even know them," Aunt Beryl had said in my most melancholy moments. "You were only three. You can't remember them enough to miss them. Life is hard, Nicole. You gotta be tougher than this."

It was easy to be strong being surrounded by beautifully sung hymns and prayer warriors in fancy hats and pristine gloves, when gazing upon stained glass Jesus at Gethsemane above the altar reminding me that He had been crucified so that I may live. It was easy to have faith and believe that it was gonna be all right, that He'd never give me more than I could handle, that all things were possible—even surviving a scuba diving accident and leaving the ocean without brain and heart damage. At home, though, another reality punched me in the face. *Truman was gone and I'd never see him again.* And I cried that night, and didn't eat dinner, and wished that it were me instead of him.

Was that being "all right"? Was that "handling" anything?

CHAPTER 2

I sat with my supervisor Jennifer in the VP of marketing's bright corner office. Stared out the office window and watched as other CelluTech employees bustled across the campus. They were laughing as they walked, enjoying the sunshine and the cornflower blue sky—two Los Angeles poseurs on a day like today. Why couldn't the weather reflect my mood? A sky the color of puke and blizzards, and humidity that pushed against eyeballs until they burst like smashed grapes.

Jennifer was scribbling on the legal pad she had brought with her, waiting for the conversation to continue. Jennifer, with her perfect blond bob, perfect breasts, and wrinkle-free Banana Republic skirt sets of every color . . . She wore enough perfume for all of CelluTech. At the end of the day, every one of us had smelled of Ysatis. Truman probably thought I had been having an affair with another woman.

I gazed at the artwork on Tharren O'Shea's walls—blown-up images of T-cells and lymphoma cells wrestling for control, test tubes holding fluorescent, life-saving drug therapies.

Tharren twisted in his chair, and stared at me. His wide, green eyes showed no signs of understanding my decision to take a leave of absence six days after my husband's accident.

What couldn't he understand? What was so hard to grasp?

Why would I want to be in the office from nine to five, consumed with lesser things—*who used my coffee creamer without asking?*—when my husband was in the *g.d. Pacific Ocean*? So I wouldn't get compensated after my vacation and sick time ran out. Didn't care. And poverty didn't scare me. Aunt Beryl had worked in a languishing health food store, and in the rough times, had often bought our groceries with food stamps.

If there was a time *not* to work, losing your husband to the *sea* was one of them.

Truman and I had done everything together. Going to the movies and taking trips to Best Buy and Big 5, to Vegas and Santa Barbara. He'd call me at work every day at noon to ask about my morning, and I'd call him from home every evening to ask what he wanted to eat. He'd always say, "You," and I'd always laugh and blush and give him what he wanted: enchiladas and me.

He had been the Auntie Mame in my world. *Life is a banquet. Do some good here and there, but stay for the awesome entertainment.* And he had married me, an anxious and reluctant woman with storm cloud tendencies, who had been left in a compromised mental state long before he and I met.

Losing someone is like burning your hand on a hot stove. At first, your skin is numb because the brain is acting as a protector, telling the body that all is well. But all isn't well. There's nerve damage, painful blisters, swelling . . . As that icy numbness wears off, your injuries are laid bare to the world, prone to infection, and the searing pain that comes with recovery seems unbearable . . .

Tharren's mouth moved, but I only heard my heart *thumpthumpthump.* What was he saying to me? *Nicole, it's not that bad? Truman will come back? What about that endocrinology report?*

Didn't care. I twisted the rings on my fingers and remembered: Truman's clothes were in the laundry hamper. What was I supposed to do with them? Wash them? Let them stay there until he returned? And what about the shirts that needed dry cleaning? Should I take them or . . . ?

Jennifer's face hid in shadow, framed by the copper morning sun. Her bright pink lips floated in midair as she said, "Nicole," then waggled my knee. "Hey. Nic."

I snapped out of my fugue, and said, "The timing of this isn't the best, especially with the annual report coming up. And I haven't even started writing the intro for that yet." I swiped at my cheek—my fingers were wet with tears. I did that a lot now. Crying without knowing.

Jennifer touched my knee again. "Don't worry about that."

I gazed down at my blouse—I had missed a button. And I wore a navy blue suit jacket with black trousers. *At least I'm wearing matching . . .* I glanced at my feet: a brown left loafer and a black right loafer.

I offered Jennifer a weak smile, then said, "I just need time to figure everything out. To focus on . . . To be honest, I don't know what I should do. But I can come in part-time to get some things off the deck . . ." I paused, aware of the unintended pun.

Tharren said, "That's not necessary, Nicole. In three months, you'll come back, and you'll, umm . . . Truman was . . . is . . . a great guy and . . ." He cleared his throat, then turned to Jennifer. "Give Peter the annual report. Give the new girl, what's-her-face—"

"Bridget?" Jennifer said.

"Yeah, her," Tharren said. "Give her the molecular immuno-therapy piece."

As Jennifer and Tharren reassigned my workload to other teammates, my breathing quickened. The runaway train in my mind gained speed, and I closed my eyes and forced myself to run ahead of it, to pass the engine, to race ahead of the grill. Soon, the train grew smaller behind me . . . smaller . . . so small that I could no longer see it. Safe again, I exhaled, and opened my eyes.

Tharren and Jennifer were staring at me.

I cleared my throat, and whispered, "I'm okay. It's just . . ." *Hysteria.* I forced myself to smile. "Bridget will be good. She really knows the CelluTech voice."

"Great." Tharren stood from his chair. "We'll be thinking about you, Nic. Let us know if you need anything, okay?" To Jennifer, he said, "Stay a moment."

I didn't say anything else as I trudged out of that office. I didn't stop in my step until I reached my car.

CHAPTER 3

Asphalt retarring on the Sepulveda Pass made my drive back to Beachwood Canyon more treacherous than usual. I didn't think of anything as I, along with three lanes' worth of cars, crammed into one lane. I pressed the brake when lights blinked red. Pressed the gas when lights blinked green. My skin burned and itched as though I had rolled on a carpet made from potato chips and smoldering wool. My head hurt, and my stomach growled since I had forgotten to eat breakfast. *Again.*

On Rockcliff Drive, a car had hit a possum, and now, the animal's bloody gray corpse was melting into the concrete. I drove past the mess, smelling the creature's death as I drove up the hill to my house. *Poor possum. Couldn't get out of Death's way.*

No one stood on the front porch.

Maybe tomorrow.

Each time I came home, my heart pounded with hope and expectation. Because maybe this time, Truman would be standing at the door, waiting for me. He would smile sheepishly, and say, "Can't find my keys." He could never find his keys. Or his phone. Or his eye drops.

A man wearing red sweats and a Led Zeppelin T-shirt darted in front of me as I pulled in front of my house. A chocolate Labrador retriever bounded by his side without a leash, but stopped in its trot once I climbed out of my car and rushed to the porch. The Lab stared at me with unblinking dark eyes—*you almost hit us*—then, he growled.

Anxious, I aimed my key in the vicinity of the lock and missed.

Up ahead, the jogger shouted, "Come, Max!"

The dog glanced at its master, looked back at me, then raced up the hill.

I saw that Jake Huston's living room windows burned bright with light—he was home. Since the accident, he had left countless voicemail, email, and text messages on my home and mobile phones.

Call me, Nic. I'm—

Hey, Nic. I'm—

If you need—

I never listened or read his messages in their entirety. Didn't really care what he had to say. So I deleted them, and refused to return his calls.

Undaunted, Jake had knocked on my door a few times.

But I never answered. I'd stand in the foyer, my arms pinned to my sides, mere feet away from him, willing him to just leave me alone, wishing that we had never met.

I shoved the key in the lock and pushed open the door.

The house was cool. Dark. Quiet.

Truman used to shout, "Hey, babe," when he'd come home. He'd find me on the couch in the upstairs den, or cooking dinner in the kitchen. He'd kiss my forehead three times, retreat to his office to connect his phone to its charger, then return to my side to talk about our day.

Nothing happened now. No one kissed me. No one called me babe.

I leaned against the closed front door and slowly exhaled, exhausted by the day.

Something thumped against the floor.

I reached for the doorknob, tempted to walk back out and not stop until I reached the Sunset Marquis and its twenty-four-hour staff. Hand on the knob and holding my breath, I said, "Hello?"

Silence.

I shouted, "Truman?" then cocked my head to listen.

The low thrum of the refrigerator. My own staggered breathing.

The living room furniture hid in the dim light. The telephone sat on the coffee table. Its antenna blinked red—a message. The telephone had become my constant companion. If I sat, I placed the phone on my lap like a Pomeranian. If I showered, I lay the phone on the counter within reach. Each time it rang (and it wasn't Jake calling), I'd say "Hello" with the hope that Truman was calling to say, "You'll never guess what happened to me."

But that hadn't happened. Yet.

I flipped the foyer's switch, and light filled the small space. That day's mail lay scattered beneath the mail slot while five days' worth sat on the small wood table. Magazines, credit card offers, bills, not-opened greeting cards that offered comfort and consolation. What would a card say? Did Hallmark publish limbo cards? *Best wishes for finding out about your situation so you can know and then deal.*

A flat box the size of a child's blanket leaned against the wall. It held a mandala brocade that Truman had purchased in Tibet. Wherever he traveled, he would bring back arts and crafts. Teddy bear paintings from Paris, a framed *mola* from Panama, a pan flute from Peru. "For Little Trumanita, whenever she comes," he'd say. Each piece sat in the guest room, waiting to be displayed in our future daughter's bedroom.

I grabbed the telephone from the coffee table and returned to the foyer. Called a number I now knew by heart. "Flex, it's Nicole."

Flex paused, then said, "Hello, darlin'."

"Did you all go out today?"

"No, we didn't."

"Are you giving up?"

"Of course we're not."

"Could he still be alive?"

He let out a long sigh.

I knew his answer—I asked him these same questions every day—then swallowed nervously. "Thanks, Flex. I'll talk to you later."

Newspapers towered in a separate pile on the foyer floor. Heavier than mail, I had kicked them to the side, opening only one with a headline that had captured my attention. Network Executive Missing After Dive Presumed Dead. Despite that word—*dead*—my future with Truman remained undetermined. "Presumed" offered hope. "Presumed" offered possibility. And I held on to that word like gold.

Since Truman's accident, time passed in muddy slices of silence. I'd sit on the chaise in the bedroom, on the couch in the living room, or in the kitchen until the light changed in that room, until the telephone rang and brought me back to the present. I avoided Truman's spaces—the state-of-the-art den downstairs and his home office upstairs. Each time I neared the closed doors to either room, my skin prickled, my mind clicked as though God had installed a Geiger counter near my heart.

Sometimes, I'd forget my life's new circumstances, and I'd call the house or Truman's office without remembering. Truman would tell me to leave a message, and promise to call back as soon as possible.

Sometimes, I would stumble across a random thing—a tub of half-empty Cherry Garcia in the freezer or a Post-it note filled with Truman's scribbling in the bedroom—and I'd stare at that thing, for hours it seemed. Even though Truman wasn't there in the house, he was still *there*, in the house.

CHAPTER 4

Monica had kept me company since the night Truman didn't come home. We ate (or Monica ate and I watched her eat) and she'd jabber about the celebrity host who had fallen off the wagon and had cursed out her staff, of the ridiculous demands of her richest clients, about old college friends she had found on Facebook. I would smile on cue, offer grunts, "oh reallys" and "wows" but my focus would remain on the phone: willing it to ring with news of Truman's return from the coral beds of Farnsworth Banks. Monica would go home close to midnight, leaving behind Tupperware filled with spaghetti, chicken, or chili. She was my Food Fairy.

And just as she had every night, she set out cartons of food on the coffee table. "Hope you feel like Thai again."

Leilani flounced through the front door. "I was on a call," she announced, slamming the door behind her. She wore a tight black skirt set with her latest acquisitions—DD breast implants—draped in black crepe. Dressed for Mourning.

She was the total opposite of her brother. After graduation, she had moved back into her parents' home with the plan to earn a master's in social work. At home, her ambition quickly waned. Tuna casserole and Salisbury steak dinners became her kryptonite. With her parents' support, she quit her jobs as an administrative assistant at Universal Music, as a management trainee at MetLife, and as the assistant secretary at her family's old church.

Men—Truman, too—often took care of Leilani's needs so she never had reason to hold a job even if it sucked. Her latest caretaker was a guy named Jonathan, one of her kinda-boyfriends-but-something-no-one-could-figure-out. Neither Monica nor I knew much about Jonathan. Not his last name. Not his educational background. Leilani had told us that he was a born-again Christian who read his Bible during breaks (breaks from what, we didn't know). But Jonathan's eyes, always red and rheumy, testified to worship of another spirit.

Truman hated Jonathan, a man who had never worked a sixty-hour work week in his life. A man who lived off a settlement against Food-4-Less, and thought that his ill-gained wealth (we're convinced that he had staged his fall) made him worth anything. Leilani thought different. Jonathan was her type: a pretty boy with wavy hair, hazel eyes, and access to every controlled substance snorted, smoked, or shot up in the Northern Hemisphere.

Leilani plopped on the couch next to me and brushed her bronzed cheek against mine. "I talked to Flex today. He said that you two had your daily call." She slipped off her sunglasses and dropped them into her giant Balenciaga bag.

"He didn't tell me anything new," I said.

"The case is closed, Nic," Leilani said. "That's why he has nothing to say."

The police department didn't conduct a criminal investigation surrounding Truman's accident. They had easily determined he had drowned, that we weren't scamming the system to collect insurance money, and that we weren't trying to dodge the IRS. Two days after the accident, Harvey Feldman, our estate attorney, petitioned the courts on my behalf. With no body or signs of foul play, a probate judge declared Truman Baxter "presumed dead," and at ten o'clock on that morning, I officially became a widow.

Harvey had called me after the ruling with a lift in his voice, as though I had reason to celebrate. I thanked him for his help and hung up. A courier dropped off a large manila envelope stuffed to capacity.

Harvey had written the note clipped to a thick sheath of legal papers. *Don't know if you have the latest . . .*

I had never liked discussing wills, estates, and life insurance with Truman. The thought of him dying made me shudder, made my brain freeze. But once he started climbing up and jumping off things, I had no choice.

Early in our marriage, Truman and I had enjoyed hiking the trails in Griffith Park. On Sunday mornings, we would set out with the sun high above us in a cloudless sky. Hawks searching for food drifted on invisible waves while lizards sunned themselves on rocks. At the top of Mount Hollywood, we'd enjoy the 360-degree view of Los Angeles. We'd share bottles of water and granola bars. We'd kiss, talk, swat at dragonflies and bees.

Truman became bored with the park, with those trails and that view. He wanted to tackle something more challenging. Something more vertical.

I had joined Truman on his earlier excursions to lesser mountains and to tourist trap caves—not to climb or spelunk beside him, but to enjoy a novel, the hotel, and the hotel spa. I stopped tagging along before his first true cave exploration to Moaning Cavern, where the Centers for Disease Control had just alerted spelunkers to an outbreak of bat rabies. Truman left without me, and promised to run from the first bat he saw.

Days before his ascent up Mount Whitney—his first "real" mountain—I had read a news article about a climber who had slipped off Whitney's slope and had fallen to his death. Truman and I had a great argument that night, awesome entertainment for our neighbors. In the end, he promised to turn around if the climb got too rough. But he didn't turn around, even after he had broken two fingers and cracked a rib.

I stopped fighting him on this—each adventure he took spoke to his unwavering determination, and each journey symbolized the Black Man's Struggle. He had something to prove—to the world, to himself. Moaning Cavern would be his last spelunk, and Mount Whitney would be his last climb, then we'd return to Griffith Park and watch the sun set over the Pacific.

But Mount Kilimanjaro followed (19,340 feet high *and* in Tanzania), and then a larger, more dangerous cave in Peru. We took fewer vacations together since he allocated most of his salary and off-time to climb, crawl, and jump.

"Not only is all of this expensive," I complained, "it's also dangerous. You can get infected with something, or break another rib or . . . You could *die,* Truman. What would you do then?"

"Nothing," he said. "I'd be dead." He smiled and squeezed my hand. "If I wanna climb the ladder at work, I gotta do more than play company softball. It's what *they* do, Nic, and if I'm with *them,* I'm right there when *they* decide to hand out promotions. We were about to jump off that bridge near San Luis Obispo when Keith offered me the EVP slot, remember?"

"I understand the importance of networking and schmoozing," I said, "but *we* shouldn't hang from bridges since *they* just stopped hanging *us* from trees."

Truman rolled his eyes.

"Since 1922, more than 200 climbers had met their fates on Everest."

He cocked an eyebrow. "Did you do some googling to prepare for this argument?"

"Yes, I did. You're a numbers guy. And I've read *Into Thin Air* four times."

He sighed. "You're right. It is dangerous. I'll be more careful. Speaking of Everest—"

"Don't even . . . Get it out of your . . . No. No way."

"Just hear me out, Nic. You won't believe the idea I had."

And I didn't.

For a year, a camera crew would follow a quartet of FSNers (including Truman) as they prepared for a climb up Mount Everest. Then, they would telecast the climbers' attempt to summit.

He grinned. "What do you think?"

I crossed my arms, fixed my jaw and said nothing.

Truman's bosses loved the plan.

Climbing made him happy, though, and I knew that he would scale Everest without my support. I also knew that he'd be distracted by my disapproval. And being distracted meant missing a step, neglecting to check oxygen . . .

Crap.

To show my support, I jogged beside him as he prepared his lungs and legs for the climb. And a month before the trip, I presented him with a gift wrapped trash bag.

"What's this?" he asked, poking the bag.

I shrugged and smiled. "Open it."

He peered at me for a moment, then glanced at the bag again.

"It's not a bomb," I said. "Open it before I change my mind."

He tore away the paper to find a down parka and a down sleeping bag. He gawked at me.

I swiped at my tear-filled eyes. "I don't want your important bits getting frostbitten up on the highest mountain in the world."

Truman left for Nepal on the first of May. I didn't sleep much in anticipation of late-night or early-morning phone calls that would announce either his death or his decision to turn back. I hated the telephone now. Its ring pinballed and echoed throughout our cavernous house, striking bare walls and Mexican tile floors, only stopping once I answered—another reminder that I lived there alone until my husband, God willing, returned to the States.

Fear (of robbers, of rapists, of everything) also kept me awake. Since we were anti-gun, Truman had bought a twenty-two-inch machete as a weapon, and while he was away, I slept with it beneath the mattress. The television played all night, and every light in the house burned bright, and I never (not once) watched news stories about young women being raped, stabbed, and murdered in parking lots, in their garages, in their beds.

I checked into the Sunset Marquis on nights when the wind shrieked beneath the house's eaves and the neighborhood dogs barked nonstop, and I glimpsed phantoms out of the corner of my eye everywhere I turned. Once, Truman had arranged to have a strawberry cheesecake and a bottle of champagne delivered to my room. The message on the dessert plate: *Sweets not shrieks. Luv u. T.*

On his tenth day away, I found a Post-it note he had slipped into my day planner before leaving the country. *Damn, it's cold up here w/o U. Tru.*

I thought about him constantly. During meetings. While taking showers. And I scrutinized every entry Truman's team posted on the network's website.

> Tuesday. Hitting base camp today. In great spirits. Never been so cold in my life.

> Wednesday. A Dutch climber had to turn back. Pneumonia.

And I read Truman's entry more times than I could count.

> Hey, everybody. It's Friday, and we're resting at Camp Two. Weather's good. Besides a few aches, doing great and have begun prep for the Big Push. Heading up to Camp 3 tomorrow (fingers crossed) and then, to summit. Check in tomorrow as we start up the hill. I love you, Nicole!

> Peace and we're out!

Truman Baxter at Camp 2

Was that true? Was the weather right for the ascent? And aches? What kind of aches? Was he following directions? Would he turn back if the team leader told him to?

Seven climbers died that season, but Truman reached Everest's peak, only suffering from a frostbitten pinky toe.

Before his return, I stocked the refrigerator with Ben & Jerry's, brie, and pounds of green apples—his favorite foods. I even drove to Costco—a store I hate more than sin—to buy a crate of Red Vines because he loved licorice. And because I loved him.

He returned to the States two weeks later, emboldened by his success, convinced of his immortality. He reminisced about the cold and the coughing, and the sound of tents flapping in thin wind. He remembered the thrill of it all, and he told me that he would return to Everest, and then, he would climb Denali, where nighttime temperatures dropped to forty degrees below.

I ignored the pad see ew Monica had dumped on my plate, and nibbled instead on a spring roll. Monica and Leilani talked and kept me in the conversation with *Can you believe that?* and *Remember him?* I would say, "Oh yeah," and "No way," not really listening.

But then, the time came and Monica retrieved the thick envelope my attorney had sent.

"Nic, I can't believe that you didn't call Harvey earlier about this," Leilani said. "You don't know when you're going back to work. You have bills and expenses you don't even know about yet. You need that money to live."

"Yeah," I said near tears. Then, I reached for the red string tied around her left wrist. "So what's this for?"

Leilani slapped my hand away. "Don't change the subject. And it's a Red String."

I offered a tiny smile. "I see that it's red and that it's a string."

"Ain't that a Kabbalah whatchamajig?" Monica asked.

"Yeah," Leilani said.

"So what's it for?" Monica asked.

"It protects me from the evil eye," Leilani said in all seriousness. "Other people's negativity can keep me from realizing my full potential. There's some other stuff about Rachel the matriarch but . . ." She shrugged. "I don't know all that much about it. Way too much stuff to read. And then they want you to go to all these classes and crap . . ."

"Amazing that you actually tied the string *around* your wrist," I said. "Seems easier if you would've just kept it in your cheek."

"Ain't all this Jewish?" Monica asked.

Leilani nodded as she plucked a spring roll from the carton.

"But you believe in Jesus," I said.

"Minor detail," Leilani said.

"Our Lord and Savior is a minor detail?" I asked, eyebrows lifted. "Is this the same woman who told me back in college that I was going to hell cuz I listened to Prince and wore jeans, and that this was a Christian country and we Americans shouldn't have to learn anything about Ramadan or listen to some heathen rant about some false god that lives in some rice paddy in the jungles of East Asia?"

"Lei, you did say all of that," Monica said.

"I'm an adult now," Leilani said. "And I believe in what I wanna believe in." Then, she turned to me, and added, "Maybe if you wore one of these, you wouldn't need to pop Paxil and Valium."

Monica smirked. "So this Red String is helping you with your . . . you know?" She sniffed with exaggeration, then swiped at her nose.

"That's for recreational use," Leilani explained. "Not for psychological issues. And I don't need drugs to function. I can stop whenever I want."

Monica rolled her eyes. "Spoken like a true cokehead."

"Stop saying things like that," Leilani said. "It demeans us all. Are you gonna read the will or are we just gonna sit here and mock my religion?"

"Yeah, Mo," I said. "Stop mockin' and lollygagging, will ya?"

"Fine." Monica pulled out the documents and began. *"I, Truman Shepard Baxter, a resident of Los Angeles, California, hereby make this Will . . ."*

He had left me both cars, audiovisual equipment, stock in FOX, Disney, and Microsoft, three insurance policies totaling a little under $950,000, liquid cash assets totaling a little over $275,000, and his 401(k) and IRA accounts. He had willed Leilani $30,000.

Leilani, eyes bulging, whispered, "Wow."

Monica turned to her, and said, "Guess you should call Harvey."

Leilani crossed her arms. "But I'll only inherit that if I find a full-time job," she said. "Truman must be losing his mind if he thinks . . . *Full*-time? My people were freed one hundred years ago." She flapped her hands near her face to cool down, then took a deep cleansing breath. "It's okay. I'm fine. Money makes people lose perspective." Perspective? She wore Dior, a perfume she couldn't afford until Jonathan's slip in Sauces and Condiments.

"Welcome to the real world, my dear." Monica glanced at me, and said, "You're not talking."

I shook my head—there was nothing to say.

Monica and Leilani went back and forth about beneficiaries and work, Truman, and the ocean. But I found interest in the tiny gray spider skittering across the face of the *New Yorker*.

Leilani grabbed her shoes from the floor. "It's Flex's fault that he's dead. Maybe we should sue him for wrongful death or something."

Blood drained from my face, and my skin turned cold and immobile as marble. "Flex is his friend."

"*Friend?* Flex was the professional on that boat," Leilani said, pointing her stiletto at me. "He should've known Truman wasn't ready to go down there. He should've put him with somebody more experienced, not with that bitch who got him killed." And then she ranted about Flex's irresponsibility, more about Truman not being on that boat in the first place, and *something something something*.

I didn't have the energy to defend Flex. Hell, I didn't even know if I *wanted* to defend Flex. Because maybe Leilani was right. Maybe all of this *was* his fault.

Before leaving, my friends cleared away the food and placed cartons filled with leftovers in the refrigerator. They offered kisses, hugs, and promises to call me the next morning, then they hopped into Monica's Range Rover.

"I'll call you when I get home," Monica shouted out the window.

I waved goodbye as the truck pulled away from the curb.

Alone again, I leaned against the front door. "What now?" My reflection in the foyer's mirror appeared fuzzy, as though God's thumb had smeared my edges.

Maybe I should stay in the foyer tonight. Why leave? Leave and do what? Shower? For whom? Watch television? And talk about it with the air? Sleep, eat, shit: That's all I did, and sometimes I forgot to do all three.

I thought of the John Denver song "Some Days Are Diamonds (Some Days Are Stone)." I forced a smile to my face, and avoided looking at my smudged reflection. *When Truman comes home, I'll make every day diamond.*

Then, I grabbed the mandala from Tibet and made my way upstairs.

CHAPTER 5

I stood at the dresser in my bedroom. Lingerie—mostly lacy things—had spilled from the open drawer. I had been pawing through the heap, searching for a pair of cotton briefs when I found a blue box. The Clearblue Easy pregnancy test.

Light-light blue because the pregnancy hormones in my body were dying.

The telephone rang, a cannon in the quiet.

Startled, I fumbled the box, and rushed down the hallway to the den and found the phone on the computer desk.

"Hope I didn't wake you." It was Monica.

I settled onto the couch and muted the television's volume. "Nope. Still awake."

"Just wanted to check on you," Monica said. "I'll let you get some sleep."

"Thanks for everything today. You're making this less painful than what it could be."

Monica told me to call her if I needed anything. "If you want, I'll drive back over and I'll sleep there."

I thanked her, but refused the offer. "I'm cool."

"I'll call you in the morning," she promised.

I tossed the phone to the foot of the couch and turned on the television.

Seinfeld.

JFK Jr. at Elaine's gym.

I lay there, waiting for sleep to come, with my protective machete beneath the couch cushion. I did this every night now: watch reruns of *Taxi* and *I Love Lucy*, *Cheers* and *Futurama*, no longer able to watch films like *Seven* and *Alien*, thrillers I had loved before life changed.

Maybe something's wrong with you. Maybe you have insomnia or something neurological and dangerous.

"Nothing's wrong," I muttered as I shifted on the cushions.

How do you know? Are you a doctor?

I kicked away the blanket and settled at the computer a few steps away. After a quick Google search—sleep disorder—I clicked on IWant2Go2Sleep.com and took the site's sleep deprivation quiz:

I wish I had more energy. Yes.

I anticipate a problem with sleep several times a week. Yes.

I often feel like I am in a daze. Yes.

I have dreams soon after falling asleep or taking naps. Uh-huh.

I clicked the last box to calculate my sleep score: symptoms of insomnia, sleep apnea, and narcolepsy.

How the hell could I be an insomniac-narcoleptic?

Get an evaluation from your physician, the site suggested.

No, thanks. Because *eventually*, I'd *have* to fall asleep, right? The longest someone has stayed awake is eleven days. I'd be asleep long before then.

I padded to the bathroom. Chugged a capful of NyQuil, then popped a Valium even though the pill had lost its potency. I returned to the den, and settled back on the couch. The midnight episode of *Home Improvement* flickered on the television screen.

The house creaked and settled into the earth. A strange, cool draft brushed across my face. My eyelids fluttered . . .

"Nicole."

My eyes popped open, and I glanced across the den.

Truman sat in the chair at the computer desk.

I shrieked, then hid my face in the pillow. After catching my breath, I peeked at the man who had been missing for a week.

Water drenched Truman's khaki shorts, making them tree-bark brown. His face glowed silver from the television's light. Swipes of blood stained his wet Body Glove T-shirt. Drops of water plinked off the tips of his bent elbows and plopped onto the floor. Ocean sand muddied his Vans and the hardwood floor, making the den smell like late-night cemetery.

My face flushed, and heat spread like brush fire across my cheeks. I forced myself to breathe slowly, but my head wobbled—moments away from fainting. I stuck my hand beneath the couch cushion and my fingers grazed the blade of the machete.

This is impossible. It can't be . . . Is it . . . ?

Truman leaned forward and exhaled. His breath smelled of seaweed and fish. A clump of sand thudded to the floor, and water dripped from his shorts on top of it to make mud. He stared at me with eyes lighter than before. Seawater beaded in his hair, and trickled down his forehead into those unblinking, strange-colored eyes.

"Truman," I whispered, "is that you?"

He said nothing.

A nervous breakdown—that's what this was. I knew this like I knew my name. And this obvious collapse had led me to hear and see strange, impossible things. And it made my heart beat too hard and too fast, causing the room to seesaw.

I closed my eyes and waited for the world to right itself, waiting for impossible things to cease.

A breeze brushed against my cheek.

I opened my eyes.

Truman had abandoned the desk.

I hopped up from the couch. *Where did he go?*

Home Improvement flickered on the TV screen. The red numbers on the clock said 3:16.

My mouth filled with spit and bile, and the back of my throat closed. I stood there with rubbery knees, unsure of what to do.

A door slammed.

Someone's here. Oh crap. Someone's here.

Another breeze drifted through the den, bringing with it the scent of citrus.

I sniffed—Truman's cologne.

My feet freed themselves, and I tiptoed to the couch and pulled the machete from the cushions. The rubber grip was notched—better to hold in my sweaty, uncertain clutch. The steel blade was clean and sharp, and glistened in the dim light. I had watched Truman swing it through the fronds of our neighbor's creeping banana palm. Effortless and uncompromising in its execution. He had grinned back at me, and had said, "It's the weapon of choice for guerrillas."

And for insomniac-narcoleptic court-mandated widows, too.

I slipped to the door and glanced up and down the corridor—empty. I crept down the hallway, sniffing like a bloodhound until I stood before my bedroom's closed door.

Wasn't this open?

I twisted the doorknob and pushed open the door. Flipped on the light switch, and the lamps on both nightstands popped on.

There he was. In bed. Hidden beneath the comforter.

The room was cold and damp, like a window had been left open during a winter storm.

I inched toward the bed, tapping the machete against my calf as I watched the sleeping figure beneath the comforter.

If this was Truman, why didn't he wake me? He knew that I had been worrying. That I was terrified. He wouldn't just stare at me, would he? Leave to take a shower, then climb into bed without saying "hello"?

I'm sleepwalking. It's the Valium and NyQuil cocktail . . .

"What, babe?" Truman asked.

I yelped, nicking my shin with the blade. I scrambled back to the door, panting as I waited there, wincing from the cut on my leg.

Breathless, I hit the light switch, and the bed fell back into darkness. I hurried to the end of the hallway to check the security panel—still armed—then rushed back up to the den, to the couch and the television.

I saw him. Truman in wet clothes at the desk. Truman in bed. He called me babe.

I stuck the machete beneath the couch, then grabbed a discarded sock to blot the pebbles of blood on my calf.

How is any of this possible?

Pills. Exhaustion. Nausea and hunger. Loneliness and uncertainty. Migraine, aneurysm, neuroblastoma . . .

How do I know I'm okay?

My mind reached for certainties.

Abraham Lincoln was the sixteenth president of the United States.

A square has four sides.

J.R.R. Tolkien wrote The Hobbit.

S-U-P-E-R-C-A-L-I-F-R-A-G-I-L-I-S-T-I-C-E-X-P-E-A-L-I-D-O-C-I-O-U-S.

If I were crazy, if my brain was, indeed, dying, I wouldn't have been able to recall any of this, right? *Right?*

As dawn crept through the curtains, I sat rigid on the couch, asking myself questions, grasping at mental touchstones—*Mick Jagger sings lead for the Rolling Stones*—to ensure my sanity, to guarantee normal brain function. The phone rang twice, but I didn't answer it either time. Could only do one thing—*Bismarck is the capital of North Dakota.* Outside, a leaf blower droned—I needed to pay the gardener. I couldn't remember how much. Couldn't write a check in my condition. Didn't even know where I had left my checkbook.

At 8:30, the den glowed with sunlight the color of flames.

I Love Lucy.

My eyes burned and my muscles ached. I stood from the couch and stretched. I sniffed the air—couldn't smell Truman's cologne. No one sat at the computer desk and chair. The hardwood floor was shiny and dry. Out in the hallway, golden light spilled through the cupola's window, and dust motes danced in the sunbeams. My dream of Truman's visit (it *had* been a dream after all) dissipated in the light, and as I stood in my bedroom doorway, my fears now seemed puny and irrational.

The bed was empty. The linens were neat and tucked.

I nodded—*yes, a dream*—then wandered back to the den and to my space on the couch.

Lucy and Ethel were stealing John Wayne's footprints from Grauman's Chinese Theatre.

The phone rang again. *Out of Area, Out of Area.* I ignored the ringing as Lucy tried to pry her foot from a bucket of quick-drying cement. I had seen this episode hundreds of times, knew it by heart, didn't have to watch to know what would happen next. My eyelids fluttered and my mind drifted toward sleep.

Beep . . . Beep . . . Beep . . .

The alarm.

One beep, then silence. The floorboards creaked.

Wide awake again, I pulled the machete from beneath the cushion and hid in front of the couch, listening to those footsteps come closer . . . closer . . . My clammy palms clutched the machete's handle. I shivered, fear chewing at my calm like termites through wood.

The footsteps stopped outside the doorway. And then, the intruder stepped into the den.

One . . . two . . . three . . .

I erupted from the floor with a scream, with the machete held high over my head.

Leilani screamed, too, and dropped a paper bag covered with grease splotches.

"Oh crap!" I fumbled my weapon, surprised and relieved to see my friend. "I'm so sorry."

Weak-kneed, Leilani scooped the bag from the floor with shaking hands. "If you don't want pastrami, just say so."

"I'm sorry," I said and took the bag from her. "I didn't know it was you."

Leilani, dressed in a micromini, a baby T-shirt, and red stilettos (you know, what most women wear on Thursday mornings), turned off the television and fell onto the couch. "What the hell are you doing with a cleaver anyway, and why aren't you answering the phone? I've been calling you all morning."

"It's a machete," I said, "and it's for protection. And I didn't answer the phone because Lucy had just met John Wayne." I took a big bite from the pastrami sandwich, then asked, "Did I leave the front door unlocked?"

Leilani shook her head. "I was scared that something had happened to you, so I used my key."

"Key?" I asked with a full mouth. "Since when do you have a key to my house?"

"Since always."

"And who told you the code to disarm the alarm? Truman?"

Leilani nodded. "When you guys moved in, remember? For emergencies. Like today."

I grunted, remembering a scene about something with some people millions of years ago.

She scanned the messy room: half-empty mugs of tea, discarded tissues, a bloody sock, and abandoned sweatpants. "Looks like a homeless shelter in here."

Before the accident, our upstairs den had been as neat as a minister's robe. Books organized by fiction and nonfiction, author and genre. A seventy-inch television sitting atop a cabinet that stored a DVD library as organized as the books. Remote controls in a wicker basket, and magazines—current issues with no perfume samples or subscription cards hanging from the pages—fanned across the oak coffee table.

In a week, that same room had devolved into an overstuffed junk box with an extraordinary view of clutter. Every day, I vowed to clean up my mess, but I'd watch reruns of sitcoms and talk shows until nightfall. Too late in the day for chores, I'd pushed the piles to the side of the room. Like a five-layer bean dip, shoes sat beneath towels, which sat beneath sweats, cups, and discarded tissues.

"Do you even know what day it is?" Leilani asked.

"Thursday," I said, chewing. "The gardener came."

"He forgot to yank the weeds from your hair," Leilani countered. "So: What's the plan for the day?"

"Finish this sandwich, then watch old episodes of *Maury*."

"We should go shopping," she said. "There's a sale at Fred Segal. Then, we can have lunch. Get out of the house and hang out. And we should do something for the Fourth of July tomorrow. Fireworks at the Hollywood Bowl."

"Don't feel like it," I said.

She peered at me in silence, then said, "I miss him, too, Nic."

I nodded, then nibbled a shred of meat.

"How are you doing?" she asked. "Really?"

"I'm popping Valium like PEZ. And I'm watching more episodes of *Home Improvement* than should be allowed, and . . ." *And Truman. I saw Truman.* My appetite vanished, and I held out the rest of the sandwich to my sister-in-law. "Want the rest of this?"

Leilani grimaced. *Girlfriend, that's* food.

I stuffed the last third of the pastrami back into the bag. "I haven't slept well all week. At first, the Valium let me sleep on and off, but now? Nothing. I haven't slept for more than—"

Leilani's cell phone chimed "Havah Nagila." She popped it open, and read the message. "It's about a job."

I said, "Answer it before they change their mind," and then stood from the couch.

She sent her thumbs flying across the phone's tiny keypad. "Sorry, Nic. One . . . moment."

I wandered down the stairs and out onto the deck. Summer sun had blistered the parched canyon, drying the wild grass into a crispy brown. Gusts of warm wind kicked up dust and shook apart chaparral, worrying every fire crew in the city. I eyed the hillside with concern. A brush fire—that's the last thing Los Angeles needed.

"Sorry about that," Leilani said, stepping out from the house. "You'll be glad to know that I have an interview at . . ." She squinted at the sun and plopped into a deck chair. "Damn, it's bright out here." She reached into her bag and found her sunglasses. "If you don't wanna shop, let's see a movie. Something fun and escapist."

I turned to her, wanting to speak but unable to.

"What?" she asked.

"I saw Truman."

She waited a moment, then narrowed her eyes. "Was that a joke? Cuz I don't get it."

I frowned: What had I expected her to say? "I saw him last night. This morning. Whenever. At least I think I saw him. It was weird."

She hesitated as shadows darkened her face. "And? Then what?"

"And then he left."

"This ain't funny, Nic."

"I'm not trying to be funny. I just . . ."

Something in Leilani's expression shifted—don't know what it was—and she slipped on her sunglasses.

"I know it sounds crazy," I said, sitting next to her, "but I'm telling you the truth. He was sitting at the computer in the den. So close I could touch him. I smelled his breath, his cologne. And then I saw him in our bed. And the covers were moving like he was sleeping and breathing, and I know what you're thinking, but he was there, and . . . and . . ."

Leilani chuckled and shook her head. "In the bed. Truman was in the . . . It wasn't just a crumpled-up blanket or something? Or Robert Downey Jr.?"

"Lei, I'm serious. You haven't . . . ? You haven't seen him? You haven't witnessed anything strange? Something that you can't explain?"

Leilani stared at me behind those sunglasses and said nothing.

I shrugged, and said, "Who's to say that he's . . . you know?"

"The judge says that he's . . . you know."

"But we have no proof that he's . . ."

"No such things as ghosts," she said, shaking her head. "I'm the crazy one. You're the smart one. You're supposed to know better."

"So what did I see?"

"Nicole, I don't know what you saw," she said, her voice cracking with tears. "You're not the same woman you used to be, you know? I'm not, either, and it hurts to even talk about this."

We didn't speak for a long time. I gazed out at the canyon, my mind still processing all that I had experienced hours before. Leilani swiped at teardrops tumbling down her cheek. She leaned back in the chair, and tilted her face to the sky.

"I'm sorry," I finally said. "I just thought . . . You're my friend, and I don't know what I saw . . . or imagined . . . or . . ."

"Have you told Mo about any of this?"

"About seeing Truman?" I shook my head, then blushed. "I don't want her to think that I've lost my mind. You're family, and I'd know you'd understand."

Leilani nodded, then took a deep cleansing breath. "I wasn't sleeping well, either. *But!*" She reached inside her purse and pulled out a business card. "I found a solution, and I'm gonna share it with you cuz you're so damn special to me." She forced a fragile smile to her face and handed me the card. "Dr. Lucas will hook. You. Up. Swear."

"I'm already on Valium."

"Guess what? It ain't working. You need rest, Nic. Obviously."

"I'm not imagining this."

"So you believe in ghosts now?"

"But he's not a ghost," I said, awed that I had uttered any of this aloud. "He's not a ghost. He's alive. He's . . ."

He had *looked* real. He had *smelled* real. But all of this was impossible, and now, all of this sounded outrageous. And my inability to determine real from imagined supported my earlier conclusions: My sanity had been shipped to Jesus, or to the saints, or to whoever owned the rights of Reason.

"You won't say anything to Mo?" I asked.

"You'll go to the doctor?" Leilani asked. "And we'll go shopping today? And to lunch and a movie?"

I nodded "yes" to everything. "And we'll find a fireworks show tomorrow, but not at the Bowl."

Didn't have the strength to return to the place where Truman had proposed to me.

"If you'll do all that, then . . ." She tightened her lips, made a zipping motion across her mouth, and tossed the imaginary key behind her.

CHAPTER 6

I stumbled into the house an hour before midnight, slightly tipsy after drinking bottle after bottle of Smirnoff Ice with Leilani and Monica on the *Queen Mary*'s lawn. When we weren't drinking, we had gazed at the sky like the hundreds who sat with us, awed by the soaring pyrotechnics symbolizing our country's battle for freedom. When we weren't drinking and gazing, we cried—our first Fourth of July without Truman. The three of us toasted him with our malt beverages until the fiery climax of red, white, and blue ended, and the sky boasted only smoke and helicopter lights.

The antennae on the telephone blinked red: a voicemail message left on July 3.

Hi, Nicole. This is Tami, the manager of Human Resources at FOX Sports. I hope you're doing better. We certainly miss Truman. We're in the middle of a reorg right now, and with everything the way it is, we've had to move ahead and . . . We're gonna need the space, and we were hoping that you could come down sometime and, you know . . . If you can't right now, we totally understand, and I can get someone else to—

I deleted the message without hearing the rest.

To the sober part of me, Tami's voicemail made sense. The network was a business, not a charity home for missing executives. With sweeps on the horizon, and the new fall season and ratings to consider, the higher-ups had to move on without him. I only resented that they wanted me to come into the office and help them do it.

The drunken widow in me, however, cursed out Tami and those sons-of-bitches at FOX for moving on after just nine days—*not even two weeks!*—and for giving his office—*his office!*—to some other guy who wasn't as smart or as handsome as Truman. How could they have hired someone so damn quick? Was this jerk waiting in the office supply closet, résumé and briefcase in hand? Bastards.

I wandered to the dining room and stood before the wine cabinet. Sixteen bottles nested in wooden cubbies. Each had come from exotic wineries around the world. I had selected two: a dessert wine from Volcano Winery in Hawaii, and a rare California Viognier that tasted like bliss. Truman had found the other wines on his adventures taken without me. His two favorites were the Shiraz he picked up in India en route to Everest, and a Merlot he discovered at a winery in Chile after a cave tour.

I pulled the Merlot from its hole, and plucked the corkscrew from the sideboard's drawer.

Truman had postponed opening this bottle. *For a special occasion,* he had told me.

Was this occasion special enough? I stuck the corkscrew into the cork and twisted.

The cork wouldn't budge.

I gritted my teeth and pulled harder. No luck.

Truman had always opened the wine. It seemed so easy—stick the thing in, twist, pull.

I tugged at the corkscrew handle again. This time, the cork twisted, but didn't lift. I pulled again—nothing—and once more. Ashes of anger filled my belly with each tug. One more pull, one more failure, and I hurled the bottle with strength I didn't know I had. It exploded against the wall, and red wine sloshed down its surface, a purple Rorschach blot on ecru paint. Shards of glass glimmered on the hardwood floor, and the aroma of ripened berries and crushed grapes filled the air.

Damn it, Truman.

Even before the dive, I had prayed every night that he would make it home safely, that some LAPD hotshot with a grudge against successful Black men wouldn't make an example out of him. Any time the police helicopter soared above our neighborhood with that damn bright searchlight invading hillsides and driveways, I had lain in bed, terrified, imagining Truman's face pressed against the asphalt, guns trained on his head.

And he had survived this city—the cops, the gangs, the freeways—only to perish in the damned *ocean*?

Why didn't he stop and think?

Why did he have to be a hero?

Damn it, Truman.

After picking up wedges of glass, I pulled on a jacket, and grabbed my car keys from the breakfast bar. I pulled at the porch door to exit, but the door wouldn't open. I turned the lock, then unlocked it again, and pulled harder at the knob. The door opened with a *whoomf*, and sent me stumbling backward.

That door had never stuck before. It was the house. It was pissed that I had vandalized its precious dining room wall.

Explosions from forbidden firecrackers boomed throughout the canyon. Bursts of purple, green, and gold exploded over rooftops and hillsides. In the middle of my street, teenage boys on skateboards vaulted over an object shooting white sparks from its belly. A kid with blond locs shouted, "Happy Bastille Day" as I drove past.

Not many people wandered the aisles of the village market. A couple of potheads stared into the deli fridge of cheese, and an old woman in a pink rain bonnet roamed Frozen Foods. I clutched a shopping basket and peered back at the millions of drug labels winking at me from their shelves. Natalie Cole's weak alto warbled from the store's speakers. "Miss You Like Crazy." Appropriate. I dumped four bottles of NyQuil and two boxes of Excedrin into the basket. I trudged two aisles over, and grabbed a box of Sleepytime tea, then headed to the checkout counter.

Arnib, the cashier on duty, was reading the *Los Angeles Times*. He adjusted his glasses and his Uncle Sam–style top hat. "Happy Fourth of July," he said as he slipped the newspaper behind the cash register. "You're in here pretty late. You usually come in around six."

I stared at him and said nothing.

"You go to the Bowl to see the fireworks tonight?"

I grunted.

Embarrassed, Arnib's chubby cheeks cranberried. He busied himself with his scanner gun and my bottles of NyQuil. "Not feeling well, huh?"

"Can't sleep," I mumbled.

"It's so loud out there. I thought firecrackers were illegal in Los Angeles. My poor dog's probably hiding beneath the bed." He stopped scanning and looked up at me. "You should try Tylenol PM. NyQuil's good, but it leaves you groggy. Hungover." He pointed to the pyramid of Tylenol boxes at the end of the counter. "We have 'em on sale. Buy two for seven dollars."

I glanced at the boxes—the sign displayed there said, SALE, BUY 2 FOR $7.

"Want them?"

I shrugged.

Arnib grabbed two boxes, scanned them, then tossed them into the bag. "How's your friend doing?"

I blinked, then said, "Which friend?"

"Mr. Huston. I see you two together all the time. Here. At the coffee shop next door. How's he doing?"

"Fine, I guess."

"He's handling all the craziness okay?"

My lips tightened into a thin slash, and I lost all feeling in my chin.

"You read the paper, right?" Arnib reached behind the register for the *Times*. "He's about to be suspended by the bar," he said, handing me the California section. "I didn't know he was a gang lawyer. He seemed so . . . I don't know. *Honest.* Guess you just don't know people."

I looked away from Arnib's fleshy purple lips to read the article:

Lawyer for Mexican Mafia Member Possibly Violates
Ethics Code

Jacob Huston, a partner at the powerful law firm
Tighe & Johns, may have violated ethics laws in defense of his client, Gustavo Hernandez. Hernandez,
23, an alleged member of the notorious Mexican
Mafia, was arrested last December for the kidnapping
and murder of 12-year old Luis Argueta. Argueta's
body has yet to be found, and Hernandez denies any
involvement in the kidnapping and death of the missing honor roll student.

"I just want closure," Avemaria Argueta said. "This
suffering is too much. My son was innocent. Just a
baby. How can that attorney defend those monsters?"

The Los Angeles District Attorney has not publicized
the well-regarded lawyer's alleged violations. An anon-
ymous source, however, recently spoke to the *Times*.
"This is a serious and troubling matter. Once the dust
settles, Mr. Huston may be disbarred."

When contacted by the *Times*, Huston offered
no comment.

Jake represented the effin' Mexican Mafia? In the last year, this
prison gang had racked up countless charges on drug trafficking,
money laundering, and murders. Everything they did—breathing,
even—was criminal.

I shook my head. There had to be more to this. Maybe Jake had
been forced somehow to get involved, and . . . Jake defended homeless
people and starlets with sticky fingers. Petty thugs caught up in unjust

Three Strikes cases. Not . . . *these* people. He wasn't Tom Hagen in *The Godfather*. But then, Tom Hagen seemed pretty nice, too. Jake and I had our personal issues, but I'd let him defend me any day. He was a great attorney. Smart. *Ethical.* The State wouldn't disbar him. He was a good guy.

"You can keep it," Arnib said. "Geez, you've been through a lot lately, huh? First, your husband, and now, your friend's . . . problems."

I muttered, "Yeah," and then, "How much?"

He glanced at the register's display. "Forty dollars and seven cents."

I found the bank card in my wallet, and with a trembling hand, swiped it through the debit machine.

A receipt spilled from the register, and Arnib tore it away and handed it to me. "The Tylenol's gonna work for you," he said with a smile. "Promise."

I'm chasing Truman across a field of poppies. The sky darkens, and I stop in my step. Truman's disappeared, but a wine-colored blob is oozing my way. I turn and run. I reach the harbor, no longer in the poppy field. The ocean undulates before me. I glance over my shoulder—the blob gains speed, oozes just a few feet behind. I run down the dock, tripping over jutting planks. I reach the end of the pier—nowhere to go. "I can't swim," I tell the blob. But the blob continues to creep, and I take a step back and—

I awakened from that nightmare sweaty and breathless. I swiped at my runny nose and glanced at my fingers. Mucus and blood smeared my fingertips. Did I give myself a hematoma? Was my brain bleeding?

Go to the doctor, Nic.

I kicked away the comforter but refused to stand. The thought of showering, dressing, leaving the house, and climbing behind the wheel again made me weary. I couldn't make a grilled cheese sandwich, I hadn't showered in days, and now, my brain was possibly bleeding, and still, I couldn't *do* anything. My energies had been expended during my tantrum in the dining room and my visit to the market's drug buffet.

I twisted tissue into my bleeding nostril, then lay back on the couch with my eyes focused on the television screen. My breathing slowed, and my eyelids grew heavy, but each time I grabbed at the promise of sleep, it moved just a little out of my reach. On the television, a commercial for *Wicked* flickered on the screen. *No one mourns the wicked.* Clips of Elphaba and Glinda, flying monkeys and . . .

What was that?

I glanced around the room. Living room couch. Carpet. Den. I glanced at the clock—almost midnight. *Growing Pains* on the television set. Bloody tissues scattered across the blanket.

What was . . . ?

A bump or a scrape or . . .

I cocked my head to listen.

Silence.

I pushed aside the blanket and bloody tissues and grabbed the machete from beneath the cushions. I tiptoed out of the den, and crept down the hallway.

The red light on the security panel shone. *Alarm armed.*

I stopped in my step.

That Tibetan mandala brocade Truman had brought back from his Everest trip? The same brocade I had deposited into the guest bedroom just a day ago? It hung next to the security panel. Wide-eyed, I stood there, trying to remember when I had done this.

Yesterday? After I . . . after I did . . . something? Or this morning?

I tapped the machete against my leg. *Had to be yesterday.* I nodded, then continued down the hallway and down the stairs, pausing every few feet to listen.

The kitchen glowed with moonlight until I flicked the light switch. Dishes were piled high in the sink. The icemaker rumbled, and ice cubes crashed into the freezer's tray. I placed the machete on the counter, grabbed a mug from the cabinet, and scurried to the refrigerator.

Light crackles blue when I dream of you
Love rockets fly twirl soar
You light my sky with languid magic

My last message to Truman . . . A message he never saw.

I squinted at those words until I could no longer see them. With closed eyes, I reached for the door handle and pulled. I grabbed the carton of orange juice, making sure to turn away before those words returned. *You light my sky with languid magic.* I poured myself a glass of juice, then guzzled it. Poured another glass, and drank half. *Maybe I hung the mandala while Lei was here and I just forgot that I did.* I placed my cup in the sink, and glimpsed a shadow near the driveway.

The hairs on my body stiffened. "Who's there?" I shouted.

Maybe it's a raccoon.

A raccoon shaped like a person?

Something rustled through fallen dry leaves.

I grabbed the machete from the counter, and crept toward the door.

Footsteps . . . Running . . .

I dropped to my knees. The machete fumbled from my hands and clattered to the tile. I crawled to the door and peeked out the window: the Volvo, the BMW, and darkness.

I opened the door—the cold air shocked me, made my heart beat faster. I looked up the hill. Didn't see anyone. As I inched back to the kitchen, a light popped on in the darkness.

Jake's house.

CHAPTER 7

Keith Ensby, FSN's executive vice president of marketing, stopped in his step once he realized that I was the haggard woman sitting on the lobby couch. He grinned to hide his shock and wrapped his arms around me. "Nicole, you look . . ." He paused, then said, "I'm so glad to see you."

My hair lived in a nappy bun. Dark circles couched my eyes. My face had puffed from not enough sleep and salty fast food. I wore deodorant; that is, if I remembered to use it, and on this morning, I couldn't remember if I had or not. I had spent a half hour trying to look *this* good.

Keith, on the other hand, resembled a middle-aged Robert Redford. Martha's Vineyard–handsome, towheaded, and cocky. And despite his wife's fears, he also threw himself off cliffs and pulled himself up mountains. He had missed the diving trip to Farnsworth Banks because of conjunctivitis he had caught from his four-year-old daughter Bella. He had forced the network to pay for that high-tech sea search for Truman.

I trudged behind Keith as he strode through the main corridor. The nape of his neck was brilliant pink, sunburned from some recent adventure. All the gray strands in his blond hair meant that he was too old for climbing, jumping, and diving, and I wanted to scream, *Don't do this to your wife. Don't do this to Bella. Stop being a selfish prick. Look at me. Do you* see *me? You want Meredith to look like this?* But I didn't. Men don't listen.

Posters of sports greats hung on the walls, and live images of some guy in a Lakers jersey, some woman swinging on parallel bars, and some giant clutching a football played on monitors no one watched. The FSNers who knew me nodded their hellos or stared as I toddled past.

"We really miss him," Keith was saying as we marched through marketing. "Especially with this China expansion coming up."

As we got closer to Truman's office, my skin prickled—the same Geiger counter sensation I experienced near his spaces at home.

"Oh. I got HR to give Leilani a job interview," Keith told me. "Nothing big. An administrative assistant position down in royalties. But it's good pay. Great benefits."

"When does she start?" I asked.

"She never showed," Keith said. "The job was basically hers as long as she passed the background check like everyone else who works here, and agreed to mandatory drug testing."

I smirked. "She must've been excited about *that*."

"She sent me this rambling email about the Constitution, the Eighth Amendment, and religious liberties." He paused, then added, "Truman was too gentle with that girl."

"*Girl?* Lei's the same age as me."

Keith grimaced. "You serious?" He used his key card to unlock Truman's office door. "We keep it locked . . . You know how people are."

A person leaves and suddenly, their stuff is up for grabs. Chairs, electric staplers, metal mesh file holders . . . Coworkers pick at the office, leaving with their arms filled, pushing chairs loaded with Post-it note dispensers, dictionaries, and dry-erase boards until their ex-colleague's office is stripped as clean as a gazelle's skeleton in the Gobi.

Keith reached across the wall to hit the light switch. "No one's really been in here since . . ."

Ratings awards and commendations hung on the walls. An original Thrilla in Manila poster signed by Joe Frazier and Muhammad Ali hung on the south wall. On Truman's desk: an open bag of Doritos, an FSN mug with its bottom black from evaporated coffee, pictures of Truman and me, as well as pictures of him and Penelope dressed in climbing gear.

Penelope. She had died that day. She had panicked and rushed to the surface without decompressing.

Keith said, "I hate to ask you this, Nic, but I just can't accept that . . . I mean, the guy's a great athlete. Strong. Smart. Are they sure?"

"*They* are," I said. "Me? Not sure at all."

Keith nodded, then said, "I'll find some boxes."

I sat in Truman's high-backed chair, and surveyed everything before me: the ivory-handled letter opener, stale tortilla chips, calendar . . . His desk looked as though he had just stepped away to make a photocopy.

Another framed photograph sat at the edge of his desk. "Your Future Kid." Truman and I had posed for this snapshot eight years ago in one of those county fair photo stations. The booth's software had combined my picture with Truman's to produce a composite of our "daughter."

We had named her "Trumanita." She had Truman's pointy nose and my almond-shaped eyes. We had laughed at the mashed-up picture, called it tacky and strange. Days later, the photograph disappeared. Now, I knew where it had disappeared to.

In real life, our daughter would have inherited Truman's broad shoulders and my cheekbones. He would have sneaked her candy and cookies after I had told her "no." He would've taken her on horseback rides and to Lakers games. Bought her climbing boots and video games. Brushed her hair into Afro puffs, and rocked her back to sleep after nightmares.

"Someone in here?" Elene Givhan stood in the doorway. She gasped seeing me seated behind Truman's desk. "Oh. Hi," she said, forcing an uneasy smile to her lips. "I didn't know who . . ."

My nerves caught fire seeing this woman again. I wanted to fly across that desk and beat her down right then, but God kept me burning in that chair.

Elene swallowed nervously—she smelled danger, but she couldn't move. "I'm . . . I'm . . ."

"Close the door." Somehow, my fingers had wrapped around the letter opener.

Elene closed the door.

"Did you sleep with my husband?" I asked.

She twitched, and ran her fingers through her hair. "I don't think that's—"

I slammed my hand against the table, and shouted, "I don't care what you think."

Elene startled from my explosion, and she eyed the letter opener.

"Answer the question," I said, standing from the chair. "Did you or did you not have an affair with my husband?"

She continued to gape at the letter opener.

I tossed the weapon to the carpet and leaned against the desk with my arms crossed.

"I cared about him," she said. "That was it. Nothing happened between us."

I shook my head. "I don't believe you."

Defiant, she cocked her chin. "That's your problem, then."

"*Excuse* me?" I saw stars—my mind had become a piñata and her words were a thick stick being wielded by an eight-year-old boy. "Wanna say that again?" I asked, my hands clenched into fists.

Elene was at least five inches taller than me, but size didn't matter today. I had enough anger to destroy an entire village.

She squared her shoulders, and said, "You need to leave."

"You don't tell me what I need to do." I took a step forward and smelled her perfume. She wore a scent that smelled like bubblegum and roses—something obnoxiously named Flirt or Temptation.

"I'll call security," she said.

"Call security. I don't care. My husband is *missing*, bitch, you think I care about—"

The door opened. "What's going on in here?" Keith stood there, boxes in his arms.

My anger continued to grow, unabated by Keith's presence. But when he dropped the boxes to grip my arms, his cool fingers tamped down some of my fire. "Nicole," he whispered, "you're upset, and that's okay. But you can't . . . You shouldn't . . ." He turned to Elene. "Why the hell did you come in here?"

Elene dropped her eyes to the carpet, then opened her mouth to speak.

Keith pointed to the door. "Get out of here."

Elene nodded, then departed in steely silence.

CHAPTER 8

Keith agreed to messenger over the artwork, and asked if I wanted to sell the signed Frazier-Ali poster. "We'll give you $10,000 for it," he had offered as he helped me load the car.

"Not right now," I had said. "Because if he . . ."

Keith nodded. "I understand."

The sun had dropped behind the hills by the time I pulled into my driveway. Once inside, I struggled up and down the dark stairs with Truman's office boxes in my arms. I nudged the door open with my foot, and kept my eyes to the floor as I stowed his effects into the closest corner. Mission accomplished, I darted out, and retreated down the hallway. Felt sick. The kind of sick Aunt Beryl used to cure with saltines and ginger ale.

I crept past my empty bed, eyes on the comforter, and prayed that Truman wouldn't just . . . *appear* like a magician's assistant in a Vegas magic act.

I reached the bathroom.

No tricks. No ta-dahs.

I cringed at my reflection in the mirror. I had been pretty once upon a time, but over the last thirteen days, my beauty had evaporated like clouds on a hot, dry day; the old me—the well-coiffed, polished, and unwrinkled Nicole—had been stolen and replaced with a hollowed-out sleepwalker sharing the same name and the same DNA.

Did other court-mandated widows look like me?

I reached for the tap—

Whiskers in the sink.

Why are there whiskers in the . . . ?

Maybe they've always been there but you're just seeing them now.

I stared at those thick short hairs as though they were poisonous barbs.

Of course they've been here. He hasn't shaved since . . .

I hadn't paid much attention to my house's cleanliness, especially the bathroom. Hell, I rarely visited my bedroom. Who knew how long those hairs had been there.

I rinsed the bowl until no whiskers remained.

The bathroom light flickered. A second later, the light popped off.

I could no longer see the sink. I could no longer see my reflection. Couldn't see anything.

I crept back out to the bedroom.

No burning lamps. No glowing digital clock. The only light in the room came from the moon.

I inched to the den.

No little green and blue lights gleaming from the computer, the stereo, or the cable box. I stood there, feeling the prickly freak-out start in my toes and creep up my shins.

It's okay. It's just a blackout. It's okay. I held my breath and listened.

No whir from the computer fan. No low rumble from the refrigerator. No buzz from the television.

I tiptoed over to the window, the den's only source of illumination. Lights burned in the windows of my Cuban neighbors. The other houses on my side of the hill also had power.

I'm on a different grid, that's all.

Arms out before me, I inched out of the den to the hallway. The security panel glowed red, powered by its own mega-battery. Moonlight spilled through the beveled glass of the cupola window. The picture frames hanging on the walls shone, the faces in those photographs hidden in the light.

I glanced at the Tibetan mandala, still unable to remember hanging it there, then tromped down the stairs. I opened the front door, and stepped out onto the porch. Cool air washed over me. The brick felt cold beneath my feet, and vibrations rumbled from deep down in the earth to my soles. The air smelled sweet. Orange blossoms instead of sage. But there were no orange trees in the canyon.

The lights were on at Jake's house. Lights were on everywhere. No blackout. Just my house.

I stood there, confused and sleepy.

A dog barked and kicked me out of my trance. I raced to the sideboard and grabbed six candles and a book of matches. A sliver of glass left from my episode with the bottle of Chilean Merlot sank into the ball of my right foot, and I cursed as pain rippled up my shin.

I darted up the stairs, my right foot bloody, and reached the hallway out of breath, my knees like rubber bands.

In the den, I lit two candles and set them on the coffee table. I placed two on the computer desk, and two on top of the television. I perched on the couch and picked the glass from my foot, then sat mesmerized by the six points of golden light flickering all around me. Four black holes had swallowed the corners of the room as imp shadows danced on the ceiling. Another shadow waxed in that candlelight. A shadow that didn't belong to me or to the television or to the bookcases.

I smelled orange blossoms again, and saw him out of the corner of my eye.

Truman sat at the computer desk, watching me.

I turned to him, but refused to respond in word or in gesture. My body shook with strained fear and frustration.

He sat.

I waited.

He waited.

"What are you?" I whispered, not wanting an answer, not even sure I had spoken aloud. "Are you real?"

He blinked.

I covered my mouth with both hands. The room spun and that vibration returned, but in my teeth this time.

Golden points of light flickered in his eyes, and he said, "It hurts."

I shrieked, and my injured foot hit the coffee table. A candle toppled to the floor, and landed on top of my blanket. The blanket caught fire, and flames brightened the den.

I'm having a nightmare. This has to be a nightmare.

But the fire possessed heat; the light was too vivid for a dream. The hardwood floor warmed beneath my feet—this fire was real.

The smoke detector started its high-pitched beeping and if it didn't stop, the security company would call, then send fire trucks rumbling up to my house.

I jammed down the dark stairs, and raced into the kitchen. Beneath the sink, I found the small fire extinguisher Truman had bought just months before from a door-to-door salesman.

The alarm keypad in the foyer chimed, and a woman's voice said, "This is APX Control Center. Is everything okay there?"

I shouted, "Yeah, I just . . . burned some . . . popcorn."

"We're not getting a message from the kitchen's sensor," she pointed out. "It's the upstairs den."

"Well . . ." I shrugged. Had nothing else to tell her except the truth, and the APX Control Center wouldn't have been able to handle the truth.

"All right, then," she said with a sigh. "I need your safe word before I note this as a false alarm."

Safe word? My mind was too gooey to retrieve something so random. I stood there, trying to remember, then imagined my books in flames. "Apocalypse!"

The woman thanked me and disconnected.

I raced back up the stairs, tripping on the last two steps. The extinguisher flew out of my hands and clanked onto the hardwood. I grabbed it, and raced to the den.

Truman was gone, but the fire continued to burn, containing itself to the blanket and to the left side of the coffee table. I aimed the extinguisher at the mini inferno and saw nothing but white. My breathing tightened—less oxygen in the room because of flames and fire retardant. In less than a minute, I had killed the blaze. Nothing left except a charred, wet mess and a half-burned wooden table.

Monica couldn't speak. Her mouth didn't even move to attempt to speak. She could only stare at the mess captured in the flashlight's beam. "Is that *blood*?" She directed the light to crimson footprints marking the wooden floor.

"Maybe they turned off the power," I said, stating the obvious.

"Do you remember paying the bill?"

I shook my head—Truman had always paid the power company.

"You could've died in here, Nicole. Candles? In your state?"

"It was dark," I said, clutching my cell phone to my chest.

And my "state" didn't cause the fire. Seeing Truman—*that's* what caused the fire.

"Here." Monica handed me the flashlight and plucked the phone from my hand. "I can't believe this."

I sat there, hypnotized by the flecks of ashes swirling in the flashlight's beam. "I need a new blanket."

Monica handed me the phone. "It's the power company."

The woman on the other end said, "Address?"

I recited my address, then gritted my teeth.

"The name on the account is Truman Baxter," she said.

"Yes."

"This account's delinquent. May I please speak with Truman Baxter?"

"He's not here right now."

"When will he be back?"

"I don't know."

"Well, his name is on the—"

Trembling, I held the phone out to Monica. "She wants to speak to Truman."

Monica paused, then took the phone.

I lay on the couch, blanket-less, and listened as Monica explained to the customer service rep about the overdue bill and the lights.

May I please speak to Truman Baxter?

No. You can't.

CHAPTER 9

I sat at the breakfast bar staring at fire-colored fruit flies that buzzed over corpse-like bananas. I lifted my coffee cup, but didn't drink, hypnotized by the magnetic hovering of insects over old fruit. Any other time, I would've gleefully smashed those annoying buggers between my palms. Now, though, I needed all living creatures—flies, roaches, and possums—to exist and to be okay because maybe then Truman would be okay.

Monica had stayed with me overnight. She had wrapped my bloody foot in gauze, and had mopped the floors. By the time sunlight cracked across the canyon, the power to my house had been restored.

Leilani had only gawked at the den's damage before storming out of the room. And now, dressed in a micromini that showed her thong, she rummaged in the refrigerator.

Monica, buttering slices of toast, noticed Leilani's wardrobe malfunction, and raised an eyebrow. "Wow. You're wearing underwear."

"Yep," Leilani said. "I have an interview today."

"With who?" Monica asked.

"These people," Leilani said. "I don't know who. My girl Keisha hooked me up."

"Here you go." Monica slipped a plate of toast near my hands. "You need to eat." She returned to the sink, and squirted dishwashing liquid over the dirty cups and plates.

"She'll eat when she's ready," Leilani said. "When she's not burning shit up."

"It was an accident, Lei," I said, then nibbled the toast. "The candle fell over."

Monica watched me over her shoulder and nodded as I swallowed the bread and sipped from my coffee cup.

But the toast was making me nauseous. I dropped it back to the plate and hid my face with my hands. "I can't eat. I'm so tired."

"And I'm tired of you being tired," Leilani mumbled.

I glanced at her and saw no emotion in her expression. No softness. No glee. No sass. She had meant what she had just said. "Am I inconveniencing you somehow?" I snapped. "Keeping you from doing something productive, like finding a job?"

Monica said, "Nic, calm down."

"Want me to throw a Mardi Gras parade?" I asked my sister-in-law. "Or maybe I should drive us all down to Hooters for hot wings and beer? What am I supposed to be feeling right now, Leilani? You're smart. You're a rabbi or whatever now. Tell me how to stop *plotzing.*"

"I don't expect you to throw parties now that my brother's gone," Leilani said, "but your attitude is getting old. And now it's getting dangerous and you need to snap out of it."

"It's been two weeks," I said. "I'm doing the best I can."

Leilani rolled her eyes. "You're not *doing* anything. Everybody's doing everything—"

"Excuse me? *Everybody?* Have I asked *you* to do one damn thing for me?" I shouted. "Have *you* offered to deal with Flex or the coast guard or his coworkers or any of that? No, you haven't. You're only interested in going shopping and eating lunch and a bunch of other bullshit that I could care less about right now."

"You wanna know why?" Leilani asked, hands on her hips. "Because *I'm* dealing with the truth: Truman's dead. Case closed."

"That's your opinion."

"That's the state of California's opinion," Leilani retorted, tears in her eyes. "He's not coming back no matter how much I want him to. And you need to stop living in denial and move on as best as you can."

I grabbed my mug and limped to the coffee maker. "You obviously don't understand."

"*I* don't understand?" Leilani screeched, her eyes bugged in disbelief. "You think this has been easy for me? Truman taught me how to *walk*, damn it. I couldn't sleep in my bed at night without him until I was seven—"

"Stop, okay?" I said, closing my eyes. "I'm not interested in comparing my grief to yours—"

"I've accepted it," Leilani continued, her face red now, that vein (like Truman's) in her forehead hard against her skin. "But you're telling me that you can't? Your future doesn't include him, Nicole. He will never get into bed with you again no matter how many times you imagine him there. He will never sit at that computer in the den. He will never say one word to you again, and you wanna know why? Cuz he was acting stupid and he didn't listen and he drowned and no one was down there to save his ass."

I glared at her, offended and disgusted. "How can you say that? Are you *high*?"

Defiant, Leilani folded her arms. "Fine. Get mad at me since you can't scream at God or at Truman. I understand that you want to but you can't. And I know that right now, you're too screwed up to accept—"

"*I'm* screwed up? What about—?" I turned to the refrigerator and froze.

Light crackles blue when I dream of you . . .
You light my sky with languid magic.

I turned back to my sister-in-law. Opened my mouth to speak, but couldn't. The words on the refrigerator—my last message to Truman—had taken my breath away.

At ten o'clock in the morning, only retirees and stay-at-home moms with sticky-handed toddlers roamed the aisles of the village market. Without the crush of the rush hour crowd, they could nibble grapes, and chat in the middle of Toiletries at their leisure. Monica pushed the grocery cart through the Bread aisle and, like one of those toddlers, I followed behind her.

On the drive down, Monica and I hadn't talked about Leilani or our argument. She had only asked, "You saw Truman again?" And I had nodded as response.

I wanted to say so much to her—*thank you* and *I love you for doing this*—but if I talked, I'd start crying, burdening her even more. Didn't want that.

Being my mother-sister-friend as well as a business owner–girl-friend had exhausted Monica, and that fatigue showed in her face, in her gait, in each sigh. Immediately after Truman's accident, she had remained the manicured bar mitzvah queen in Dolce & Gabbana pantsuits, but two weeks later, the woman now selecting a loaf of sourdough had pimples on her forehead and chin and dark circles beneath her eyes. Her acrylic fingernails needed filling and polishing. Her dry lips needed moisturizer and lip gloss. She was starting to resemble me.

Leilani was right—my anger at God frightened me. Wasn't being angry at Him sinful and fundamentally wrong? And being mad at Truman—wouldn't that be blaming the victim? *If you, Truman, hadn't done x, y, and z, then* . . . Was it my parents' fault for driving in the rain that morning? Was it Aunt Beryl's fault that a gene had mutated in her body and cancerous cells took over her pancreas? I didn't blame them for dying.

But the circumstances surrounding Truman's accident differed from those of my kin. He had played an active role by going diving one Tuesday afternoon and never coming home.

Monica pushed the basket toward the floral shop. "Some fresh irises will cheer us up."

I wandered to Frozen Foods, and stood in front of the ice cream case. The linoleum was dry and polished. Of course, the store's janitor had mopped up after my accident. I gazed at the shelves of Ben & Jerry's. Cherry Garcia. Truman's favorite. My shoulders hunched as memories of that day returned. I closed my eyes and forced back the urge to scream, to break the case's glass and throw cartons of ice cream at the walls.

Breathe . . . Breathe . . .

The aromas of sunscreen and oranges, seaweed and ocean wafted down the aisle.

Truman's reflection gleamed in the freezer. He stood over me as he stared at the tubs of ice cream.

I didn't move. The air around me had chilled, and I closed my eyes again.

"Nic? You okay?"

Jake's reflection had replaced Truman's.

"I stopped by the other day," he said. "You didn't answer."

I took a step away from him.

He tilted his head, and his dark eyes narrowed. "Why are you ignoring me?"

"What do you want?" I asked.

"I just want to talk to you," he said. "I'm worried about you."

I shook my head and said, "Not right now."

"Why are you acting this way?"

I gawked at him. "Are you really asking me that, after all that's happened?"

He frowned. "I'm just asking you to pick up the phone when I call or open the door—"

I took another step away from him. "I can't do that right now. I know you care, but I can't . . ."

"Just give me five minutes," he said, reaching for my arm.

I twisted away from him, then darted down the aisle. I didn't look back as I escaped to Ethnic Foods to catch my breath.

CHAPTER 10

Nothing much had changed in the waiting room of Orleigh Tremaine Newman—A Whole Person Corporation. There were fewer stacks of paper on the credenzas, and Thai food aromas had replaced the smells of onions and french fries. Another group of patients sat in those seats—Wednesday morning regulars, I suppose, including a tight-lipped pale woman dressed in a pink velour sweat suit; a Black woman with long, gray French braids; and a willowy blonde staring into her cell phone.

Piper told me that I owed for two missed appointments. "You never called to cancel," she said.

I scowled at her as she processed my debit card.

Dr. Tremaine's eyes widened as I walked into her office. "Hello, there, stranger. I saw that you had changed your appointment time today, but I still didn't know if you'd show."

I shrugged. "Here I am."

She slid my folder before her and said, "Now, on our last visit—"

"On our last visit, my husband was alive," I blurted. "And now he's not." I paused. "Or he is. Or . . . I don't know."

Dr. Tremaine peered at me over the tops of her glasses.

"I guess I should start at the beginning."

She nodded, then sat back in her chair.

I told her about Truman's accident, about the search, about the probate judge, the wine, and the fire. Then, I added, "I think he's haunting me."

Dr. Tremaine chuckled and shook her head. "Don't be silly, Nicole. What you're experiencing—"

"Silly?" I screeched. "You're not very good at this, are you?"

She held out her hands, and said, "Oh, sweetie. I didn't mean—"

"I come here for help because I'm seeing and experiencing things that are freakin' terrifying and you tell me not to be *silly*? What the hell?"

"I didn't mean . . ." She sighed, then touched her temples. "I was careless to use that word, and I apologize. What I mean to say is this: You're mourning. It's easy to accept that and do nothing, but you've taken the opposite route. You've come here, which must have been difficult for you.

"First things first: Anger and grief are attached. You should never force yourself to only think so-called 'good' thoughts. *Never.* You are entitled to scream, to throw dishes, to *feel*. To see strange things that you can't explain. It's honest, it's healthy, and it's human. Shakespeare wrote, 'Give sorrow words. The grief that does not speak whispers the o'erfraught heart and bids it break.'

"Hallucinations," she continued, "and that's what I think you're having—are very normal after the death of a loved one."

I twisted my fingers, then whispered, "Maybe I'll stop having them if I sell the house, move somewhere else."

"But that won't lessen your pain," she said. "And you shouldn't do something as major as selling property right now. You've had enough of a life change and you don't need another one. If, in a few months, you feel the same, then go for it. But let some time pass first."

"I miss him," I said. "It's hard living there without him. Life's changed."

"Change can be painful, but it's not a bad thing. It's the only constant in this world." She leaned forward in her chair and smiled. "Life has a beginning and an ending. Everything in between those points shapes us, shapes our relationships. His death will help you figure out your own life's purpose. It will move you to live more meaningfully, allow you to reflect upon what matters most to you. I know this has all been stressful and over-whelming, but I'll help you through it."

I tugged at the ragged seam on my jeans. "When his parents died, he didn't know what to do. I'd find him sitting in a dark room, wanting to cry but unable to. He didn't want to see a therapist or talk to a minister or . . ." I closed my eyes and remembered sitting beside Truman on our bed. "I told him that I knew how it felt not to have parents. Told him that the pain was normal.

"He told me that I was lucky. That I'd never know if my father was a mean bastard like his. His father never saw value in him, and didn't consider him a real man because Truman didn't play football. Because Truman called the plumber sometimes instead of fixing it himself. A tiny part of him was glad that Douglas Baxter had died."

"He didn't go to a therapist because he had you," Dr. Tremaine whispered. "You helped him cope."

I hugged myself, and tried to smother that ache in my heart. "That night, I knew without a doubt that we were supposed to be together. That we were supposed to help each other survive."

"But he's gone now."

I nodded, tears burning in my eyes.

"What do you miss about him?"

Everything. "Sitting beside him on the couch with a game controller in my hand . . . Swatting his hand as he picked at my plate of french fries . . . Watching him walk across the mall, across the street or anywhere. Driving up to Santa Barbara, hanging out in Vegas . . ." I chuckled then added, "I miss his snoring. How he'd grind his teeth sometimes while he slept."

Dr. Tremaine placed her chin in her hand, then said, "What *don't* you miss?"

I frowned, startled out of that blissful place of shared french fries and road trips.

She nodded as encouragement. "It's okay."

I took a deep breath and closed my eyes. Many of the qualities that I had liked about him had pushed us apart. "He was a flirt . . . He could be too ambitious . . . He always wanted excitement, and he got bored quickly." A tear slipped down my cheek.

This time, Dr. Tremaine offered me tissue from the box on her desk. She pulled the folder back in front of her and made a note as I dried my eyes.

"Do you know why you're crying?" she asked.

"It just doesn't seem fair. He was a good person. And I know that rain falls on the just and unjust, but . . . There was so much more he wanted to do in life. He wanted to buy a motorcycle. He wanted to learn Japanese. He wanted to take me on a hot air balloon, and he wanted to retile the bathroom. He hated that tile in our bathroom."

"I know you may not see this now," Dr. Tremaine said, "but one day you'll look back on your relationship, warts and all, and you'll say to yourself, 'what a wonderful life we had together.' And you won't be sad for what you lost. Instead, you'll be happy for what you had. So many people in this world miss out by not enjoying the here and now, wishing that the world could give them more than it can."

I nodded, twisted the tissue, and ignored the tears slipping down my cheeks. "So what do you do with the bad times? Do you just overlook those?"

She cocked her head. "What do you mean?"

"We had problems. I lied to him about some things."

"Like?"

I rocked back and forth in my seat as my mind continued offering "things" that I hadn't planned to utter aloud. "I got pregnant without him knowing. I never told him, even after I miscarried."

"So sorry to hear that."

"And I feel guilty for . . ."

"Go on."

I swallowed, then forced myself to say, "I had an affair with our neighbor."

Dr. Tremaine didn't blink or show any hint of surprise. "Did you tell him?"

I shook my head. "I had planned to, but I didn't get the chance. I didn't want him distracted during the dive. Not that it mattered in the end. But that's driving me crazy the most: knowing that I didn't get to tell him, but being relieved that I didn't have to say such awful things to him." I glanced at her. "That's bad, isn't it?"

"It's normal," she said. "And you're being honest. That's what our time together is about. I don't judge you for your actions. I'm here to help you understand yourself and your relationships with others, including your relationship with Terry."

My mouth opened, then closed. *Who?*

"Do you think Terry would've asked for a divorce had you confessed?"

Speechless, I could only stare at her. I had said my husband's name at least five times since I had sat down, and somehow, to this woman, "Truman" had become "Terry."

And there we were again. Just like our first visit. I didn't want to talk anymore, especially since I had said too much anyway. God knew my thoughts, yes, but voicing them scared me. My words were now fully realized demons that taunted me and teased. *You'll never be good. YHWH will never forgive you for being so evil. For doing evil.*

The clock chimed. My half hour was up.

"I think we covered a lot of ground," Dr. Tremaine said, pulling her prescription pad from the desk drawer. "Valium and Paxil, right?"

I left the psychiatrist's office with a stone in my belly and two prescriptions for drugs that no longer worked.

I hated doctors' offices, and avoided them as much as possible. No matter the economic status of the patients sitting with me, HMO waiting rooms always made me feel hopeless and poor, quick to apologize for catching whatever ailment that had forced me through double doors, and into Mercy Health Group's waiting room where hundreds of patients battled for care, and vied for the attention of anyone wearing a badge.

On this day, the waiting area was beyond crowded and more than loud. Two televisions at opposite ends of the room blasted at full volume—a Spanish telecast of a soccer match, and an English telecast of a Dodgers game. Children with various injuries and sicknesses, in varying degrees of filth and cleanliness, climbed on chairs and on tables. Their parents, dull-eyed and spent, stared at the yellowing linoleum, or at one of the two television sets bolted to the walls. The busted air conditioner offered no relief, and the hot room reeked of cheap pine cleaner, sweat, and desperation.

But if I wanted to get well, I had to deal with the crowds and the germs and the two-hour wait.

By the time I reached the exam room, it hurt to see, and I kept my eyes closed as I took off my shirt and bra as instructed, and pulled on the white paper gown. I climbed onto the exam table and studied torn posters taped to the wall as I waited.

Have You Been Vaccinated?

What is a Virus?

Nutritional Facts Every Parent Should Know!

Outside the room, doors opened and closed. Patients spoke to nurses in broken English. Laughter too loud for a doctor's office echoed down the hallways. I lay back on the table, eyes closed, and debated. *Stay in the room? Or hop off the table and leave, never coming back?*

"Somebody's not gettin' no rest."

I opened my eyes—I had fallen asleep.

A large Black woman dressed in pink scrubs gathered sticks and swabs onto a steel tray. She smiled at me, showing the gap between her two bottom teeth. "What's the problem today?"

I whispered, "I can't sleep even though it looks like I can. And I'm starting to have bad headaches."

The nurse rested her tongue in that gap. It resembled a moray eel. Pink and black, blotted like she had dipped it in ink.

"Basically, I need something for pain and insomnia," I said.

She cocked an eyebrow. "Really?" Not *"Really? That's awful,"* but *"Really? I call bullshit."*

"I haven't had a full night's rest since . . ." I stopped to think. "I don't remember when I had a full night's rest."

The nurse smirked, and headed for the door. "All right, then. Dr. Lucas will be here in a minute."

My headache took on audio. Sounded like an organ playing chords. *Free. Free. Free.* Over and over again. But as Dr. Lucas held open my eye with his cold, pink fingers, those blasts hushed into whispers. The pain was hiding from the brightness.

He stepped away from me, and clicked off his penlight. "Well, Mrs. Baxter, I don't *see* anything abnormal." He was a handsome man with eyes the color of blue steel. He was tall and wide—a middle-aged football player's body. More play-action pass and leaping over buildings in a single bound than performing rectal exams and poking around in people's mouths.

I rubbed swirling dots out of my eyes, and said, "My therapist prescribed Paxil for anxiety, and Valium to help me sleep. But one: I'm still anxious. And two: I'm not sleeping."

"Got it," he said, then scribbled on a prescription pad. "I heard about Truman. I'm terribly sorry. Leilani adored her brother. I saw her the other day. She's not handling it well, either." He tore out the prescription. "Grief and depression: That's probably why you're getting the headaches. But the pain won't go away until you get some sleep. Until you find some stability."

I offered a weak smile. "Stability? What's that?"

He squeezed my shoulder. "Klonopin is a wonder drug. One pill, twice a day, and you'll be a new person in no time. Or, you'll be the old person you were before."

The old person I was before. That's all I wanted.

◆　◆　◆

Arnib saw me standing in the pharmacy's line and pushed his stock cart toward me. He grinned and said, "Did that Tylenol work out for ya?"

Were we homies now? And I didn't remember if the Tylenol had worked or not, but I said, "It worked okay."

He nodded with enthusiasm. "Good, good. I'm glad. Anything to help." He gasped, then whispered, "Did you read the article today about Mr. Huston? His client? That gang-banger who murdered the twelve-year-old? Got shot yesterday. He's on life support and may die. Serves him right."

"Next in line." The Korean woman behind the pharmacy counter motioned for me to come forward.

Arnib said, "Can you believe that? So now, the judge is trying to force Mr. Huston to spill everything the guy told him. But Mr. Huston still won't talk—"

"Next in line," the pharmacist repeated.

"Mr. Huston had to get his own lawyer, isn't that crazy?" Arnib said. "I still can't understand how someone so nice can represent gangs." His eyes shifted to brown customers roaming the aisles. "I've seen a few of them around here. I think they're visiting Mr. Huston at his house, getting his advice. One was in the store just a minute ago. We're not supposed to do racial profiling, but this is a nice neighborhood, you know?"

I caught the pharmacist's eye, and told Arnib, "I should probably . . ."

"Oh. Yeah," he said. "Don't mean to keep you. I just wanted to say 'hi.' See if you're doing better." He blushed. "Catch ya later." Then, he wheeled his cart down Paper Goods, and threw one last glance in my direction.

I raced to the car from the village market, not caring about Jake, the Mexican Mafia, or a judge's orders. I dove behind the steering wheel, tore open the bag, pulled out the vial of Klonopin, and popped the top.

I shook a pill onto my palm, swallowed it, then took long pulls of Diet Coke. Once again, science had offered a promise—*new person in no time.* I sank into the seat and waited for my change to come.

Two parking spaces away, a Latino kid wearing sagging jeans and a pristine white T-shirt leaned against a tricked-out Escalade. His forearms were covered in tattoos, and the diamond and gold watch on his wrist looked more expensive than all of the furniture in my house. He was staring at me, and nodded when I realized that he was standing there. He opened the truck's door and climbed behind the steering wheel. He glanced at me again before placing a cell phone against his ear.

I started my car.

He started his truck.

Nervous, I backed out of the space, almost ramming an old man driving a scooter.

The driver in the Escalade waited. He pulled out as I moved forward.

I made a left, and decided I would not drive up my street if he was still following me.

The man in the Escalade turned left.

Crap.

At the street before Rockcliff Drive, he turned left again and disappeared down the hill.

The City had blocked off the bottom of my street—retarring and pothole work. I drove past my street and made a left at the next block. I rarely drove home from the east side of the canyon, and most of the houses on these winding streets hid behind high shrubs and gates. As I continued up and west, the neighborhood became familiar again. I slowed as I reached the blind curve before my Cuban neighbors' place.

Jake Huston was standing on my kitchen porch, one hand on the doorknob, the other hand clutching a stuffed trash bag. The door was ajar, and golden light from the kitchen gleamed from behind him.

What the hell is he doing?

I jammed on the brake, and clicked off the car's headlamps to stare at him with disbelief.

Jake threw a glance in the direction I usually took. Seeing no one, he retreated from the porch, bag in hand, and raced up the hill.

Nauseous, I rounded the bend, and eased into my driveway. I climbed out of the car and gazed in the direction he had run.

No Jake.

A breeze passed through the canyon, bringing with it that stink of dead things. And, in that fleeting moment, I wondered: Did Jake and his clients dump that poor dead boy somewhere on the hillside?

My kitchen door was unlocked, and the security alarm pinged once—I hadn't armed it before leaving the house.

Or maybe I had.

I grabbed my cell phone from my purse and punched in Jake's number.

No answer.

I gripped the phone tighter as his voicemail told me to leave a message. I wanted to say *What the hell were you doing at my house? Don't come here anymore.* Instead, I ended the call without saying a word. I tossed the phone on the breakfast bar, and took several deep breaths to stop shaking.

What did he want?

Maybe he's planting evidence somewhere in my house, a place cops wouldn't think to look.

What was in that trash bag?

Maybe he's hiding something that belonged to that dead boy . . . Like a shoe or the boy's jacket . . .

I shook my head, refusing to continue down Tinfoil Hat Alley.

He must be hiding something.

Because why *had* Jake been calling so much? And why wouldn't he tell the judge where the dead boy was buried? And what the hell was in that trash bag?

What did Jake Huston want?

CHAPTER 11

Six hours.

That's how long it took for the Klonopin to kick in, aided by an early-morning episode of *Family Matters*. I lay on the couch, my mind twisting around my flight from the village market's parking lot. *Who was that guy in the Cadillac? Was he following me? Did he work for Jake? And what was Jake doing at my . . . ?*

My eyelids drooped, and I heard myself snoring, drifting toward sleep . . .

The phone rang.

Startled awake, I grabbed the telephone from the floor and shouted, "What?"

The den bloomed with sunshine. *Designing Women* had replaced *Family Matters*.

"I know what will make you feel better."

I squinted at the clock: 7:17 a.m. Asleep for five hours. "Leilani, what the hell—"

"Pack a bag. We're going to Vegas!"

Maybe leaving Los Angeles would do me good. Sleeping in a bed instead of sleeping on a couch. Watching people guzzle margaritas by the mile as they pretended to be someone else. Losing myself in the

,neon distractions of slot machines and the click of roulette wheels. Spending time with Leilani. Spending time away from the house. Away from Truman.

Outside, a car's horn blew. I grabbed my overnight bag, and took one last look at the den and that couch as though I'd never return. Was I selfish leaving like this? What if Flex called? What if Truman called?

I sighed, frustrated with having to play "What If?" before making every decision.

The horn blew again, and I ran down the stairs to the kitchen. I grabbed my cell phone from the counter and selected, "Forward All Calls." Any call from my home telephone would now hit my cell. A good compromise, I thought, as I stepped out into the warm sunlight.

Leilani sat behind the steering wheel of a cherry red convertible BMW.

I stood on the porch, gaping at her.

Dressed in tight white jeans and a tiny tank top, she smiled and said, "Like it?"

"When did you buy this?"

"Yesterday. After my fight with you, I needed something to cheer me up."

"Usually people buy shoes or an iPad or . . ."

"I'll pay for it with the money Truman left me," she said with a shrug. "As soon as I get a job, of course. Think he'd like it?"

"He'd think that you're throwing your money away."

Leilani scowled, then slipped on her sunglasses. "You getting in or not?"

I tossed my bag into the trunk, then climbed into the passenger seat.

"It's cute," I told her.

"Yeah," she said.

Not many cars were leaving Los Angeles, and so we jammed out of the city in less than an hour. The Beemer's stereo blasted 50 Cent, but the thrum of the wheels against asphalt lulled me into a deep, dreamless sleep.

Go, go, go, Shorty!

My head rolled to the side and hit the BMW's door. I opened my eyes.

50 Cent was still shouting about someone partying like it was her birthday.

A passing highway sign said LAS VEGAS—75 MILES.

Leilani, zooming east on Highway 15, held her cell phone to her ear. "I did not," she was saying. "He's a total li . . . I'd never blow a guy in a bathroom stall. Maybe in an elevator . . ." She laughed and the car picked up speed.

I sat up and winced—the July sun had burned my neck and face.

Leilani glanced at me, then told the caller, "My sister-in-law's making faces. I'll hit you back when we get there." She pressed a button, then tossed the phone in her purse.

I stretched, and asked, "Was that Monica?"

"No. My girl Keisha."

"Keisha from school?"

"No," Leilani said. "You don't know her."

We rode in silence for three miles.

"You still with what's-his-face?" I asked. "Food-4-Less Guy."

"Jon?" Leilani smirked. "We're off and on. Off right now."

"I saw Keith over at FOX a few days ago. He mentioned something about you coming there to work."

"He was offering me some low-level job," Leilani said. "I can't be thirty-seven years old, being somebody's *assistant*."

But at thirty-seven, Leilani had never been anybody's anything.

"So what are you gonna do?" I asked. "Maybe you should—"

"Damn, Nic," she snapped. "I'll figure something out, all right? I have to. It's not like my darling brother left me much of a cushion."

"We're riding in your cushion."

"Fine. Whatever."

"You're in a mood."

"I'm entitled."

"Enjoy."

"I will."

We didn't talk as we raced past dusty green Joshua trees and rocks the color of Mars.

◆　◆　◆

The Palms' Rain nightclub was filled to capacity, and the crowd's noise competed with Jay-Z's "99 Problems" blasting from the club's speaker system. Revelers cast in fuchsia and yellow lighting shouted and rapped along to the song. Girls in tiny skirts and tinier shirts clambered into private cabanas and onto the laps of guys who'd be called "gross" in another town and at another time of day.

Body shots up in the DJ booth.

Unofficial go-go dancers writhing on raised platforms around the dance floor.

Vodka, Goldschläger, and Heineken everywhere.

I sat at a small table near the entrance and sipped Pellegrino. I tugged at my black wrap dress and slipped off my heels. With the magic of makeup, I had pulled it off, and looked as hot as an insomniac widow could. All around me, people ten-plus years younger than me grooved on the dance floors and the bar tops. Leilani, dressed in a whisper of a dress, writhed in the middle of the madness and drank Cristal from the bottle.

Truman and I had loved dancing together. At clubs, at weddings, at FSN's Hollywood Holiday Party. Our sweaty clothes would stick to our skin as we grooved to old school LL Cool J and 2 Live Crew. We'd bump and grind to the beat as though we were teenagers again. We didn't care if we didn't know the latest steps. We'd ignored the burn in our knees, backs, and in our throats as we shouted X-rated lyrics to the sky. We'd leave the dance floor spent, thankful that the DJ had played something stupid from the Spice Girls or Foo Fighters.

Four guys seated at a table across the room ogled me. I ignored them and glanced at my cell phone's clock: 11:38.

Back at the table, the shortest guy in the world quit his staring and strolled over to me. He wore a mustard three-piece suit and more jewelry than I owned. He pointed at me, and said, "*King* magazine, right?"

I silently regarded the munchkin in his tiny yellow suit. Truman didn't own a single piece of yellow clothing. And despite threats of piercing his ear, he never did. He wore his wedding band and a watch—either the titanium TAG Heuer he bought for his thirtieth birthday, or the diving watch I gave him for Christmas.

"You was Miss February," the munchkin was saying. "Am I right? I know I'm right. Wanna know how I know? The legs." He licked his lips as he peeked under the table at my legs. "Baby, I'd remember your legs—"

"I really don't feel like talking right now," I said. "So if you don't mind . . ."

He glanced over his shoulder to his friends. He threw them a thumbs-up, then turned back to me with a scowl. "That magazine's a piece of shit, and your legs ain't shit, either. You have a good evening, miss." Then, he toddled back to his table.

Thanks to the power of grief combined with modern medicine, I couldn't work up the interest to be offended. I sipped my water, saying nothing as Leilani fell into the chair beside me.

"Who the hell drinks water in Las Vegas?" she asked.

"Me," I said. "Cuz your doctor gave me pills that would make the Pope jump off a bridge. I'd start running through the casino naked if I drank a martini right now."

Leilani cocked an eyebrow. "Are the pills working?"

"Oh yeah." I nodded at the munchkin and his friends. "Ask the little guy over there. I'm a joy to be around." I tilted my face to the sky as mist sprinkled from the scaffolding. "This place is crazy. I've never been to a club with special effects."

"Only in Vegas, baby," Leilani shouted. "Wait until they make fire shoot across the ceiling. You dance yet?"

I shook my head. "Not yet. Just enjoying the view."

"I have something for you." Leilani pulled a blue velvet box out of her clutch.

"Are you about to propose?" I asked, smiling. "Because it's yes! We're in Vegas. Let's be crazy kids and get married! Right now."

"Open the box, you nut."

I opened the box to find a red string and a business card.

"The String protects you from the evil eye," she said.

I glanced at my friend. "Evil eye . . . Right." I pulled out the business card and read: "*Zephyr Tott, Spiritual Adviser.* You want me to see a *psychic?*"

"She's an *adviser,*" Leilani corrected. "Zephyr's totally helping me deal with Truman's death. I see her two or three times a week. We talk, and I cry, and it's working. I'm gonna help her expand her business. Get her up on Facebook. Help her redesign her website so she can do web-cam consultations or whatever."

I shook my head, and placed the card back in the box. "Kabbalah, Lei? Psychics?"

"You went to a psychiatrist before everybody thought it was fashionable," she said. "Back when you were a kid, seeing a shrink was taboo, wasn't it?"

"Yeah, but—"

"I'm telling you, Nic. Zee's so *wise.* She can totally see other dimensions of existence."

"*Other dimensions of existence?* I don't believe in that crap."

"*Crap?*" Leilani screeched. "You're insulting my beliefs."

"Which you pick up like a box of tampons from the store." I shook my head. "You're going from one religion to another but you're not giving any belief enough time to—"

"Since when do you have the answers?" Leilani asked, her eyes hot with anger. "Has Jesus told you why Truman was killed in some freak accident? Or why you think he's haunting your bed? Or why you can't sleep, or why you have headaches—"

"I was doing fine until we strolled into the Sexy Second Circle of Hell."

"What-the-fuck-ever, Nicole. You sit here and be miserable. I don't care anymore. I can't care cuz you know why? I have to start healing. If you wanna pick at your scabs, go ahead. But I can't let you pick at mine." She left the table, and returned to the bar top to wiggle along to Beyoncé's "Get Me Bodied."

Yeah, like Bey, I also wanted to be myself tonight, but who was that? *Scab-picker*, according to my sister-in-law.

Yeah: what-the-fuck-ever.

I chugged my glass of water, then headed back through the mirrored entrance to the casino, and into the smoky air. Older gamblers crowded the slots and video poker machines. The younger ones—faces flushed from scotch and Cosmopolitans—hung over blackjack tables and roulette wheels. Tourists wearing ill-fitting shorts and damp T-shirts raised their cameras to take pictures of big-boobed coeds writhing to Duran Duran's "Rio" and performing body shots on a bar counter.

I glanced at my cell phone. Fifteen minutes before twelve.

Just make it to midnight, then call it quits.

I trudged toward the center of the casino, following the music of a live band playing Blondie. I plopped down at an empty table. A pretty waitress wearing a laced-bodice dress swiveled to my table. Her plastic nametag said "Satin." She shouted over the music, "Can I get you something?"

I shouted back, "An Amaretto Sour, please." So much for the ban on booze. Times like these called for something stronger than water. Times like these actually called for something stronger than Amaretto. But I was medicated.

She nodded at a menu card that stood on my table, and asked, "Anything to eat?"

I didn't move to pick up that card but saw "Quesadilla." And that's what I ordered.

As that invisible band played "Heart of Glass," Satin returned with my Amaretto and quesadilla. She slipped my bill beside the plate, and as I handed her two twenties, a square of paper slipped from my wallet.

After Satin left, I unfolded that square torn from *National Geographic* eight years ago. *A beaten wood plank-way cutting across shallow turquoise waters, and ending at a white sand atoll in the middle of the Laccadive Sea.*

"That's where we'll retire," Truman had promised, tapping his finger on the picture.

Since then, I'd take out that photo and long for the day we'd reach those sandy beaches and pristine waters, hard work and everyday life a part of our past.

I slipped the picture back into my wallet and sat silently for a moment. After taking a deep breath, I devoured the greasy tortilla in seven bites, then guzzled my watered-down drink. The band started "Raspberry Beret," and I stood up from the table to begin my march toward the elevators.

Glanced at my cell phone again: six minutes to midnight.

I wandered to a blackjack table, and with the encouragement of the four other players, found myself seated in the first position. A Black guy with a graying goatee occupied the seat next to me. He smiled, and I noticed his chipped front tooth. His body reminded me of Mike Tyson's—bulldog, stocky, short. His features—eyes, nose, mouth—sat too close together, as though God had decided against using the entire canvas.

He said, "How you doin' tonight?" Stacks of chips towered near his thick hands.

I said, "I'm okay," then nodded at his pile. "But I think you need one hundred more."

He winked at me. "Maybe you'll bring me luck."

I slid fifty dollars to the dealer. "I'm as lucky as a cricket."

His eyebrows scrunched—*huh?*—and he offered me his hand. "I'm Chris."

"Nicole." We shook.

His eyes were kind, his handshake firm. He gazed at me and I busied myself with chips.

The dealer slipped two cards before me—*eleven.*

I turned to Chris, and said, "Is it me, or does the dealer look like Captain Picard?"

He laughed. "You a Trekkie?"

"Kind of. You?"

He shook his head. "Hate that show. All of 'em. But you know what?" He held up his beer bottle. "Here's to the next generation."

"So, Chris. What do you do for a living?"

He doubled down on my bet, then said, "I'm an electrician."

I nodded. "So you give people power?"

The dealer slipped a queen of clubs on top of my eleven.

He motioned to my cards. "And I got you double your money."

"Appreciate it," I said. "And where do you light up lives?" My cheeks flushed. *Was I flirting?*

"Tennessee. I'm here for a bachelor party. We're leaving tomorrow. I started not to sit down and play, but I'm glad I changed my mind."

Chris had recently divorced. He had one child—a seven-year-old boy named Jalani. His ex-wife worked as a letter carrier. He missed being with someone, he said, even if it had been someone he couldn't stand. "I still don't get that." He nodded at the rings on my finger. "What about your husband? Looking at those rings, I see he's a big baller."

I shrugged as my mind filled with explanations. Instead of saying, *My husband died and I haven't slept since June 26 and I'm on Klonopin for anxiety and I can't take off my rings yet because that's like giving up,* I said, "Not too different from your situation."

After he had won all he could, Chris suggested that we find a place to talk. He took my hand and led me to another lounge. We ordered drinks—Midori for me and Bailey's for him. The more we talked, the closer we sat.

I liked *The Simpsons.*

He watched mostly sports and news channels about sports.

I liked playing video games.

He stopped playing them once the era of Pac-Man ended.

I read one hundred books a year.

He flipped through *Sports Illustrated*, and the sports page of the newspaper. "Wow," he said. "This is crazy. Can't believe I'm sittin' here with a nerd."

Wide-eyed, I grabbed his arm. "Oh, crap. The dress didn't fool you?"

"You're a sexy nerd, though. That's kinda nice."

I smirked.

"But you are," he said. "Don't act all nonchalant about it."

I dropped my eyes to the unnaturally green drink in my hand.

"Why do you do that?" he asked.

"Do what?"

"Look away. Every time I compliment you, you look away. I'm flirting with you now, and you're shutting me down. Is it my breath?"

I laughed, then met his eyes. "I've been through some things lately."

We gazed at each other silently. Don't know what he saw in my face, but he took my hand. He leaned forward, and as he moved to kiss me, someone shouted "Chris!" A chubby guy hoisting two beer bottles plopped in the seat across from us. "What's up, man? We've been all over the place looking for you." He nodded at me, and said, "How you doin', miss?" Before I could answer, he said, "Sorry for interrupting, man, but time to hit the next *spiz-zot!*"

"Dang. Already?" Chris glanced at his watch. "Y'all give me a minute." As his friend danced back to the waiting revelers, Chris stood and said, "This is depressing. We were just getting to know each other."

"It's not depressing," I said. "You have no idea what you've done for me."

"Call me if you want to light up your life." He placed his business card in my palm, then kissed my hand, "Good night, Nicole."

I watched him join the group, and waved to him before he disappeared into the crowd.

Exhausted and thrilled, I retreated to the elevator banks that would take me to my room. My feet hurt and my face ached from smiling. Two hours. That's all it had taken for someone to make me feel something other than pain. Had to be a record *somewhere.*

From our suite's window, I glimpsed the neon-hot Strip only a mile away. *America's Playground.* Truman and I would always stay at the Mandalay Bay. We would eat at Emeril's or Nobu, and drink martinis and red wine by the bottle. We'd stagger to the roulette wheel or to the blackjack tables, and play until our eyes and lungs could no longer take the cigarette smoke. Then, we'd return to the suite—always a suite—and we'd . . .

I yanked the curtains together and stepped away from the window.

I exchanged the dress for shorts and a T-shirt, and then, I washed my face. I settled into the king-size bed and clicked off the lamp.

Complete darkness.

I sat up and listened.

Silence.

I yawned, then lay my head on the pillow. My eyes closed. I dreamed of slot machines and green bottles of Pellegrino floating in the Laccadive Sea.

CHAPTER 12

I awoke to silent darkness—the blackout curtains had helped me find sleep and stay there. The digital clock said 10:11 a.m., and I sat up in bed, more refreshed than before. Las Vegas was a magical city. By the time we returned to Los Angeles, and with the help from my new drug, I *would* be my old self again.

I padded to Leilani's room, and whispered, "Lei, you're a genius." She didn't answer and I flicked on the light switch.

Her bed was empty.

Maybe she had come to the room late and left early this morning, I thought. Klonopin and fatigue would've prevented me from hearing the Macy's Thanksgiving Day Parade marching past the foot of my bed.

But the gold comforter was tucked, and the pillows were still high and fluffy.

I wandered around the suite. She wasn't standing out on one of the balconies, or relaxing in the sunken bathtub. The half-full bottle of Moët we had popped open before going to Rain remained on the tray, untouched.

I showered and dressed.

Leilani was still missing.

She's an adult, I told myself. And I'm an adult. We don't have to babysit each other.

At a café downstairs, I ordered breakfast without her. Eggs. Corned beef hash. Toast. Cups of rich, brewed coffee. I ate as though I hadn't eaten in months. In many ways, I hadn't. I had stuck pasta or chili or grits into my mouth, and I had moved my jaws to process it, but I had tasted nothing, and had enjoyed it even less. Now, though . . .

My cell phone rang and I glanced at the display before answering. It was Leilani. "Where you at?"

"*Girl,*" she said. "Where do I even *start?*"

"I'm having breakfast at the café downstairs," I said. "But I'll sit with you if—"

"On my way."

Five minutes later, Leilani stumbled to my table. She wore the same skank-wear from the night before. Her bloodshot eyes were rheumy, and the insides of her nostrils were crusted. She smelled like she had been baptized in Courvoisier, then forced to run ten laps. "What are those?" she asked, then stabbed a fork into the middle of my plate.

"Eggs." I stared at her as she continued to eat. "You can order your own, you know. They serve Blacks now."

She winked at me. "Where's the fun in that? And I don't have time. We need to get back to LA."

"What? Why? We just got here."

She stuffed her mouth with toast, then said, "I know, but I got a call about a job. Interview's tomorrow." She paused, then added, "Are you keeping me from fulfilling my brother's last wishes? Are you keeping me from reaching my full potential? I have a BMW to pay for."

Disappointed, I shook my head.

She took a few more bites of egg, then stood. "I need to wash up. Meet you back in the room."

I sank in my chair and wished that Monica had come with us. I would've stayed then. Caught a Cirque show. Had a fancy dinner, maybe at Nobu. Shopped at Caesar's and the Bellagio. Maybe even played a game of roulette. Put it all on black in Truman's honor.

Another time. Soon.

I strolled through the bustling casino, its air swirling with clouds of cigar and cigarette smoke. Barely legal waitresses in short crimson dresses shouldered trays of scotch, Bloody Marys, and Coronas through the already-boozy crowd. Smoking geriatrics with glazed eyes threw their Social Security checks down the gullets of slot machines. Many had been seated there a while—several drained cocktail glasses were stacked near their liver-spotted knees.

I sat at a Blazing 7s slot machine and slipped a twenty-dollar bill into its mouth. On my fifth pull, a trio of red, white, and blue sevens slammed into the slot window—500 quarters. I giggled and my heart leaped at winning $125. As I waited for my voucher to print, I watched a group of giggling girlfriends pull their veiled bride-to-be pal through a bank of video poker machines.

Used to be Mo, Lei, and me. Young, beautiful, easy to please. Excited about our futures, about our careers. So eager to become adults, to find husbands, to start our happily-ever-afters. Too eager to even think about worst-case scenarios, like our Prince Charmings dying at forty.

I drove as Leilani slept off her sex-booze-coke-filled night. Didn't mind the quiet—I enjoyed the quiet and the vast desert stretching into the horizon. Maybe Lei could drop me off at the airport, I thought. I wouldn't even go home. Straight to LAX. Vegas or bust.

Having fun, Nicole? Flirting with electricians and gambling away your husband's hard-earned money? Is that what you're about now? Truman is out there somewhere . . . not *having fun.*

I turned onto Rockcliff Drive.

The house was waiting.

I pulled into the driveway, and shook Leilani from her sleep.

She yawned. "We're here already?"

I grabbed my bag from the back seat and climbed out of the car. "Thanks for the getaway. I needed it."

Leilani scooted over to the driver's side. "Are you gonna make an appointment with Zephyr?"

I shrugged. "I'll think about it."

"Trust me. She'll change your life."

My life was waiting for me on the other side of the front door.

I disarmed, then rearmed the burglar alarm, and dropped my bag in the foyer.

Now what?

The silence made my skin prickle and my face flush. My shoulders had tensed in less than ten seconds, and I stood rigid against the door. I took a deep breath, then kneeled beside that growing pile of mail. Tasks, even stupid ones, offered moments of not thinking, not fearing. I sorted through bank and credit card statements, subscription notices, direct mail appeals . . .

Nope. Couldn't do it. But closer to doing it than before.

I shoved the pile of mail to the wall, then roamed through the living room, dining room, and hallways, deciding at each whether to turn on the light or leave it off.

Turned all of them on.

I climbed the stairs, but halfway up, I froze in my step.

Crap.

The Panamanian mola that Truman had brought home for Baby Baxter, the mola that had been left in the guest room, now hung on the wall. Breathless, I stared at that framed piece of cloth, know-ing—*absolutely certain*—that I had not—

What was that?

I snapped my head to the left and looked up the staircase.

Heavy, rhythmic breathing . . . Snoring . . . Someone was sleeping in one of the rooms.

An intruder?

Impossible. I had armed the alarm before leaving for Las Vegas. It would have had to be deactivated because the security company would've called otherwise. Leilani was the only other person who knew the code, and she had been in Vegas with me.

Does Jake know the code? Did he sneak in?

Why would Jake break in and fall asleep in my bed? That didn't make sense.

I plucked the mola from the wall, then marched up the stairs to grab the mandala near the security panel. I deposited both in the guest bedroom, then trekked down the hallway to the bedroom.

A figure hid beneath the covers. The comforter rose and fell with each breath.

I yanked at the comforter, and something icy grabbed my fingers and slashed through my hand like a frozen knife blade. I shrieked and twisted away, stumbling to the floor. I scrambled toward the nightstand, then covered my head with my hands. I hid my face in my lap. Eyes squeezed shut, I stayed in my protective armadillo ball until my mind cleared.

It's okay. You're okay. Look again. Just look again.

I loosened from my clench, and peeked out.

A bed. An *empty* bed.

With weak arms, I crawled over discarded shoes, jeans, and sweatshirts to the bathroom. I grabbed the sink and pulled myself up from the floor. I opened the medicine cabinet: Paxil. Valium. NyQuil. Neosporin. Dental floss. Zaditor . . . No Klonopin. Crap. The Klonopin vial was still packed in my overnight bag. And my bag was downstairs. Too far. I needed something *now*.

I grabbed the Paxil vial, and popped one, then another. I turned on the tap to wash away the bitterness and—

Whiskers in the sink bowl.

I paused, then splashed water around the bowl until it was clean again. I charged back to the bedroom, and scooped a pair of dirty sweats and a T-shirt from the floor. I changed clothes in the hallway, starting a new pile with my discarded jeans and shirt. I could sleep downstairs in the living room. Or I could check into the Sunset Marquis. But as I negotiated the stairs, my knees wobbled and my pulse raced—I was now under the influence of two hastily swallowed Paxil. Too high to drive.

The kitchen was empty and silent. No snoring. No ghosts. No shavings left in the sink. The metallic taste in my mouth remained and I wobbled to the cupboard for a drinking glass, but stopped in my step.

My last refrigerator message to Truman had disappeared. Almost all of the magnetic words sat on the left side of the door. Only a few words remained in the center.

> Storm watch for frantic princess
> She lies to live smooth
> Hide goddess
> For I want the mountain castle

I stepped back and squinted at those words, at a message that had not been there before. Blood flooded my head, and I lost all feeling in my face. Numb, I gazed at that poem, then touched the word "storm." I plucked it off the steel door. Barely felt it between the pads of my damp fingers. I slipped "storm" between "smooth" and "hide." "Castle" between "want" and "the." I moved each word into a new place until no coherent message remained.

PART III

CHAPTER 1

The Santa Anas had returned to Los Angeles, forcing hot, dry winds and dust across the Basin. I tried to lose myself in *Anna Karenina* and Tolstoy's Russia, but any time the wind blew, any time the loosest ceramic tile on the roof jangled, I glanced anxiously at the ceiling. I had burned through ten pages of the novel, but had only comprehended two. Couldn't focus—the wind shrieked like banshees between houses and down hillsides, carrying with it the threat of explosive fires.

I tossed the novel to the floor, untangled my legs from the blanket, and wandered to the window. No birds soared across the darkening, dirty sky. The setting sun threw purple shadows across the canyon's face, and pewter ashes stuck in the screen's mesh—a massive brush fire had engulfed the San Gabriel Mountains less than fifty miles away.

A door slammed.

I spun around. My eyes skipped across the empty den.

You heard that. Don't pretend that you didn't.

"It's the wind," I said aloud.

Unconvinced, I crept to the couch and pulled the machete from beneath the cushion. I tiptoed over to the door and peeked out into the hallway.

Each room's door was open.

"Lei? You here?"

No answer.

I crept toward the staircase, stepping in puddles of water—

What the . . . ?

I stopped and flipped the light switch.

Wet footprints trailed from my bedroom down the hallway, and down the staircase. Wet footprints that I hadn't made since my feet were dry. Wet footprints that were several sizes larger than my feet.

I stooped and reached out to touch the water, but I stopped with my hand still outstretched.

If it's water, what will you do?

Because how did it get there?

If you touch dry ground, what will you do?

Because what, then, was I seeing?

I lingered there for a moment, and nibbled at the ragged cuticle around my thumbnail. I muttered, "Okay," then followed those footprints down the stairs, one step at a time, careful not to step in the . . . whatever it was.

The wet prints, lighter now, led to the kitchen, and stopped in front of the refrigerator. The chaos I had created among the magnetic words on the fridge door had found order.

Frantic princess lies
I want the mountain castle

With trembling fingers, I reached out to scramble the words again.

"Tonite" blasted behind me. *DJ Quik.* Truman's ringtone.

I whirled around—my cell phone was sitting on the breakfast bar.

Frozen in place, I stared at the phone in disbelief until it dropped into silence. A moment later, the phone chimed. Heart pounding wildly in my chest, I grabbed it, and peered into the display.

What . . . ?

1 NEW TEXT MSG.

I retrieved the message, but dropped the phone before I could finish reading.

◆　◆　◆

I thrust my cell phone at Leilani and Monica as soon as they returned to the dining room table with filled dinner plates. "Explain this," I demanded.

"Can we eat first?" Leilani asked.

I held out my phone as the answer.

Leilani took it from my hand. Monica leaned over and squinted into the cell phone's screen.

I stared at the flickering candles sitting in the center of the table.

"*Babe,*" Leilani read, "*U have something 2 tell me. Cant rest til U do.*" Leilani stared at the phone with wide eyes. "What the hell is this?"

Monica cut into her steak. "It's called a text message. You send them all the time. What's the big deal?"

My hands shook as I refilled my glass with wine. "It was sent today."

"Okay," Monica said. "Again: The big deal is . . ."

Leilani and I glanced at each other; then, she dropped my phone as though it had stung her.

"Look at the caller's number, Mo," I said. "It came from Truman's cell phone."

Monica studied the message again, and then shrugged. "Where's his phone?"

I shook my head. "It wasn't in the dive bag. Flex told me that he put it in there right after he called me that day."

"Maybe he's wrong," Monica suggested. "Maybe somebody's messing with you cuz they know that Truman's . . . That you're . . . Someone on the boat could've found the phone."

"I don't know," Leilani said as she rubbed her arms. "This is just weird. Reading that message . . . It sounds just like my brother." She shivered, then pushed the phone back to me with the tip of her finger.

"And what about the art?" I asked.

Monica and Leilani glanced at each other, then gaped at me.

"The mola and the mandala that I found hanging on the walls?" I said. "I didn't nail them there."

"Maybe Truman did," Leilani offered.

"When?" I screeched.

Monica peered at me with narrowed eyes. "You think that he hung those *after* the accident?"

"I'm saying that they weren't hanging there before the accident," I shouted. "And now, I'm getting a text from his cell phone?"

"Calm down, Nic," Monica warned. "Repeat after me: Occam's razor."

Leilani frowned. "Monica, what the hell are you talking about?"

"The simplest explanation is most likely the correct one," Monica explained to her, then turned back to me. "Nicole, do y'all have Sprint? Because Truman could've sent that message six weeks ago, and you're just getting it now."

Leilani nodded, brighter now because of Monica's explanation. "Their service sucks. That's why I switched to T-Mobile . . ."

As my friends continued to complain about Sprint's service, I heard faint music playing in another room.

I cocked my head: Peter Gabriel's voice. "Do you guys hear that?"

Leilani and Monica continued to compare their cell phone plans.

I left the table and stood in the dining room's entryway. "Signal to Noise" was playing.

"Hey," I said, "did either of you turn this on?"

"We've been sitting here all this time," Monica said with a lifted eyebrow. "How could we—"

"How did it come on?" I asked. "It's one of Truman's favorite songs."

Monica said, "Maybe it came on by itself. Don't stereos have timers now? Don't you guys have that fancy audio system or whatever?"

Footsteps pounded above us. *Running.* A door slammed.

"What the hell?" I shouted.

Leilani screamed, "Somebody's in here!"

I darted out of the dining room and ran up the stairs, stumbling and hitting my forehead on the next step. I wobbled some, but crawled to the landing.

Wet footprints glistened on the hardwood floor.

My gaze followed those prints until . . .

Truman stood in the middle of the hallway, in a pool of seawater. His back was turned to me, but I knew that wet Body Glove T-shirt and those wet khaki shorts. Threads of water coursed down his calves—calves that sagged and melted into his muddy Vans.

I flattened my body against the stairs, and muttered, "Shit, shit, shit."

Leilani and Monica huddled behind me. Leilani whispered, "Who is it?"

I nodded in Truman's direction. "Look. Just . . . See." I don't know if my friends looked—I couldn't take my eyes off the man standing just a few feet in front of me.

"Umm . . . ," Monica said. "What am I seeing? Other than a hallway?"

"It's Truman," I said, gawking at her. "He's right . . ." I turned back.

Truman was gone. The floor was dry.

"He was right there," I said weakly. "I swear he was. I know I sound crazy, but . . ."

But there was no good way to finish that sentence without sounding crazy.

"Someone's here," Monica said. "Even I heard that door slam." She jogged down the stairs and disappeared into the kitchen.

Leilani, wide-eyed and pale, inched down the steps.

Monica burst back into the foyer with a meat cleaver in her hand.

Leilani shrieked and said, "What the hell are you doing with that?"

"I'm going outside," Monica said, opening the front door.

I rushed down the stairs, and said, "What if he's out there?"

But Monica had already disappeared.

Leilani looked spooked as she stared out the open door. "I probably shouldn't say this but . . ." She turned to me, her mouth fixed into a grim line.

"Say what?" I said.

She whispered, "I think Monica . . . I think something's going on with her."

I gawked at Leilani, and a strangled chuckle came from my gut.

Leilani nodded and rubbed her temples. "I know. That's why I didn't want to say anything, but I can't shake this feeling, especially with everything that's going on with her company, you know?"

I blinked—I didn't know. "What's going on with her company?"

Leilani glanced at the door—no Monica—then took a step closer to me. "It's not doing well. Since the stock market's all crazy, people can't afford big parties, and Mo's been racking up credit cards, taking out business loans . . . She told me that she had to pay, like, a shitload of back taxes, and there was some other weird crap that I can't even wrap my mind around. She may have to sell her condo."

"Monica?" I shouted.

"Ssh!" Leilani said, glancing at the door again. "You don't have to tell the world, do you?"

"She's the most responsible person I know."

"And that's why she hasn't talked to you. You tend to get all sanctimonious and patronizing and disappointed. And with Truman gone . . ."

I narrowed my eyes, then asked, "But what does any of that have to do with me?"

"Money, sweetheart," Leilani said. "You have no heirs. If you flip out and put her in charge of your estate, guess what happens? You'll be like Britney Spears and her dad." She waited a beat, then said, "Monica would control the money Truman left you. And she could embezzle that money to keep her company afloat."

I shook my head, my throat now closing. "Why would she do that to me?"

Leilani shrugged. "You can take a girl out of Watts, but you can't take Watts out of the girl. Money makes people do strange things, Nic, and you're vulnerable right now. Near the edge, and you only need a little push to just completely . . . Don't tell her that I told you about any of this." She paused, then added, "I may be completely wrong, and really: I hope I'm wrong, but I just wanted you to—"

Monica rushed back into the foyer and closed the door. "No one's out there. Maybe we should call the police."

"The cops won't do anything," Leilani offered. "We didn't actually *see* anyone. Anyone alive, at least." To me, she said, "Maybe you shouldn't sleep here tonight."

"Come stay with me," Monica said. "Hang out until all this blows over."

"All *what?*" I asked. "Until all of my life blows over?"

"Nic," Monica said, then stopped. Ellipses and redacted boxes of text hung in the air between us, creating an anxious quiet. "Well, I won't be okay with you being here alone."

"I'm fine," I said. "I'm terrific. I'm cool."

Monica shook her head. "I'll go home, grab some clothes for my brunch with Magic Johnson tomorrow, and I'll spend the night."

"I'm not an invalid," I snapped. "I'm gonna have to learn how to be alone."

"But you're not alone," Leilani said. "I'm here."

"I am, too," Monica said, then touched my shoulder.

I jerked as though I had been shocked by an eel. "I'll be fine." I attempted to smile. *See? Would I be smiling if I wasn't okay?*

"I'm gonna give you something," Leilani said. "You need it more than me, especially after what just happened." She reached into her giant bag and pulled out a pistol.

I gasped, and took a step back.

Monica shouted, "Why the hell do you have that?"

"I've had this thing forever," Leilani said, offering me the gun. "It's just a .22."

"*Just?*"

"She needs protection," Leilani said.

"And you give her *that?*"

"What do you want her to use? A potato peeler?"

I hugged myself to resist temptation. "I have a machete."

Leilani rolled her eyes. "You wanna be that close to whatever it is that wants to hurt you? I don't think so."

Monica shook her head. "This is a bad idea."

"Spoken by someone who isn't being terrorized day and night," Leilani snapped. She turned back to me, and said, "Don't worry. It's not one of those black market guns that blow up in your face. I got it at Walmart."

"Oh. Well. Then it's okay," Monica said, rolling her eyes.

I reached for the weapon, and Monica said, "Nicole, you hate guns." I took the pistol from Leilani's grasp. I had never held a gun in my life, not even a fake one. It was heavy. Oily. Cold.

"It's already loaded," Leilani said. "I don't know how it works, but the internet probably has instructions somewhere."

Monica muttered, "I can't believe you did this."

Leilani sucked her teeth. "At least I'm doing something to help the situation. Doing something besides acting like a bitch."

Monica said something else to Leilani, but I didn't hear. The roar inside my head had reached a deafening pitch. As though I sat inside the Staples Center during Game 7 of the NBA Finals, and the Lakers were winning. Yeah. Like that. But without the ecstasy. And with a gun.

At 8:15, it was still hot out. There was a rumor that rain would come on Sunday afternoon; but this evening sky—clear of clouds but filthy from the fire—signaled that there would be no rain on Sunday, or on any other day.

I waved as Monica and Leilani pulled away from the house.

"I'll be back in an hour," Monica shouted out the window.

I returned to the dinner table. Someone had snuffed out all the candles, and now, the dining room smelled of burned cinnamon and crushed cloves. Soft yellow light from the chandelier shone down on half-full wineglasses rimmed with grease and lipstick. I fell into a chair, placed the gun on the table, and stared at the ruins of the evening.

"Tonite" blasted from my cell phone.

The ringing stopped; then, after a minute, it chimed.

Maybe Monica was right. Maybe someone had stolen the phone.

I glanced at the display: 1 NEW TEXT MSG.

I jabbed a button.

Babe. How R Mo & Lei? I miss dinners w/U 3. I luv u.

Something rumbled outside, near the kitchen, then hit the side of the house.

My pulse thundered and without thinking, I grabbed the gun from the table, and muttered, "I'm ending this bullshit right now." I stomped through the kitchen, but faltered in my step when whatever it was struck against the house again.

As soon as I opened the door, I smelled fire. Ashes drifted from the sky, and my eyes burned from the filth. A large black trash can now sat behind my parked cars. The container had been filled with so many trash bags that the lid could not close.

I aimed the gun toward the receptacle, and waited for it to move again.

"Nic?"

I jerked and swung the gun to my left.

Jake stood there. He saw the .22, and the newspapers he carried fell to the ground. With his arms raised and face white with fear, he tried to speak but couldn't.

I kept the gun pointed at him and said, "What are you doing?"

"I . . . I . . ." He swallowed and his nostrils flared. "I was pulling out your trash cans."

I cocked my head and smirked. "Do I look stupid to you?"

Arms still raised, he shook his head. "I'm just trying to help. I've . . . Nicole. Put down the gun."

"No."

"Then aim it somewhere else."

"Kiss my ass." My finger—the one on the trigger—flexed.

Jake noticed. He paled more as he realized that a crazy widow, not his thug clients, would kill him today. "Who do you think has been picking up all the old newspapers and circulars and crap around here? Me, Nicole. I've been paying your gardener, putting out your trash cans, washing your cars, just so that your house looks lived in." He took a deep breath, then whispered, "I left you messages, telling you that I was doing all of this so that you'd know. I'm just trying to help. Do you hear me? Are you there?"

The gun shook in my hands and my arms wobbled with fatigue. I had never listened to his messages. I had erased them as soon as I could, as though his voice emitted poisonous gas. And I hadn't paid the gardener since the accident. And I had walked past delivery menus on the walkway and porch without stopping to pick them up. Monica had gathered all the trash in the house and had placed the bags near the kitchen porch, probably assuming that I could handle stuffing the bags into the cans and taking out the cans once a week. But I hadn't. The person who claimed to have done all of that stood in front of me, staring into the eye of a box store pistol.

Unless he was lying . . .

Disoriented now, I let my arms fall. The gun hit my thigh.

Jake slowly dropped his hands. "Nic—"

I turned away from him and stumbled back to the kitchen.

"Nicole, wait!"

I slammed the door, locked it, and slid to the floor. I would wait there until Monica returned, and if Jake tried to enter, I would shoot him.

CHAPTER 2

Google offered six pages of results for "Zephyr Tott" including a link to a website—awakeningbyzephyr.com—with sections titled "Visions to the Heart" and "Inspirational Insights That Lead to Conscious Awakenings."

> See and understand yourself.
> You don't have to be scared anymore.
> Awakening brings liberation.

Any other time, I would've snickered at this language soufflé. But now, in these circumstances, one word—*liberation*—resonated with me, a glimmer of light in sulfurous fog.

An hour later, I stood before the front door of a whitewashed cottage on Highland Boulevard. An ornate sign hung across the cottage's face. ZEPHYR TOTT ADVISERS. A neon sign in the bay window glowed OPEN. I had stopped at an ATM—I would pay for this visit with cash. I didn't want a check or a credit card statement linking me to Zephyr Tott. And I would use a fake name to keep other "advisers" from seeing "Nicole Baxter" on their psychic-friend mailing lists.

I glanced over my shoulder to my getaway car. *You can leave this place right now.* My underarms prickled, and beads of sweat trickled down my ribs. Was I really about to do this? Was I really about to walk into a psychic's—*no, adviser's*—business? I exhaled, and told myself that if it got too weird, I'd leave and never drive down Highland Avenue again.

Zephyr Tott's waiting area was a mash-up of a mortuary's family viewing room and my aunt Beryl's library (a room that had been filled with forty editions of the King James Version of the Bible, back issues of *Cat Fancy*, and hundreds of bottles of expired vitamin E). Gewgaws of unicorns, angels, and toddlers hoisting umbrellas sat in bookshelves, cubbies, and glass cases. Pictures of Jesus, the Dalai Lama, and Martin Luther King, Jr. were nailed to the walls. An old Black man in need of a shave and a bath sat in an armchair and stared into space.

Compared to Dr. Tremaine's office, this place felt like . . . *home.*

A skinny Black woman wearing purple velvet sat at the reception desk. Her hair was a patchouli-scented casserole of locs, shells, and beads. She closed the book she had been reading (*The Art of Tarot*) and smiled at me. "Welcome to Zephyr's. I'm Trish. Do you have an appointment today?"

I stepped away from the counter and said, "Oh. No. Did I need to call first?"

"We usually like appointments, but—"

"I can come back." *Yeah. Make an appointment and never come back.*

"No," Trish said. "Don't you dare leave."

Piper, Dr. Tremaine's receptionist, would have growled at me for making a last-minute appointment. Scratched my eyes out with her shiny black fingernails.

Trish picked up the telephone receiver and punched three buttons. After a moment, she said, "Can you squeeze in a new client?"

I glanced around the waiting room to confirm: There was one old man in an otherwise-empty waiting room. *Squeeze?*

Trish hooked the phone on her shoulder. "What's your name?"

"Emma."

"Nice to meet you, Emma." To the person on the phone, she said "uh-huh" a few times, then hung up. "She can see you right now. The consultation fee is $150."

Zephyr Tott's office didn't smack of New Age Freak, nor did it smell of Thai food or Burger King. Where papers had covered Dr. Tremaine's credenzas, potted plants sat on Zephyr's. A few diplomas hung on the walls, along with tasteful paintings one purchases at World Market or high-end swap meets. Yanni played on the stereo—no judgment from me. I had watched "Yanni Live at the Acropolis" on PBS three times.

Zephyr seemed young—late twenties or so. She was tiny in stature, barely hitting five feet, with sandy brown locs, mint green eyes, and skin the color of buttered toffee. Jada Pinkett Smith in Mrs. Roper's fire-colored caftan. She handed me a cup of tea, and unlike Dr. Tremaine, joined me on the couch. "If it helps you feel more comfortable," she was saying, "I was a psychiatrist in my former life. I published a few papers, wrote three books on loss, spoke at thousands of conferences. Made my momma proud. But my gift didn't mesh well with the . . ." Fingers hooked. "*Traditional* types."

I sipped the bitter liquid. Its warmth relaxed my shoulders and uncurled the spaghetti strands in my mind.

"To my esteemed colleagues," Zephyr continued, "my gift was witchcraft and voodoo. At first, their dismissal hurt me. But then, I thought about it—most of them discounted the existence of God, so why would I want acceptance from people who didn't believe in souls and soul givers?"

I took a longer sip, and eased back onto the couch. After getting past the tea's sharp taste, I found lavender, honey, mint. It was more soothing than the so-called Sleepytime variety I guzzled at home.

"You like it?" Zephyr asked.

"The tea?" I nodded.

She rose, and strolled to the credenza. "Lavender has its medicinal uses, you know. Insomnia, anxiety, depression . . ." She returned to the couch with a big bag of tea. "It's nature's sedative," she said, handing me the bag. "And it's yours."

I shook my head. "Oh. No. I can't—"

"Please. It will help you."

I said, "Thanks," then stuffed the tea into my purse.

Zephyr watched me for a moment, then said, "Tell me, Emma. What do you want? Why are you here today?"

I stared into the fragile cup as though the answer floated in the amber-colored tea. "I'm lost right now. I'm seeing things I never thought I'd see. Scary, dangerous things. And it's challenging everything I believe. I need to get back on track before I completely derail, but I don't know how to do that on my own."

"Do you have a church family?"

"Kind of, but . . . My situation's unique, and the people there are older, you know? They would offer the same three Bible verses that wouldn't apply to what I'm going through, and then . . ." My cheeks burned, ashamed from betraying the church with this admission. "I still believe, but right now, I need more than 'Have faith.'"

Zephyr took my cup and placed it on the coffee table next to hers. "May I take your hands?"

I hesitated, then nodded.

Zephyr rubbed my knuckles, then closed her eyes.

I waited silently, puzzled. *What do I do now? Are we praying?*

Zephyr opened her eyes and said, "How long has he been away?"

I flinched and pulled back, caught off guard.

But Zephyr didn't release her grip. She smiled, and said, "Emma, death is merely existence in another realm. There's nothing to fear from death. Or from those who have left us. Now. How long?"

I swallowed, then said, "Three weeks tomorrow."

"You had so many things to say," Zephyr said, then closed her eyes. "You had so many issues left to resolve, but . . ." She tilted her head as though she was listening to something. Her eyebrows crumpled. "But it was sudden and you didn't get a chance to talk about those things that were tearing you both apart.

"You weren't proud of your behavior," she continued. "You betrayed him. After promising yourself that you'd never betray him like that. But you did. Right before he died. With a very dangerous, very powerful man."

I snatched my hands away and glared at the tiny woman seated beside me.

Zephyr shook her head. "Emma, what we discuss here is private. Consider this like you would any traditional doctor-patient relationship." She cocked an eyebrow. "You can even give me your real name if you'd like."

Name? I didn't care about . . . How did she . . . ? I shook my head, my mind at once dull and sharp. "How did you . . . ? Doesn't it like, take three sessions or something before you . . . ?"

She said, "I'm not a psychiatrist anymore, sweetheart. My gift's bigger than that. You want answers. I give them to you. But my question to you is this: In order to be free, are you willing to deal with the pain that comes with acknowledging your part in Truman's death?"

I hopped off the couch, and shouted, "How do you know his name?"

Zephyr's eyes sparkled. "Because he's here with us. Right now."

Freaked out beyond freaked out, I whirled around. Saw no one except the woman in the fire-colored caftan.

"It's okay if you can't see him," Zephyr offered.

"No . . ." My eyes darted to the credenza, to her desk, to the open window and its silent wind chimes. *Why couldn't I see him?*

Zephyr said, "Emma, just—"

I raced out of the office, and darted down the hallway to the waiting room.

Trish was lost in her book.

The old man was snoring loudly, his chin resting on his chest.

I ran through the waiting room and out the front door.

The sun had seared the blue sky white, and its heat slowed my step. Blood had drained from my face, and my shaking had tightened to become shivering. I collapsed near the Volvo's tires and hunched over the pavement as the eruption bubbled first in my stomach, then erupted from my mouth. Fear, anxiety, tea—all of it spewed out and onto the concrete in a frothy, lavender-scented mess.

I couldn't see him. Why couldn't I see him?

CHAPTER 3

How could she know his name?

I hadn't given Zephyr *my* real name, even though she had "sensed" Emma was a fake. Still: I hadn't made an appointment, and I had paid cash so that no one could discover my true identity through banking information. And still, she knew . . .

This shit was scary, and the tiny part of me that still prayed and believed and didn't eat pork or say words like "shit" regretted transgressing against the Bible and seeking counsel from someone who sees dead people.

I couldn't go home now. A rip in the space-time-life-death continuum had occurred, and an empty house with strange drafts and eerie creaks was the last place I wanted (or needed) to be.

Leilani didn't answer the phone the ten times I called her, and as the sun dipped toward the ocean, I had no choice but to pull into Visitor Parking at Monica's condo in Marina del Rey—as far from Benedict Canyon as I could drive in my state of mind.

I offered Monica no explanation for my visit, and let her guide me to the guest bedroom. I'm sure my ashen face and the stench of sweat and vomit told her plenty.

Monica left me a cup of peppermint tea and clean towels, then closed the door behind her.

What should I do?

What should I believe?

Should I sell the house?

Or should I keep the house and let Leilani live there while I find a smaller place?

I lay in Monica's guest bed, unable to answer these questions because I had become imprisoned in an everlasting paralysis dream. I couldn't move. Couldn't scream. Told myself to wake up, to wiggle a finger, to do *something*, but I couldn't, no matter how hard I tried.

Truman was everywhere. At home. At Zephyr's. I couldn't escape him even though my heart had longed for him since that day in June. Strange and sad, I know. Pushing and pulling. Wanting him near, yet fearing him and running away to keep my secrets secret. Knowing that each time he visited meant one more dodge.

U have something 2 tell me.

What would he do to me if I told him the truth?

That night, I didn't see Truman again after doubling my Klonopin dosage. Safe in a drug-synthesized cocoon, I slept without dreaming, and resented the sun's morning light forcing my eyes to open. The new-day noises irritated me: the pounding surf, Monica's rumbling clothes dryer, the roaring crane at the condo construction site next door.

I trudged to the bathroom. Closed my eyes as I leaned against the towel rack, my mind and body noodle limp. I twisted the shower knobs, and hot water blasted from the silver nozzle. I turned back to the sink, and stared at my reflection in the mirror as steam clouded its surface. I pulled off Monica's T-shirt and boxers and stepped into the shower. I stood there, not moving, as water beat against my body.

I dunked my head beneath the stream, then scrubbed and lathered with Monica's fancy shower gel. My muscles appreciated the movement and the manufactured scent of Clean Linen. My mind cleared, and oxygen shot through my invigorated limbs. I could've stayed in the shower forever . . .

I rinsed off, twisted the taps, and stepped out into a cold, foggy world.

Words had been written across the mirror's steamed surface.

I'LL LUV U 4EVER. TRU.

Monica didn't speak as she poured coffee into three mugs. Leilani stood at the countertop and silently spread blackberry jam on toast. Moments before, I had burst into the kitchen, wet and naked, demanding that my friends see the message written in steam. By the time Monica and Leilani reached the bathroom, the words on the mirror had evaporated.

Monica slipped a cup of coffee near my hands, then sat at the tiny dining room table. "Don't get mad at me for saying this," she said, "but you need help. Maybe you should go someplace."

I glared at her. "What do you mean by 'someplace'?"

Monica hesitated before saying, "There are very nice centers or whatever that can help you figure all this out and help you get the rest you need. Don't worry about the house, or the bills, or any of that. I'll take care of everything. Just say 'yes' and I'll get everything in place."

Leilani smirked at me and cocked an eyebrow.

Monica touched my wrist, and said, "I'm only saying this—"

"Because you think I'm crazy," I said, snatching away from her.

"*Ghosts*, Nicole?" Monica said, wide-eyed. "Ghosts that send text messages, hang paintings, and write on mirrors? Does that sound normal to you?"

I glared at her and said, "Of course it isn't normal."

Monica said, "Lei and I don't want you picked up because you broke down on the 405. Do you want The People carting you off to some asylum so that we'd never see you again? The State can do that, you know."

"Yeah, a seventy-two-hour hold," I said, "but I'm not—" *What? Crazy?*

Leilani reached into her handbag and pulled out a silver flask.

Monica watched as Leilani poured bourbon into her mug. "It's eight in the morning."

Leilani ignored her, and turned to me. "Didn't Dr. Lucas give you something?"

"He gave me pills for anxiety." I lay my head on the table, confused by Monica's offer to help.

Monica smirked. "We should sue the Einstein in the lab cuz them pills ain't working."

Leilani said, "You can come stay with me since Mo's obviously tired of you."

"I'm not tired of her," Monica snapped.

"Why are you trying to foist her off on strangers, then?"

Monica slumped in her chair. "I didn't mean it like that. I just . . . Nicole, if you're not ready to go, please stay. I just want you to be okay. But I also want you to be able to sleep and not be afraid."

Leilani poured bourbon into my mug. "This will make the freak-outs go away."

As Monica and Leilani prepared to leave for the day, I trudged back to the bedroom, my belly warm with Irish coffee, and climbed into bed. I burrowed deep into the comforter until I could no longer hear jingling keys and dishes clinking in the sink. I barely heard my friends shout their goodbyes.

The telephone was ringing.

Knocked out of sleep, I sat up in bed. The comforter now lay crumpled on the floor. My shirt stuck to my skin, and I tugged at it with thick, sausage-like fingers. I glanced at the clock in the DVD player. Almost noon.

The telephone kept ringing and I ran to the living room to answer.

"May I speak with Monica Gladwyn?" a woman asked.

"She's not here," I said. "May I take a message?"

"This is Terese at Rayo del Sol. I was calling because Miss Gladwyn called earlier today. She wanted more information about our services."

"Rayo del Sol," I said, scribbling the message on a notepad. "And that's . . ."

"We're a mental health retreat located near Santa Barbara," Terese said. "It's a beautiful facility, gated and very private. Extremely discreet. Please tell Miss Gladwyn that she and her sister are welcome to visit this week, if she wants. Who am I speaking—"

I slammed the phone back in the cradle.

Monica didn't have a sister. The only person she'd want committed still wore pajamas at noon.

Crap.

I closed my eyes and imagined being connected to wires, jerking from electric shock therapy, thrashing around in a straitjacket with stringy hair, using my feces to write "Truman" over and over again across the walls of my padded cell. Slowly and painfully dying while trapped in my twisted imaginations. *Discreetly.*

Monica wanted to put me away. And if I proved to be a danger to myself (almost burning down my house with candles was a decent start), she'd have Section 5150 of the California Welfare and Institutions Code to help her.

I rushed back to the bedroom and threw my clothes and shoes into a plastic grocery bag.

But now you know: You can't trust anyone. Not even Monica.

My world was shrinking.

CHAPTER 4

Dr. Lucas didn't ask me to undress. He listened as I told him that the Klonopin wasn't working, and that I was still anxious, that my panic attacks were worsening.

"Strange," he said. "It usually does wonders for people. Let's try something else, then." He pulled a drug catalog from his coat pocket and hummed as he flipped through the book. He grunted, then scribbled onto a prescription pad.

I waited, and peeled dry skin from my lips and watched the flakes gather on my knees.

He handed me the slip of paper. "This should do it."

I studied his scribbles. "Does that say Xanax?"

He nodded. "It's more powerful than Klonopin. Trust me: Xanax will *definitely* do something about your anxiety."

"Will it help me sleep?"

He slipped the pen back into his smock pocket. "A fortunate side effect is drowsiness. You'll be too sleepy to worry."

I considered the prescription again. "What about the *unfortunate* side effects? Doesn't Xanax . . ." I could only remember drowsiness, sleepiness, and weight gain, two of those three I didn't mind.

"You mean nervousness, diarrhea, blurred vision?"

Diarrhea? What the hell?

Dr. Lucas waved his hand. "Only a small number of patients experience that." He squeezed my shoulder, then strode to the door. "Xanax is very powerful, and those side effects are real, but I don't think you have to worry. Next week this time, you'll be thanking me."

Arnib had been assigned to work in the pharmacy, and he kept glancing at me as he processed my Xanax prescription. "I had your order handled as a special urgent rush," he said. "Usually, it takes longer than fifteen minutes. You buying this Coke, too?" He held up the soda bottle.

I stood at the counter, a zombie with a crooked ponytail.

"We have to stop meeting like this," he said. "In the store all the time, I mean. Hard to believe, but I look different out of this smock."

Is he talking to me? I blinked at him and shook my head. "Huh?"

The clerk smiled, and his clear braces glistened in the fluorescent light. "I said, 'We have to stop meeting . . .'" He cleared his throat and tried another approach. "There's this café? It's called Luna? It's down on Sunset. Good muffins, great coffee. Better than the coffee next door. And this guy? He plays Spanish guitar on Thursday nights. I was wondering if, you know, you'd like to, you know . . ."

I blinked at him again. *Is he asking me out on a date?*

He blushed, then rushed to close the deal. "I'd pay for you of course. But maybe it's too soon. My sister waited six years to start dating after her husband died."

I shook my head. "What are we talking about?"

"Café Luna. I don't wanna pressure you, but . . ."

"How much?" I opened my purse and startled at the sight of my gun. *When had I put it in there?* Couldn't remember. But then, I didn't remember much. I touched the cold weapon, and thought of shooting Arnib and the shelves of medicine and the speakers now playing Al Jarreau. My cheeks flushed as panic found me at the pharmacy.

"You paying cash or credit?" Arnib asked.

I exhaled slowly, then reached for my wallet. "Cash."

Before leaving the pharmacy, I cracked open the Coke and popped a Xanax. My stomach growled, warning me that it would not suffer through another night of tea and microwave popcorn. I wandered over to the market's food bars, and my stomach flipped, jubilant from the aromas of fresh, hot food. After filling a container with angel hair pasta and grilled vegetables, I paid the cashier and found an empty table near the windows.

As I finished half of my meal, I stopped gobbling noodles and stared into my container. The back of my neck tingled. *Someone's watching me.* I wiped my mouth with a napkin and looked up, pretending to casually gaze with disinterest at the yuppies eating dinner, the moms feeding toddlers Cheerios, the friends chatting over salads.

Truman stood near the coffee bar.

I shrieked, and a mother with a towheaded boy she called Tucker glared at me.

Dressed in his wet clothes, Truman grinned and seawater dribbled from his mouth. He beckoned me with his bloated, bloody finger. When I didn't move, he bared his teeth—sharp silver fangs that glistened with goopy spit.

My hands shook as I closed my dinner container as normally as I could, no longer hearing laughter, cell phones, "Tucker, stop that and sit down." I grabbed my box of pasta and beat it out of there, not looking in Truman's direction again. Back in the Volvo, I sat in the driver's seat, still shaking, unable to fit the key into the ignition, staring in the rearview mirror at the store's entrance to make sure—

What? That he doesn't walk through it? That thought—*he's a ghost and doesn't need a door*—made my hands relax. It was, in its way, reason at work.

Calmer now, I pulled my cell phone from my pocket and called Leilani. "I'm seeing him again. Seeing Truman, I mean."

"Where are you?" Leilani shouted over music, laughter, and talking.

"The village market. In the parking lot."

"I'm at Sony with Mo right now. She's doing the premiere of that stupid Jessica Alba movie tonight, remember? But I'll come get you if you need me to."

I nibbled at my thumbnail, feeling childish for calling. "No. That's okay. I just . . . You told me to call whenever, you know . . . I'm sorry."

"You never have to apologize to me. You should come down tonight. They have baby lamb chops and those shrimp things you love."

Tears filled my eyes as I remembered parties, martinis, and those shrimp things I loved. *Premieres and openings.* Lifetimes ago. "Maybe I will. What time?"

"Get here for nine," she said. "And put on something sexy. Something I would wear."

"So . . . naked and wearing a pair of Manolo Blahniks."

She laughed, and I promised to drink three martinis and eat a bucket of shrimp as soon as I drove past the studio gates.

I slipped the key into the ignition and started the car. Before backing out of my space, I glanced in the rearview mirror.

There he was again. Standing among the pots of orchids, gazing in my direction, baring those glistening fangs. He didn't do anything else as he stood there. And as a family of six passed in front of him, he disappeared.

Don't know why I drove to the San Pedro pier. Don't know what I expected to see. I only knew that Truman—corporal Truman—remained lost in that piece of the Pacific.

Somewhere in the fog, ship horns blasted and harbor seals barked. The western slice of the sky glowed brilliant orange—the color of romantic walks along the beach and candlelit dinners. To the east, the sky had darkened to a steely, dangerous blue. The blue of an endless universe and of Langoliers, creatures that gobbled up the present and left behind a void as sinister as this sky.

Tell me what to do.

I stood there as seagulls swooped overhead, as seals barked on faraway buoys, waiting for God to give me a sign. But He sent no column of smoke or no burning bush, and the ocean refused to surrender my husband.

It was easy for the world to move on. But I couldn't. No one had loved me like Truman had, and I could never say that he was no longer alive until someone proved otherwise.

You don't have to wait. You can join him, you know. If you jump off this pier, touch the ocean's bottom, and just keep walking, you'll find him . . .

If I jumped in feet first, I wouldn't have to struggle to stand once I reached the ocean floor.

I gripped the wooden handrail, and splinters pricked my palms. I placed one foot on the bottom slat, and lifted myself from the pier.

A damp breeze from the Pacific washed over me, and I shivered.

What am I doing?

I peered at my feet, just inches off the wooden planks.

I don't wanna die.

I stepped back, stumbling away from that vast, gray ocean, and raced toward the parking lot. I glanced back over my shoulder like Lot's wife as the dark sky continued its approach.

I climbed back into the Volvo, and closed my eyes. My nerves cracked beneath my skin like eggs against tile.

Deep breath. Deep breath. Deep . . .

I imagined sinking to the bottom of the sea, wandering past coral beds and shipwrecks in search of my husband.

My eyes snapped open—I was still sitting in my car.

The sun had set and the emptying parking lot glowed beneath the streetlamps.

How long have I . . . ?

Three spaces away, a group of cholos loitered around a tricked-out Monte Carlo. The one wearing a Dodgers sweatshirt was staring in my direction.

I touched the auto-lock button, and all the door locks clicked. Sounded so loud in the quiet that I prayed that the men hadn't heard. The gun was still in my purse, but against the quartet near the Chevy, my .22 had the same power as cotton balls.

A Mustang pulled out of the space behind me, and the Volvo's cabin filled with golden light from its headlamps. The four men lifted their middle fingers at the driver in the Ford, then threw beer bottles as it rumbled past them.

Crap.

Glass continued to crash behind me, and I glanced in the rear-view mirror.

Truman sat in the back seat.

I sat there, breathless, convinced that if I didn't appear frightened, he wouldn't speak.

Another car's headlamps shone into the Volvo, and Truman shimmered in its light.

I whispered, "What do you want?"

He smiled, and water trickled from his mouth down his chin.

"You show up now?" I asked him through gritted teeth. "*Now*, Truman? When you were alive, did you show up when you were supposed to, huh?" I clenched my jaw as my body vibrated with anger. "Did you show up for Valentine's Day? No. Did you show up for *Wicked*? No. Cuz you were a ghost then, too. I'm not scared of you. Why don't you go straight to—"

My neck tightened, and my body filled with ice . . .

Couldn't breathe.

Truman hadn't moved—he sat there, staring at me.

I coughed, struggled for air, kicked at the gas and brake pedals. I reached for the door handle and pulled. The door swung open, and I threw myself out of the car and onto my hands and knees, vomiting and coughing.

"You okay, miss?" Dude in the sweatshirt was kneeling beside me. He turned to his buddies, and said, "Maybe we should call 9-1-1."

"Naw, man. Fuck the police."

"Since when you give a fuck about niggas, homie?"

"This *buey* just shot some up yesterday, and now he all Martin Luther the King and shit."

Sweatshirt said, "But she's having seizures."

"She can suck my big fat *bicho*, *ese*. Matter of fact . . ." He lifted his shirt to show a tatted-up abdomen, then tugged at his belt.

Sweatshirt said, "That ain't funny. Not her, holmes."

Not caring about the very real danger I faced, I croaked, "Someone's in my car."

One man turned to glance inside the Volvo. He sported a tattoo of a black hand on the back of his head. "Ain't nobody in there."

Sweatshirt helped me stand, then offered me a bunch of napkins. "Too much tequila, eh?"

"Something like that," I whispered as I dabbed at my mouth. "Did Jake Huston tell you to follow me here?"

They stared at me with wide, blank eyes—each looking like the twenty-year-olds they were.

As the group wandered back to their car, Sweatshirt said, "You sure you okay?"

I nodded, then clambered back into the driver's seat. I glanced in the rearview mirror: No one sat there. I was alone. But as I crept out of the parking lot, I saw him again.

Truman, one hand held up, wishing me farewell.

Cory B., the curly-headed sales associate at Best Buy, thought I was just another weary-eyed customer who had had a long day at work. And my request—*Sell me an in-home surveillance system*—had sounded simple enough. "Oh yeah," Cory said. "I can help you with that." He smiled, then added, "And I'll make sure someone comes out to set it up for you."

"But the equipment needs to be powerful enough to pick up ghosts," I said. "Because my husband is haunting me, and I need to capture him on tape."

Cory B.'s eyes widened a bit. "Okay."

I followed him through the store, watching his long curls bounce with each step. He tried several times (unsuccessfully) to pass me off to other salesmen (*Ain't my department, man,* and *You got that covered, bro*) until we reached the audiovisual department.

He muttered, "Any of these are good."

I studied him, and he fidgeted under my stare. "But *which* is best?" I asked. "I'm here with you, Cory B., cuz you know more than me. I could've grabbed any of these and paid for it, but I didn't. I came to you cuz you're the professional. Now which is best? Which system will do what I need?"

"To see ghosts."

"Uh-huh."

Cory pointed to the most expensive system on the shelf. "This one's pretty powerful. You got your small video receiver, your sensor that detects motion whenever something moves. You get four in-door cameras, four outdoor cameras, a 160GB hard drive, and a seventeen-inch color LCD monitor. But if you have an alarm system already installed, I'm sure it may be cheaper just to ask your security company to—"

"Takes too long," I said. "And I'm not trying to look at someone breaking in. He isn't breaking *in*. And I need something now. And I don't wanna take all day straightening out wires and hard drives."

"So you *don't* want a real surveillance system?" Cory said.

"I want *cameras that record*," I said. "Strong enough to—"

"I know," Cory grumbled. "See ghosts. Right."

Minutes later, I headed to the exit with four boxes of high-definition video cameras.

The teenage greeter said, "Have a good night," and I contemplated running her over with my car.

I hid one camera in the bookcase, between *Troilus and Cressida* and *The Complete Works of John Milton.* Slipped another camera into the bathroom cabinet, nestling it between stacks of towels. I placed another camera on top of the refrigerator, between a box of Special K cereal and a bag of stale barbecue potato chips. I returned to my bedroom with the last camera and placed it on top of the armoire.

I've finally done it. I've crossed the line. This can't be real.

But real and imagined no longer existed as separate ideas, and had been compromised so much that I wondered: Was there really much difference between the two? Or was it just a matter of perspective, or circumstances?

With aching shoulders, I hopped off the chair and lumbered to the bathroom. I wouldn't make the Sony party. I had depleted the stores of adrenaline that had fueled my drive to the harbor, and then, to Best Buy. I popped another Xanax, realizing (too late) that I had already taken one.

Oh well.

I floated back to the bedroom, and changed into shorts and a tank top. I needed to sleep. But instead of sinking to the couch, I lumbered down to the kitchen. My limbs had gained weight, and now, I struggled to stand. I slid against the cabinets and sank to the cold floor. I sat there, staring at the brown, curled twigs attached to the ends of my feet. Don't know how long I stayed there, but the light changed all around me, and I could no longer see my toes.

My head rolled forward until it touched my bent knees. Heard myself snoring, and my head snapped up, awake again.

So warm in here.

Beads of cold sweat trickled down my spine, making my tank top stick to my skin like caramel.

I crawled over to the kitchen door, and pulled myself to my feet. I stepped out into the cold air. My bare arms prickled, and I hugged myself for warmth.

The dog up the hill was barking again.

I took a few steps to the driveway, the asphalt like hard, scratchy ice beneath my bare soles.

I staggered on to the strip of land between my house and the Cubans'. Could hear the theme song from *Six Feet Under* coming from their second-story window. The moon was almost full on this night, and the canyon shone with silver, bright light. Magic.

"Lord of the rings," I muttered. "Elf woods."

I stepped forward and the canyon swung to the left, then returned to center. I swayed, then closed my eyes. Kept them shut as I wobbled forward, stopping once my toes met dirt.

Into the brush . . . Burrs and sharp twigs stuck my skin. Winced once, then . . . numb. Didn't hurt.

The land sloped and the wild brush rose higher than my hips. Something glowed in the deepest reaches of the canyon.

A key.

Like in World of Warcraft. *I need that key. Keys open treasure chests. I want treasure. Or maybe it'll open a door and Truman will be standing there and then it will open another door, and God will be there, seated on His throne, and the angels and Jesus and Moses will be there, too, clapping for me, smiling, because I'm home . . . And then . . .*

I stumbled about in the tangle of chaparral, tripped, and fell forward. My hands landed on something sharp. "Ow," then . . . numb. Didn't hurt. I held my hands out before me. In that silvery light, beneath that silver moon, the blood on my palms glistened like magic elixir, full of life power.

The key kept blinking farther down in the darkness and I crawled toward it, stumbling most of the way. Dry brush scraped my face, and dirt filled my mouth. I spat it out and sat up on my knees.

No twinkling key.

Another player had grabbed it.

I moaned, and a sob broke from my chest.

The canyon tilted again, and I closed my eyes. *So tired.* I lay back in the brush, not caring about rattlesnakes, fire ants, or coyotes. Gazed up at the sky. Bright stars. Silver moon. Dark woods. So quiet . . .

◆ ◆ ◆

"I found her!"

I opened my eyes to a clear turquoise sky.

"Down there," a man shouted.

I sat up and blinked. *Where . . . ?* I gawked at the brush around me, at my filthy shorts and tank top, at my bloody hands, my red, bite-ridden arms, my bare feet. My mouth tasted like dirt and squirrel.

The sheriff's deputy working his way down the hill toward me was panting and sweating.

I tried to stand, but every muscle in my body screamed.

"You okay, miss?" the deputy shouted.

I swiped at tears tumbling down my cheek.

The deputy reached me and dried his sweaty forehead with his arm. "What are you doing down here?"

I stared at him, then said, "Don't know."

He helped me climb back up to the street. A sheriff's patrol car sat in front of my house, its red and blue lights swirling, its police radio crackling. My Cuban neighbors and Jake huddled together near my driveway. Monica, her cheeks wet with tears, rushed to hug me.

"She was passed out," the deputy said.

"I got here and the kitchen door was wide open," Monica said. "And you weren't in the house, and I didn't know what . . ."

My head ached from all the talking, from the hum of cicadas in the trees, from the clicking of the police lights. I winced and crumpled to my knees.

Monica and Jake rushed to my side.

Jake said, "We should probably take her to the—"

"I'm fine," I said. "I wanna go home."

No one spoke. The squawk of the police radio echoed through the canyon.

My stomach twisted and threatened action.

Jake said, "You need help carrying her?"

Monica said, "No, I got it." But she struggled as she tried to help me stand.

Jake slipped one arm on the back of my thigh, and the other behind my back.

I caught air then, and the world rocked all the way around this time, and then I saw blue sky.

Hot water. Shea butter soap. Warm soft towel. Strawberry-scented lotion.

Third time Monica had helped me shower.

My limbs felt goopy. Blinking sent sparks blasting through my head.

Antiseptic. Bandages.

Jake sat at the edge of the chaise, one hand covering his mouth.

Monica guided me toward the bed.

I stopped in my step. "Not in here." I was out of it, but not *that* out of it.

She led me down the hallway to the den.

Jake followed.

My quilt. My pillow. My remote control.

I settled into the couch cushions.

"Nic," Monica whispered, "I don't think . . ."

I pressed "Power" on the remote and the television popped to life. *Maury. Who is my baby daddy?*

"I know we joked about this, but now it's not funny," Monica said. "We think you should get help. Like in a supervised environment."

ShaQuan said Little Kenyon had Big Kenyon's eyes and the *same exact* birthmark on his left calf. *There ain't no way that baby ain't his,* she claimed. *I ain't lyin' about this.*

"Nicole," Monica said, firmer now. "Are you listening to me? You're starting to endanger yourself."

I shook my head—didn't care what she had to say.

"Sweetheart," Jake said, "something could've happened to you down there. Coyotes, mountain lions . . ."

Big Kenyon was *not* the father, and the audience went wild.

Right as ShaQuan ran off the stage, Monica grabbed the remote from my hand and jammed the power button. "Nicole," she shouted, "do you wanna die?"

My body hurt. My mind hurt. Life hurt. And all of it made that question so easy to answer.

"Well, I'm not gonna let you," she said, grabbing the telephone.

"Who are you calling?" I asked, interested now.

"Harvey Feldman. If you won't get help, then—"

"I'll never forgive you," I shouted, sitting up.

Monica turned to Jake. "Are you gonna say something or just stand there?"

Jake stood there, mouth open, confusion painted on his face.

"I'm fine," I said. "I wanted fresh air and it was so quiet out there and I fell asleep. After all that's happened, is that so hard to believe?"

"I'm moving in, then," Monica said as she threw the phone on the desk.

"I don't need a babysitter," I said. "I just want . . ." My throat closed, and I couldn't speak.

"What?" Jake whispered.

I just want to be free. To know that God cares about me, and not in a theoretical sense, but is actively trying to find a way out for me like hostage negotiators did for those people in Iran.

I shook my head. "I swear I don't know what happened. I didn't mean to be in the canyon. Maybe I was sleepwalking. I don't know . . ."

Monica was crying now.

"I'll get better," I said. "Okay? I won't leave the house like that again. I promise."

Monica nodded, but her eyes said something different.

CHAPTER 5

I closed my eyes as Zephyr made a pot of tea. On this day, I had followed Dr. Lucas's directions—one Xanax a day. The drug had smoothed me out some, and had made me less prickly just as the doctor had promised. Still, talking to Zephyr seemed so outlandish. Sure, she was more attentive than Dr. Tremaine, and since we had no past together (like I had with Monica and Leilani), she could offer advice without beginning or ending every sentence with "I know how you are." And unlike Dr. Tremaine, Zephyr knew Truman's name without me having to tell her five times. She knew it before I had even said it. *Still* . . . She was a psychic, and that little bit of truth scratched at the back of my mind.

Zephyr's pink and gold caftan billowed behind her as she returned to the couch with two teacups. She handed me one, then sat beside me on the couch. "I know it's different and can be startling, but it's a blessing. Many people would love to have a visit from a loved one who's away."

"But these visits scare me," I said. "And I can't tell if he's real or not."

Zephyr cocked her head. "Oh, Emma. Of course he's real."

"He's getting violent," I said, then rubbed my neck—still sore from the struggle at the pier two days before.

"He cannot be violent," Zephyr said and dropped two sugar cubes into her tea. "Truman is not a poltergeist."

"How do you know?"

"Poltergeists don't exist. God wouldn't allow it."

I narrowed my eyes and cocked my head. "But God allows regular ghosts?"

She smiled and stirred her tea. "God allows things that our itty-bitty brains could never comprehend. You're projecting your anxieties about something else onto your husband, and it is manifesting itself through the physical world."

"Maybe if circumstances had been different," I said. "Maybe if there had been a body, some sort of closure . . . I hate this. Not being in control of my environment. Truman knew that. *Knows* that. Whatever. That's one reason we had problems. He was selfish sometimes. And I hate saying this, but if I had acted like him, we'd both be . . ."

"Dead?" Zephyr placed her teacup on the table. "I know this will sound harsh, but you're gonna have to be aggressive about moving on. You have to start removing some elements of Truman out of your path to recovery. I'm talking about painful reminders: houses, cars, designer clothes . . . Even money. If it's keeping you from living a full and healthy life, then you need to give it all to charity, or to family members. Bury it if you must." She paused, then added, "Then you must say your final farewells. It is part of the healing process."

"My sister-in-law wanted to have a memorial service," I said. "It just seemed premature."

"I think it's time," Zephyr said. "Even if it's a private service just for you and his sister. This way, you can tell Truman that he's your past, and that you have to heal, that his visits scare you. Let him know that you love him but your life together is over. Confess whatever sins you've committed against him, and then, move on. It'll hurt, but I'm here to help you. For as long as you need." She took my hands and squeezed. "You have big things ahead of you, Emma. A new world with new challenges, with new friends. Maybe even a male friend. Don't worry: It's all a part of moving on."

She stood and retreated to her desk. "Your assignment for the week is this: You must engage in an activity that represents the start of your new life." She smiled, and added, "You can do it. You must do it. It's a matter of life and death."

Moving on.

Moving on meant more than just rearranging closet space, and no longer buying Cherry Garcia. *Moving on* meant changing the name on the phone bill, and on the title of the house. Erasing the voicemail message and recording a new one that said "I'm not home" instead of "We're not home." *Moving on* meant going to movies and eating at restaurants and planning summer vacations . . .

Too much to ask. Too much to do.

But I had moved on before so it *wasn't* too much to ask. After Aunt Beryl's death, I had moved on. After my parents' accident, I had moved on. I would have to do it again.

Jake was jogging up the road as I climbed out of the Volvo. He slowed as he neared my driveway, unsure of whether to speak or shrink from bullets.

Something inside of me popped, seeing him again. Don't know what I felt, but it wasn't fear. I waved to him, and said, "Don't worry. I'm not armed."

He stopped in his step, and took a moment to catch his breath. "You feeling okay today?"

I shrugged.

"You really scared us the other day."

I grunted as response.

"I don't know what I did," he said, "but your opinion of me has changed, and I'm sorry, okay? But I'm not out to hurt you, Nic. I'm not the bad guy."

I smirked at him. "Okay."

"What does that mean?"

"Nothing." I turned to walk back to my house.

He grabbed my hand. "Don't go. Talk to me."

I pulled out of his grasp and backed away from him. "I've seen you sneaking around my house. Not just that one time when I came out with the gun. Other times. Sometimes late at night."

"*Sneaking around?* We're neighbors. And I told you that I'm cleaning—"

"And when you're not sneaking, your little Mexican Mafia posse is following me around the city."

"*What?*" He laughed. "You're joking, right?"

I glared at him.

"Nic, I haven't asked the Mexican Mafia to follow you."

"So you just defend them, then, right?"

He blushed and said, "You read about all that, I guess. My client—my *dead* client now—had bragged to me that he had killed that boy and that he knew where the boy's body was. I couldn't tell anyone. Even though he was an awful human being, it was my job to defend him."

I folded my arms, and said, "I'm not stupid, Jacob. I know all about attorney-client privilege."

"And you also know that as a criminal defense attorney, I can't say, 'This guy is yucky, I'm not gonna defend him.' It's my job."

"Did you have to take this case, though?"

His eyes widened. "Yes. Who am I supposed to represent, Nic? Only the innocent? Don't forget that we're all innocent until a jury and judge says you're not."

"I know that," I said with a sigh.

"Believe me, Nic," he said. "A part of me wants to tell, especially to help that boy's poor mother . . . But I can't. Even when Hernandez died a few days ago, I still couldn't say anything. Attorney-client privilege lasts forever. At least for now. The courts are trying to figure that out now." He shrugged, and placed his hands on his hips. "It's the moral thing to do, telling everything I know, but it's still unethical. I'd never be able to practice law again."

My eyes burned with tears, but I shook my head anyway. "None of that has anything to do with you sneaking around. I saw you leaving my house with a trash bag—"

"You left the door open that day," he said. "And the trash bag . . . Someone had run over that chocolate Lab near your driveway, and I didn't want you to see it."

I opened my mouth, but couldn't speak.

"Look, Nic," he said. "Truman was my competition, but I knew that you loved him. I'm not a mob lawyer, okay? I didn't put a hit on him, or have him kidnapped. I'm the jealous type, but I'm not the murdering type, and with everything that's going on with me, I'm sure you think I'm a thug in lawyer's drag, but I'm not. And I wish Truman was still alive because then I'd still have you in my life."

Don't believe him. You can't trust anyone.

"You know me, Nicole," he said with a fragile smile. "I'm the same guy who takes you to lunch and sends you flowers. And because I'd do anything for you, I'll take a lie detector test if you want. Go on one of those court shows just for you. I have the time nowadays." He took my hands again and squeezed them. "Can I take you down the hill for coffee? Just to talk. That's it. No shenanigans."

I smiled.

"What?" he asked.

"I like that word," I said. "Shenanigans. It's the writer in me." I shook my head and turned back toward the house. "I should go."

"I won't let you," he said.

What if Truman comes and you're not there? And all this is Jake's fault anyway. You can't trust him.

"Please?" he said. "Let me take a shower and we'll walk down together."

He was offering a cup of coffee, not a wedding ring.

So, I nodded, and said, "Okay," before I had the chance to change my mind.

CHAPTER 6

I showered in the guest bathroom even though Truman had already proven that he could travel anywhere to write messages on any steamy mirror in the world. I exfoliated, then shaved hairy armpits that had grown as wild as a jungle, stopping short of attacking the chimp farm covering my legs. My heart hammered as I slathered lotion on my calves and belly. Tried to relax, and act nonchalant as I groomed, but all of it made me anxious.

It's not a date. It's coffee. With an old . . . friend.

I sat in the den and waited for Jake to arrive. The setting sun had painted the room bronze. Soon, the sun and the light would disappear altogether, and it would be dark and I would be out with a man.

If it's dark, it's a date. You can't do that.

I grabbed the phone from the computer desk, and pushed 6-7-3, the starting sequence of Jake's cell phone number.

The doorbell rang.

Too late.

Jake stood on my porch, more tanned now than he had been back in June. Since then, he had probably vacationed in the Bahamas with a cute blond paralegal named "Jen" who sunbathed topless and pretended to read *One Hundred Years of Solitude.*

"Ready, Nic?" he asked.

His deep voice rumbled in my belly, and I remembered the way my skin tingled any time he said my name. In that fleeting moment, I envied Jen the Paralegal.

We walked down the hill without talking. The neighborhood sat silent. No birds chirped. No cars zoomed up the hill. Only the sound of our shoes tapping against the sloping asphalt. Somewhere, someone barbecued, and smoky, sweet air tweaked my nose. *Ribs.* I wanted ribs. And grilled sweet corn. And a pitcher of sangria.

As usual, dogs and their owners crowded the coffee shop. Jake joined the long line to order our drinks, and I wandered around until two teens with skateboards abandoned their window table. I slumped in the chair, smiling within, cheering myself for wanting ribs and for sitting in a coffee shop.

Moving on.

Jake, two cups in hand, slipped into the chair across from me. "Am I old," he shouted, "or is this place louder than usual?" He considered the rowdy crowd and mindlessly touched an angry-looking scratch on his neck.

I winced, and pointed to the mark. "Must've been some night. She jacked you up."

He smirked. "Love letter from Inmate 43986. She's a wildcat. I had to get a tetanus shot and an HIV test. The glamorous life of a high-price lawyer, right? I'll miss it." He leaned forward. "So, Nicole Baxter: How are you getting through all of this?"

I sipped my coffee, then shrugged. "Other than holding you at gunpoint, and my friends thinking that I'm crazy, with one of them wanting to commit me and the other one giving me a gun, and a bunch of other freakish, unimaginable things happening, including almost burning my house down? Other than all that, I'm great, just fantastic."

He reached across the table and grasped my hand. "First: I doubt your friends want to put you away, even after that episode in the canyon. Remember: You also thought I wanted to kill you, and that's far from the truth. Life's changed, you know? And I know it seems like you can't trust anyone because it's all so different. It'll take time to adjust, but you aren't alone, Nicole. We're friends. You'll always have me."

My skin warmed with this touch, and my pulse quickened as I imagined the feel of muscles beneath my hands, stubble against my cheek, another warm body—any body—pressed against mine . . .

My face flushed, and I pulled my hand out of his grip.

What did the other customers think, seeing us there? That we were lovers? That I was happy? What would Leilani think? Worse: What would Truman think?

"It's been three weeks," I said, "and I still don't know . . ." Defeated, I pushed away my coffee cup.

Jake peered at me in silence, then said, "My first wife, Heather, died of leukemia. She was only 26."

I cocked my head. "I didn't know . . . You told me about Dana, but not . . ."

"Because I don't talk about it much." He gazed out the window. "I couldn't understand it. How a healthy, vital woman could just . . . *die*, you know? She jogged. She ate better than most people. And then, she caught a cold except that it wasn't a cold. We sat in the doctor's office in total shock because we thought that leukemia was a kid's disease.

"It made no sense to me, and I tried to find the answer. Not the chemical, biological reasons why she got cancer. Understanding *how* she died was easy—leukemic blood cells overtaking good white blood cells. But I wanted to find *the* answer, you know?"

I nodded.

"I guess that's what drew me to you," he said. "What you do for a living. Helping people find the answer."

"How did you handle it?" I whispered.

"I was raised Catholic," he said, "and before Heather passed, I had been a pretty good one. Went to Mass every Sunday. Took Communion . . . I tried hard to stay faithful and to believe that it would all work out, but each day she got sicker, and I prayed a little less. One day, I stopped praying altogether."

An old couple—regulars who the baristas called Mr. and Mrs. Gudger—passed the window, holding hands and walking toward Sunset. Since Truman's accident, I no longer enjoyed watching them (or couples like them) in their matching tracksuits stroll hand in hand. Caught myself thinking, *That won't be me, so why should it be them?*

Resentments are quiet, evil things—snails in a vegetable garden. They chew away at your heart and you never realize that you're the mean old lady who never smiles and yells at kids to stay off her lawn.

"When you're young," I said, "you think you'll have at least fifty more years with this person. That you'll both die quiet deaths at ninety-eight. Some people do, I guess. Not everyone, obviously."

He gazed at me with brown eyes darkened by death memories. "For a long time, I couldn't move past that void. Actually, I kept falling in that void and when I was there, I wondered if God ever existed. That scared me.

"But then, I realized what a wonderful time she and I had together. She'd hate to know I was shutting myself up in the house. That missing her was making me miss life."

"How do you miss her and still function, though?" I asked. "It feels like a betrayal."

Jake shrugged. "You do small things, I guess. Make it a point to laugh at least twice a day. Go out for drinks with your friends once every couple of weeks . . . I'll always love her but that love doesn't shackle me. It's not this prison that keeps me from the world."

He offered me a small smile. "Love is like big country. Endless, unpredictable wilderness. You have some rough times, but then, you stumble on unexpected beauty and you wonder if anyone else has ever stood in that same spot . . ." He chuckled, then shrugged again. "I never felt that way with Dana, and she knew it and that's why we didn't work out."

"Our wedding anniversary's on Saturday," I said. "We would've made twelve years." Tears stung my eyes as I took his hand, needing that human contact again. "I wasn't ready, you know? It was so abrupt and . . . No goodbyes. No nothing. That was it. He was gone. And it feels like years have passed since that day, and each time I fall asleep, I wake up and wonder, where is he? Is he working late again? And then I remember . . ."

All around us, people laughed and talked. The espresso machine hissed as it steamed milk.

"It's hard being alone in this city," I said, tearing at a napkin. "Everyone's so carefree and sexy . . . Like the folks here."

Jake cast his eyes around the room. "I see scared, confused people hiding behind designer clothes and tattoos."

I considered the young faces around me.

Since Truman's death, I had marveled at the well-groomed homes in my neighborhood. I had envied the living going on behind those beautiful doors. Attractive Angelenos with shiny cars, wearing crisp, fresh clothes. They had it all.

But once upon a time, someone had looked at me, too, the way I now studied my neighbors. Someone in the world had thought I lived a pain-free, fabulous life with my man in our gorgeous home. They didn't know about our betrayals and inattentions, about that gorgeous house with its mysterious drafts and creepy rumbles. They didn't know that I lay awake at night, tired and sleepy but unable to rest, pondering whether my dead husband was actually dead and haunting me while prescription drugs coursed through my veins like blood.

No one's grass is greener. Just different shades of brown.

Not that my life was a complete wreck. Not that my situation was comparable to those women suddenly widowed with three kids and no money. But I had *planned*. I wasn't supposed to be punished anymore because other than that one time with Jake, and a secret here and there, I had colored inside Life's lines.

Jake and I trekked back up the hill in silence. Streetlamps buzzed as fog crept up the sides of the canyon. The moist night air smelled of sweet earth, wild sage, and lavender. Up ahead, my front porch glowed with golden light, and this time, I didn't feel so awful not seeing Truman standing there, waiting for my return.

At the front door, I offered Jake my hand. "Thanks for this."

"Can we see each other again?" he asked. "We can go someplace without skateboards, iPads, and Chihuahuas in sweaters. Dinner wherever you want."

I smiled. "I'd like that. My couch is about to file a restraining order against me."

He squeezed my hand before letting go. "I'll call you later." As he strolled down the flagstone pathway, he turned back to say, "If you need to talk before then, remember that I'm here, okay? As a friend." He blew me a kiss, then jogged up the hill.

Seconds away from closing my eyes, I realized that I had forgotten to take my dose of Xanax. I turned over on the couch, not planning to leave the warmth of my quilt, and watched the opening credits of *Seinfeld*. Before the first commercial break, I had already fallen asleep.

CHAPTER 7

This time, a ringing telephone, and not a nightmare, startled me from sleep. On the television screen, a young Black woman ran off the stage because the no-good now performing an elaborate dance with a white handkerchief was *not* the daddy. *Chiantay's Fifth Visit: Who's My Baby's Daddy?* Maury Povitch followed the hysterical chick backstage. "We'll find little DeVaughndre's daddy no matter how many shows it takes," he assured her.

I smiled, then glanced at the clock.

Minutes before ten o'clock.

Asleep for twelve hours.

I sat up, meeting resistance as I turned my neck. Stiff from sleeping in one position all night. Didn't mind the pain, though. I had slept for twelve effin' hours—a modern-day miracle.

I stood and stretched, my mind light, my hands aching to *do* something. Having coffee with Jake had incited some kind of mental breakthrough.

I ambled to the bathroom without casting an anxious glance at my bed. I took a shower, then considered my reflection in the mirror. No message written in steam.

I pulled on swanky jeans *(They still fit!)* and my favorite *Star Wars* T-shirt. No phantom blocked me from my drawer of clean clothes.

I made a small breakfast of toast, eggs, and coffee. No strange messages composed on the refrigerator.

After eating, I stood in the middle of the kitchen—a strange place in the daytime. With all that midday sunlight, I saw dried juice staining the grout between the tiles. I discovered grape tomatoes rotting in the back of the refrigerator's crisper. Old prints of basketball shoes—size 11—dirtied the Mexican tile floors. "I'm living in a hovel."

I grabbed the tub of bleach and a sponge from beneath the sink. As I scrubbed and wiped, bleach splattered all over my True Religions.

I'll buy another pair of jeans. Maybe I'll call Leilani and we'll make a day out of it.

After cleaning the kitchen, I grabbed a new trash bag and retreated upstairs. I stood before the closed door of Truman's home office and tried to ignore the Geiger counter sensation that came with standing so close to this room. I hesitated—didn't want to do this. Because what would I find as I cleaned? Receipts to romantic dinners with another woman? A hidden box of love letters? Condoms?

My hands balled into fists, my jaw clenched, and I backed away from the door.

You'll have to do it eventually. Just get it over with.

I took several cleansing breaths, and my hands relaxed and my teeth stopped grinding against each other.

I opened the door, then crept over to his desk.

Found a package of now-stale licorice. An empty can of Red Bull. Dusty computer monitor. Pens. A glossy box—*World of Warcraft: The Burning Crusade* expansion set—remained unopened and ready to install onto the computer. My hands shook as I plucked the can, and then the licorice, from the desk and dropped them into the trash bag. I left the *WOW* box there even though he'd never open it, even though he'd never reach level 68. I had teased him about his alter—a warlock-class gnome he had named Omemo. On the night he acquired the Field Marshal's dreadweave robe, the last piece to complete his epic armor set, he had bragged, "I'm pretty badass now." I had rolled my eyes, and called him a *WOW* nerd. He laughed and called me Nerd Princess for loving someone with an alter named Omemo.

A jumble of his climbing gear—ropes, picks, his beaten burgundy backpack—sat in the corner with the FOX Sports boxes and the framed Frazier-Ali poster.

All of that stays put for now.

I opened the blinds to allow more light, then opened the top desk drawer. Post-its, paper clips . . . A picture of Truman and me making goofy faces as the ocean twinkled behind us. *Whale watching, Santa Barbara.* I closed the drawer, then eased out of the room. *No more of that.*

Back in the foyer, I sat on the floor and transformed the massive pile of mail into three lesser piles of mail. Junk. Bills to Pay. Mail to Review.

In our bathroom, I tossed Truman's shaving kit, his allergy medications, and his deodorant. I kept his toothbrush, hairbrush, and his favorite pumice stone. Personal things. DNA things.

I peered beneath the bed. Socks. Cups. Scarves that had slipped off my hair. The Clearblue Easy pregnancy test I had dropped a hundred years ago. I shook the box—the used sticks rattled inside. We were gonna fly to Barbados. He'd dive, I'd worry. We'd get drunk and make a baby. He wanted to have a child with me.

I shoved the box into the trash bag.

In our bedroom, I threw open the walk-in closet. My wardrobe and endless parade of shoes occupied the closet's south side. Truman's clothes—blacks and khakis—hung on the north. After his last promotion, he had ditched most of his jeans and T-shirts (my favorite: I IS A COLEGE STOODENT) for business-casual wear from Armani Exchange and "grown people's shoes" from Cole Haan.

Like the downstairs den and Truman's office, I had avoided opening the closet that we had shared, preferring to wear clothes found in heaps around the house. No longer.

I stepped over the threshold.

I pulled a blue hatbox from a top shelf and opened it: three paperback relationship books. *How to Have a Passionate Marriage. Loving the Man You're With. Boosting Your Marriage Libido.* Also in the box: goodies we had purchased at the HUSTLER store one Saturday night. "To keep it interesting," I had told him with a wink while slipping tubes of Motion Lotion into the basket. We had played with our toys three times a week, and then, twice a week, and then, not so much. I didn't worry—we were experiencing normal life, that's all. Our Hustler box would find its way off the shelf, and back on the nightstand once we worked through our issues . . .

I placed the box back on the shelf.

Despite its age, Truman's MIT sweatshirt hung among his newer, more expensive wardrobe. *I'll give it to Trumanita,* he told me once. I had joked—*What if she goes to Northwestern instead?* Truman had faked a Fred Sanford heart attack and collapsed on the bed.

I coaxed the sweatshirt off its hanger, then brought the worn cotton to my face. Citrus, sunscreen, and Tide. I folded it, and placed it on a shelf on my side of the closet.

You can't do this. You can't. It's too early. You're betraying him.

I stared at that sweatshirt until that critic in my head hushed. Then, I returned to Truman's side and piece by piece, removed his clothes from hangers. I rifled through pockets and found crumpled dollar bills, receipts to GameStop, and clear candy wrappers.

By three o'clock, I had packed most of Truman's wardrobe into six suitcases. I kept the parka he wore in Nepal, the suit he wore on his last birthday, the pair of blue boxers I bought him after our first date, and the I IS A COLEGE STOODENT tee. All of it sat on my shelf, prizes to treasure until my own death.

"Nic!" Leilani shouted. "Where you at?"

I shouted, "In the closet."

"I knew you were a big lez—" Leilani popped into the closet's doorway. Her smile died once she realized what I was doing. "Nicole . . ."

I stood and said, "I know, Lei. But it was time."

Leilani shook her head.

"I had to. Maybe I'll stop seeing him now. Maybe I'll be able to move forward."

Leilani offered a curt nod. "Guess you can check off Step Three on your little list. Is all this going on the lawn tomorrow?"

"No. There's this program that clothes the homeless and poor people going on job interviews. I'm thinking of donating all of it to them."

"How noble." She darted out of the closet.

I followed her out to the bedroom. "Look through and take some things, okay?"

"That's so *sweet* of you to think of me," she said as she stomped to the hallway. "I would've hated fighting a *crackhead* for my brother's Rolex."

"Zephyr suggested that I do this. I didn't mean anything by it. Lei, don't be mad at me, okay? I really didn't want to do this."

Leilani headed down the stairs and to the kitchen. She threw open cabinets, and grabbed ingredients to make a pot of coffee.

"It's all meant to help me move on," I said. "And it's working because I'm also . . ." I swallowed nervously, then whispered, "I think I'm gonna adopt a baby."

Leilani's eyes widened.

"I'm surprised, too," I said. "I wasn't really planning anything. I hadn't even thought it through until I started cleaning up around here. But we wanted to have family, and I think . . . I think he'd be happy knowing that I . . ."

Leilani gawked at me.

I twisted my fingers and shifted my eyes to the floor. "It's just a thought. But the more I think about it and talk about it, the more I want to do it."

Leilani attempted to smile. "You can't even take care of yourself right now."

I nodded. "I have to pull myself together. I know that."

"And when you pull yourself together, you'll be able to handle raising a child alone?"

"Women do it all the time. And I wouldn't be alone, *Aunt* Leilani."

She cocked an eyebrow and chuckled. "And what did Zephyr think of that?"

I shook my head. "Haven't told her yet. Speaking of Zephyr . . . One-fifty a session? She's good and all, but Dr. Clark? My old psychiatrist? She only charged seventy-five dollars for people who didn't even have insurance. I'm not saying that Zephyr hasn't helped me. Cuz she has. I just cleaned up the house because of her. But I'm thinking maybe of going one more time and then stopping."

Leilani rolled her eyes, then jammed the "Brew" button on the coffee maker. "What do you want her to do, Nicole? Pull rabbits out of a hat? Turn water into wine? She's an *adviser*, not Jesus."

I sat at the breakfast bar. "You're right. I guess I'm expecting something phenomenal. I mean, that first visit was wild. The 'Truman is here' thing? That was crazy."

Leilani said nothing as she watched coffee drip into the pot.

"And really: It's not the money. I just feel uncomfortable going to a psychic."

"Adviser."

"Whatever."

"But you just said that she's helped you."

I nodded. "Even though something works doesn't mean that it's good for you."

"So now you're a good Christian?" Leilani asked.

"I never said anything about being good. But I don't feel nervous sticking with what I believe, even if I'm not the best at it. Nor do I feel this constant need to justify going to God. But with Zephyr, I'm constantly rationalizing my time with her. I know I'm probably not making sense to you, but I'm actually relieved that I decided to stop seeing her."

"Guess your conscience is working, then. Congratulations."

"You said Zephyr's helped you," I said. "How?"

Leilani grabbed a mug from the cupboard.

"How has she—"

"I can talk to her and she won't judge every single thing I say."

My cheeks burned at the insinuation. Still, I said, "I like her, and I like that she has an open mind, but—"

"But what?" Leilani shook her head, and muttered, "No wonder Truman never came home."

I jerked, smarting as though she had gouged my eyes.

She poured coffee into the mug, and continued: "Everything has to be Nicole's way. If it doesn't make sense to Nicole, well then, it's just stupid. While the rest of us soar, she stays on the ground, telling us that we're flying crooked." Her shoulders slumped—out of steam. "What-the-fuck-ever, Nic. You're an adult. See her. Don't see her. Adopt fifty babies from Vietnam. I don't give a . . ." She dumped cream and sugar into her cup.

I studied the countertop—what should I say? "I wasn't attacking you. Just being honest. I'm sorry that you're upset."

She grunted, and threw the spoon in the sink. "I'm sorry, too."

I climbed off the stool and headed to the door. I opened my mouth to apologize again, but stopped. There was nothing left to say.

CHAPTER 8

Back in June, my hairstylist had called after I had missed my standing hair appointment. Monica had called Phillip back, and told him about Truman's accident just two days before. As an expression of sympathy, Phillip sent me a gift basket of shampoo, conditioner, and hair gloss. I had used the shampoo once. After that, though . . . We (Black girls) don't wash our hair every day, usually every other week; but I had even broken *that* rule. I hadn't washed my hair *at all*, and now it smelled like burning leaves and sour milk. So, when I called Phillip and asked him to squeeze me in between his other appointments, he shouted, "Yes, Lord."

Once I sat in his chair, though, and told him all that I wanted, he uttered, "Get out of my chair right now and don't come back until you can think straight."

"Seriously," I said. "Cut it off."

"But it's so pretty and long," he said, hooking a finger around my formerly pink scrunchie. "When it's washed and combed."

"I need a change."

"Adopt a poodle," he said, his lip turned up in disgust. "Does Mo know that you're doing this?"

"Doing what?" I asked, eyebrow cocked. "Cutting hair that belongs to me?"

He crossed his arms. "Nope. Not doing it."

"It's my hair. Not my uterus."

Phillip draped a leopard-print smock around my shoulders. "Whatever, little Nikki. For what you pay, you *are* the boss of me."

Phillip worked on my hair as well as a middle-aged lady's weave, a chubby teen's purple cellophane, and a grumpy senior citizen's wet set. As he worked, I flipped through magazines, and caught up on Britney Spears's antics, Jennifer Aniston's love life, and Mariah Carey's sober journey.

"You can put *People* down now," Phillip said as he swiveled my chair to face the mirror.

There I was—the one with the short, boy-hair. The one with sharp cheekbones and big brown eyes. I hadn't had a drastic cut since college, when derring-do pumped through my body like oxygen. "I can't believe I did this," I whispered, wide-eyed.

"Me, neither," Phillip said as he sprayed oil sheen over my shorn hair.

"Truman's gonna *hate* this," I said, still unable to take my eyes off the woman in the mirror. "He's such a hair freak, and . . . Oh. Yeah. Forgot for a moment." Truman would not hate this or anything else now.

"Do you like it?" Phillip asked. "Not that I can do anything about it if you don't. Unless you wanna spend another three hours in this chair, getting extensions sewn onto your scalp."

"Don't worry," I said, raking my fingers through my hair. "I love it."

MO Parties was located on Hollywood Boulevard—high visibility, higher rent. I had tried to persuade Monica to perch at a cheaper locale, like in the Crenshaw District or in Koreatown. Monica had snorted at my suggestion, and now paid over $7,000 a month just to exist. Before the economy started its Death March, she could afford that. Her firm organized major events: post-Oscars parties, movie premieres, and high-end coming-of-age soirees. Back then, people had money for chocolate fountains, ice sculptures the size of VW Bugs, and thirty buffet stations. Now that the economy had zombied off the cliffs, companies had abandoned fancy fountains and filet mignon puff pastries for fake flowers and rubber chicken.

Jewish children still turned thirteen, though, and those mitzvah events were now Monica's steady gig.

Clear-headed again, I couldn't understand Leilani's fear—Monica stealing from me to save her business. Then again, I was sober today, and the thought of needing a conservator was as crazy as the thought of me pointing a gun at Jake or snoozing half naked in the canyon.

Monica sat at her desk, her fingers flying across the computer keyboard, listening to one of her clients in her headphones. Blown-up photographs of studio lots and movie premieres hung between calendars and whiteboards. The carpet hid beneath gift boxes, metallic wrapping paper, and jewel-colored goody bags—shrapnel of manufactured Joy. Monica finally looked away from the computer, and saw me posing in the doorway. "Oh. My . . . I need to call you back, Mrs. Schwarz . . . Of course . . . Yes. 50 Cent loves to perform at bar mitzvahs . . . Absolutely . . . Bye now."

I smiled, and said, "Guess what I did?" I sashayed into her office, then twirled. "Tell me you love it."

Monica playfully shoved me. "Let a few days go by without seeing you, and you get all Posh Spice on me."

I giggled. I hadn't giggled in weeks.

The tables at the Ivy were crowded with Ladies who Lunched gossiping over Caesar salads and iced tea; agents and lawyers striking deals over burgers and scotch; and C-list actresses nibbling on club sandwiches and waiting to be noticed. Monica and I ordered salads, then talked about the Schwarzes, and plans for Labor Day.

"You really look different today," she said, narrowing her eyes. "Beyond the haircut. What's up with you? And why'd you leave the house on Monday without telling me first?"

My cheeks warmed as I remembered the phone call from the rehab center. "I'm trying to pull it all together. My old life with the new. Guess I'm doing it wrong. And don't worry: You aren't the only friend I've offended. Lei isn't talking to me right now. I guess I should probably call her."

"And apologize like you always do?"

"I do not." I scrunched my nose. "I do?"

Monica nodded. "She told me something about you wanting to have a baby?"

"*Adopting* a baby. I'm not buying cribs and diapers or anything. It was just a thought."

Monica grunted. "Sorry. Sounds crazy."

"Why? It's not like I can't afford it. And it's not like I'd be the first woman on the planet to be a single mother. Your mom didn't have any help."

Monica popped a crouton in her mouth and crunched. "Yeah, and you see how my four brothers turned out."

"Why are you calling rehabilitation centers?" I blurted.

Monica paused, then said, "Huh?"

I sat on the edge of my chair, with my hands gripping my plate. "Rayo del Whatever, up in Santa Barbara."

Monica slowly shook her head, and said, "I have no idea what you're saying to me. Words are coming out of your mouth, but . . ."

I stared at her, and tried to determine if she was lying.

Monica grimaced. "Can you explain to me what you're talking about instead of looking at me like I stole something?"

I bit my lip, then said, "The day I left your place, this woman from some psychiatric facility up the Coast called." I waited—no reaction from Monica. "She said that you were looking for a place to put your sister."

"I don't have a sister."

"You have *me*."

Monica peered at me, then her eyes brightened. "You think I wanna commit you?" She laughed.

I sat back and crossed my arms. "I don't think any of this is funny."

Monica's laughter ebbed, and between chuckles, she said, "I admit. I have thought about kidnapping you and flying to Borneo until all of this drama passes. Get you away from the crap that's killing you on the inside." She shrugged and stared at the remains of her salad. "I worry about you, Nic, so don't be surprised if you do wake up in Borneo. I'll do what I need to do to protect you from yourself."

"You didn't call Rayo del Whatever?"

"I clicked on a bunch of websites the night you came to stay with me. Maybe one was Rayo Whatever. But I swear I didn't call them. Again: me worried, you cuckoo."

"It's just strange . . ." I paused, then added, "And business is doing okay?"

Monica laughed again. "Business sucks, but that's another lunch at the Ivy."

I futzed with my straw. "I have something to tell you. You're gonna be pissed, though."

Monica sensed my apprehension, and said, "Spill it."

"Last week, Lei referred me to this spiritual adviser—"

"You're seeing a *psychic*?" Monica screeched.

Other diners glanced in our direction.

I shushed my friend, and whispered, "Not anymore. And she's a spiritual adviser."

Monica shook her head. "Semantics make it legitimate? How did this even . . . ? What the *hell*?"

"And what did I expect from you?" I said. "Support?" I told Monica about my conversation with Leilani at Rain in Las Vegas, about my desperation for an answer, *any* answer, and about my two sessions with Zephyr Tott. "I didn't even say anything that first visit, but she knew I was in mourning, and she knew Truman's name without me telling her. How did she know all that?"

"Cuz you probably looked like a complete mess," Monica said with a shake of her head. "And you don't suspect she's tricking you?"

I sipped my iced tea. "I don't see the world that way."

"Since when does an Adventist-raised science writer adopt unorganized religion as a path to understanding?"

I glared at her, and said, "That Nicole died when her husband didn't leave the ocean, and when her dead husband started popping up all over the city. *This* Nicole now knows that life is all about disorder and dealing with the unexpected and . . . Okay, I'm not totally comfortable with it. Seeing someone like her. And it's kind of a hokey idea."

"It's a dangerous idea," Monica interjected. "And it will lead you straight to hell."

"Stop freaking out. I'm not throwing séances."

"You say that now," Monica said. "Next week you'll be throwing séances, writing self-help books, and buying crystals. A total cheerleader for this crap. How much is all this costing you?"

"She hasn't asked me for anything other than the consultation fee. She doesn't even know my real name."

"But you said Leilani referred you."

"She'd know me as 'Nicole Baxter,' not 'Emma.' That's the name I'm using. And I paid cash."

"But you said she called Truman by his name."

"She did." I chuckled, then said, "Will you stop?"

Monica cocked an eyebrow. "Again: How much are you paying, what's her name? *Zephyr?*"

"Doesn't matter," I said, slipping three twenties inside the billfold. "I won't see her again. And I feel good, and I'm moving forward. That's more important to me than money."

"But you're *supposed* to mourn," Monica said. "Shock. Denial. Guilt. You're supposed to go through all those steps, aren't you? You've lost someone you loved, Nicole. Hurting is normal."

"Seeing your dead husband in bed, and in the hallway? Not normal. As far from normal as you can get."

"Ghost husband." Monica sat back with a smirk. "And *that,* my dear, is simply guilt. You're seeing Truman because you didn't tell him the truth before he died."

My heart thudded so hard in my chest, I coughed. I caught my breath, and managed to say, "*What* truth?"

Monica leaned forward and cocked her head. "Trying to get pregnant without him knowing. Oh. And your *thing* with Jake Huston."

My mouth opened. Words fluttered around my brain, but refused to fall into a coherent sequence.

"You slept with him," she whispered. "I know you did cuz I've known you for almost twenty years now and you'd never let anyone that extraordinarily gorgeous and that attentive and that accessible pass you by. *Especially* when your husband's being a jerk and isn't home and possibly having an affair with every attractive woman who isn't you."

I grabbed my purse and popped up from the table. Speechless, I stormed through the restaurant with my stomach twisting, with the rush of blood in my ears drowning out all sound.

Monica and I didn't talk as we waited for the parking attendant to bring around the Volvo. Ten minutes passed in this silence until Monica flipped down the vanity mirror and slid lipstick across her bottom lip. "I haven't said anything to Lei," she said, "so don't worry: I won't tell her. But I've been thinking about this for a long time, and now, I need to say it.

"You're *making* Truman haunt you. This way, you get to torture yourself about Jake and never experience happiness again because in your mind, you don't deserve it."

I glanced nervously at my friend, then whispered, "It was just one time. With Jake, I mean. I didn't want a relationship with him or any-thing. Or maybe I did, I don't know. I had a weak moment and . . . I loved Truman, Mo."

Monica nodded. "I know."

"And I was gonna confess to him the night after the dive, but . . ." I took several deep breaths, then slumped in the driver's seat. "I hate myself for all of that." My eyes filled with tears, and the road before me shifted. I gripped the steering wheel tighter, and said, "I can't forgive myself. I don't think I ever will."

Monica squeezed my arm. "You will, but I think you need to talk to someone. And not some Hollywood psychic. You have to move past this so you can be healthy. The state won't let you adopt that Laotian baby if you're not."

I nodded, and slowly exhaled, loosening my grip on the wheel.

"Have you seen Jake again?" Monica asked. "Socially, I mean."

"We had coffee on Wednesday," I said. "Nothing romantic. Please know that, okay? I'm trying to move forward and it was a good day and I saw him and he asked me and I said 'yes' and it was just coffee—"

"Nicole, I believe you."

"It was nice being out. Talking." I turned to her and whispered, "Do you think Truman slept with Penelope? Or Elene? Honest opinion."

Monica thought for a moment, then shook her head. "He knew you were crazy and insecure. He knew if he did and you found out, you'd short-circuit and chop his head off with that machete."

We tried to laugh.

"Seriously?" Monica said. "Even when he was being an ass, it was still obvious to the rest of the world that he loved you. I could tell by the way he hugged you. By the way you guys were always laughing . . . You were best friends, and that's why you felt betrayed when he started hanging out with Penelope. You weren't used to it, like the rest of us are. We're used to mediocrity and being ignored. Not living life together." She grinned, then added, "I envied you for landing him after graduation. But then, I thought, 'That's the kind of relationship I want.' I'm sad to say that me and Gary aren't as tight as you and Truman were."

"Gary's nice," I said. "A Honda of a man. Much better than the Yugos you used to date."

She smiled.

"Do you think Truman suspected anything?" I asked.

"He probably knew you were attracted to Jake," Monica said. "And I think *you* knew that *he* knew, and so you're making him into this ghost."

"Say that you're right. Say that I *am* manifesting these visions of Truman. Explain the snoring. Explain the whiskers and the cologne. The thing in the bed. All of it."

"Phantom pain," Monica said. "The same sensation veterans with amputated legs feel. Some of them say that sometimes, their legs ache, but that's impossible cuz they don't *have* legs anymore. Maybe you're seeing Truman or smelling his cologne anytime you think of his favorite dessert or about your honeymoon or something."

"And the hairs? I actually *see* the hairs in the sink. And the words on the refrigerator. And the mandala and mola on the walls. And the wet footprints . . ."

Monica shrugged. "Sometimes I find sand in my shoes three months after going to the beach. And maybe you are sleepwalking and composing those messages and hanging pictures. I don't know. I'll admit: The fridge and text messages are throwing me, too. Maybe he is a ghost." She paused, then added, "But it would be the first time I've heard of a ghost texting."

◆　◆　◆

Phantom pain.

Maybe Monica had pinpointed my problem.

I sat at the computer and typed "physical manifestation guilt" into Google's search bar. Over two million results. I clicked on a Baylor University article titled "Grief" and scanned the page.

Grief after death is felt not just for a person and love; but for love unexpressed, anger unresolved, or a relationship unfulfilled.

I read that sentence six times before moving on.

Disturbing thoughts/experiences: hallucinations . . . strong sense of the presence of the deceased . . . bereaved person losing her mind . . .

Physical manifestations of grief commonly include fatigue, insomnia, anorexia, feelings of choking, shortness of breath, tightness in the chest, menstrual irregularities, and gastrointestinal disturbances . . .

I muttered, "Wow," as I sat back in the chair. It was as though the author of the article had lived on my shoulder since June 26.

Anger unresolved. Truman and I had both been pissed at each other. He blew his anger off on his adventures. I blew my anger off with the neighbor.

I picked at the dry skin on my lips and stared at the computer screen.

If Monica knew about Jake, who else did? The guy at the market knew, and if that was possible, could Leilani have suspected something and just hadn't said anything?

But I knew Leilani well. She had never held her tongue before, so why would she now? What if Monica—in all of her righteous Baptist-ness—had a burden placed on her heart, and the Lord instructed her late one night to tell Leilani about my transgression? Leilani would flip—her best friend had cheated on her big brother—and our friendship would end.

The internet offered no immediate solution to that problem. *Talk to a professional.*

Yeah. Been there, done that.

CHAPTER 9

Sharp peals of thunder rumbled and echoed across the canyon. Drawn from sleep, I opened my eyes and glanced at the den's window. No sunshine. More thunder. I shivered from the chill in the gray den. Twelve years ago on this date, Truman and I had married.

To his parents' dismay, we had held our ceremony at Descanso Gardens in Pasadena. *You're not getting married at a church,* they kept asking. Because we prefer a church. I preferred Descanso's fragrant gardens of lilacs and roses. I preferred standing beneath those grand magnolias, a vision in white silk and satin, cutting my wedding cake as the sun set behind the camellia forest. Dancing with Truman beneath the stars.

"If that's what you want," Truman told me, "that's what you'll get. It will be a perfect day."

Truman cut his cheek shaving that afternoon. Wesley, his best man, forgot the marriage license, making it to the gardens twenty minutes before the ceremony. Ninety degrees that day, but by evening, the temperatures dropped to a perfect seventy-six. The photographer arrived on time; our florists brought the right lilies, and the minister didn't ramble.

Monica and Leilani, maids of honor in champagne-colored Grecian gowns, walked last down the long, blossom-bedecked aisle. I followed them, unescorted, to meet my husband-to-be. *July 21. My anniversary forever.* Just as I had dreamed, Truman and I danced beneath the stars.

During "You are the Sunshine of My Life," he kissed my neck, then boogied away. I laughed at his awkward flailing and off-key singing.

During our honeymoon to the Virgin Islands, Truman and I had talked about future trips to Paris, Venice, and Fiji. Having a houseful of kids. Retiring early and traveling around Europe. Growing old together. Wearing matching MedicAlert bracelets.

But now, twelve years later . . .

I had cleaned all the closets. Organized the kitchen cabinets. Cleaned the wet goop from the refrigerator trays. I had scrubbed all the grout and tile in the house, sorted the mail into manageable piles, and had caught up on back issues of *Vanity Fair* and the *New Yorker*.

I was keeping my promise to Monica. I was back on the road to Ordinary.

As I fried an egg, Tim from Great Escape called. "Just confirming your hot air adventure for four o'clock today."

I paused, then said, "My what?"

"We have you and Mr. Baxter scheduled for your anniversary flight package. Oh. Was I supposed to say that? Did I ruin the surprise?"

Hot air balloon. Wine. Sunset. A diamond maybe.

I told Tim that Mr. Baxter and I would not be joining them today, and apologized for not canceling sooner.

Tim made sad noises, then said, "That's too bad. Next time, then?"

"Next time," I whispered.

"I hope you have a wonderful anniversary," he said, then hung up.

After breakfast, I settled at the desk in the den. Wiggled the mouse to yank the computer. I logged onto my email account.

Bigger Penis in 30 Days!

Lose 50lbsin a wk!

Sexy Girls Want 2 Meet U

Waiting—E-Card from Blue Mountain Greeting Co.

An e-card? I clicked on the link.

The screen filled with a wiggling cartoon heart. Minnie Riperton sang, *Loving you is easy cuz you're beautiful . . .*

The cartoon heart *bubumped-bubumped,* and grew larger . . . larger . . . until *POP!* It exploded, and heart fragments settled into a message.

LOVING YOU. MISSING YOU.

A cartoon janitor pushed a broom across the screen. As he swept away the shredded words, he left behind another message.

I LOVE YOU, NICOLE. HAPPY
ANNIVERSARY. TRUMAN.

My stomach dropped, and I pushed away from the desk. And just like that, Ordinary hovered over a needle, and threatened to burst like that animated heart.

The doorbell rang.

I hopped up from the chair, grateful for the distraction. Before leaving the den, though, I peeked back at the message on the screen.

Happy Anniversary. Truman.

A delivery guy dressed in blue stood on the porch. He held a clipboard in one hand, and an elaborate arrangement of Casablanca lilies in the other. "You Nicole Baxter?"

I nodded.

He handed me the vase, and said, "These are for you."

I carried the bouquet to the living room and sat the vase on the coffee table. I plucked the small card from its plastic holder, and read:

I LOVE YOU, BABE. HAPPY ANNIVERSARY. TRUMAN

I paced the living room with the telephone to my ear and my eyes glued to those lilies. "Explain it, then," I demanded. "Go ahead. I'm listening."

Twenty miles away, Monica was stuffing goody bags with green tea lip balms, Adele CDs, and tickets to the Laugh Factory. "Truman probably planned this back in June," she said. "Just like he'd already planned the hot air balloon thing. His assistant probably had a calendar of important events and a standing order at a florist. That way, if he forgot about your anniversary, it wouldn't look like he forgot."

I stopped in my step. "I'll accept that answer."

"Makes more sense than him calling FTD from the Pacific. Not to be glib or anything."

"He *was* in Nepal when he sent me the tennis bracelet for my birthday. And those lilies were waiting for me on the day of the accident."

"See?" Monica chirped. "Mystery solved. Let's have dinner tonight to celebrate what would've been Number 12. I'll see if Lei's around, and we'll stay the night so we can drink Pinot Noir-in-a-box and braid each other's hair."

We chatted a few minutes more, and I volunteered to help at her next big event. "Maybe I'll see a movie today," I said, climbing the stairs. "Roam the Beverly Center. Buy a mandoline from Williams-Sonoma."

"And Truman would want you to have exquisitely sliced zucchini."

"I'm glad I called. You're always so clear-headed. So wise. You're my Yoda."

"Comes from growing up dodging bullets and Crips, young Jedi. Promise me that you won't freak out anymore today? Unless it's absolutely necessary."

"Only in a dire emergency," I said, wandering down the hallway. "For now, I'm cool. I'm chill. It's all good and a host of other urban state-of-mind clichés."

"Dy-no-mite," Monica said. "I'll see you around seven, sweetie."

I entered my bedroom, and froze in my step.

A large box wrapped in green and silver paper sat on the bed.

That wasn't there last night.

You sure?

Last night, I had scooped dirty clothes from the floor, and had stuffed them in the washing machine. I came back to the room, and grabbed *No Country for Old Men* from the nightstand. Before leaving for the den, I had passed the bed—the *empty* bed—a final time to pop a Xanax from the medicine cabinet.

No gift wrapped box.

So how did it get there?

I crept closer to the bed, and poked the package. Hard. Slick. Real. I tore away the paper to find an orange box with brown letters printed across its top. LOUIS VUITTON. A small card was taped in the middle of the box top.

ONE OF YOUR FAVORITE THINGS. HAPPY ANNIVERSARY.
LOVE, TRUMAN.

The black Lockit MM Vuitton purse sat among take-out cartons on the breakfast bar. Monica chomped on tempura carrots, but I couldn't eat—the $3,000 bag from my dead husband had hijacked my appetite. My heart beat so hard and fast that my pulse was pounding in my toes.

Burn down the house, I thought. For real this time. *Burn it down and salt the earth.*

"I stick by what I said earlier," Monica said. "He's bought you handbags for Christmas and Valentine's Day before, and he probably saw this one and said, 'Nic would like that,' and arranged for you to get it today." She paused, then added, "And you've seen those guards at Louis Vuitton. I don't think a ghost could sneak past those goons."

"But *how* did it reach my bed?" I screeched. *"How?"*

Monica stopped eating and considered me. "What do you want me to say? That Truman's not dead? That he's hiding somewhere and torturing you for the hell of it?" She grabbed a shrimp from the carton, and said, "Did you ask your spiritual *adviser*? Doesn't she know all and see all?"

"Don't do that. Not right now."

"Six hundred dollars later, and you're as paranoid as you were before."

I shoved the bag in Monica's direction, then wiped my hands on a napkin. "You take it. I don't want it. It's evil."

Monica gawked. "You're giving me a haunted handbag?"

"Louis Vuitton bags just don't buy themselves, first of all. And then they don't walk themselves up to somebody's room and plop down on the bed like they're on vacation. I'm either losing my mind, or . . ." Or . . . *No, that's it. Losing my mind.*

I retreated up the stairs to the bathroom, only hearing my frantic heartbeat and labored breathing. I dumped a Xanax onto my palm, then forced my hand to my lips. The pill melted on my tongue and bitterness filled my mouth. I balled my hands into fists and willed the drug to work faster, to make my nerves as soft as cotton. Soon, my hands relaxed and my shoulders drooped. Then, my lips tingled, my nose, my cheeks, and then . . . Cold . . . Numb . . . Nothing . . .

Happy anniversary.

I trudged back to my room and stared at the empty bed.

Crimson comforter as red as blood. Sheets with fuzzy stripes undulating like caterpillars. Pillows shaped like jumbo marshmallows.

I slipped beneath the covers. I had bought four pillows at Target. Two for me. Two for him. He always tossed his on the ground and took mine, and . . .

The mattress dipped, and I opened my eyes. The lamps on the nightstands still burned bright. I tried to swallow, but I had no spit because of all the cotton stuffed into my mouth. The comforter rustled, and I muttered, "Mo?" I rolled over.

Truman lay in bed next to me. He was shirtless, but wore blue-striped boxers.

I hid my face in a pillow, and whispered, "It's not real. It's a manifestation of guilt. It's all in my head."

"Babe," he said, "what are you talking about?"

"If I just wait," I said, face hidden, eyes squeezed shut, "it'll stop. It'll stop and it'll go away." I took a deep breath, then peeked out.

Truman lay there, studying his dive watch. "In two minutes, our anniversary will be over." His arm fell up over his head. "This watch you got me last year? Still works. You always gave the best gifts. Like these boxers."

Wide-eyed, I whispered, "No."

"Whenever you bought gifts, it was obvious that you thought about the person," he said. "Who they were. What they liked. You didn't want me to climb Everest, but you still gave me that parka and sleeping bag. You still supported me, and I love you for—"

I clamped my hands over my ears. "I'm not seeing him. I'm not hearing him. He's not here. He's not here."

"I *am* here," he said. "I got home early just so we could talk. You always complain that I'm never here. I am now." He paused, then said, "Why are you so far away?" He reached for me.

An icy blade stabbed through my shoulder and I cried out in surprise. I scrambled out of bed, and clutched my injured arm.

Frowning, Truman sat up in bed. "Aren't you gonna speak? Aren't you gonna say 'I love you, Truman' or 'I'm sorry, Truman'?"

I shook my head, my mind tangled like fishing line.

He reached for me again, but I kicked at him.

His frown softened. "Just tell me the truth, Nic. You'll feel better."

"Go away," I said, eyes still closed. *"Please."*

"I can't go away," he said, easing off the bed. "I told you I'd love you forever. I said that on the day I died."

I hugged my knees to my chest, and covered my head with my arms. "Go away," I repeated. "Please. Please. Please . . ."

Monica found me on the bedroom floor, muttering to myself. She dropped beside me, and pulled me into her arms. Held me tight as the clock struck midnight.

CHAPTER 10

I bolted upright in bed. My sweaty T-shirt stuck to my skin. Sunlight reflected off the shiny wood floor and I squinted at the digital clock: 1:08. My mouth tasted coppery, as though I had sucked pennies all night. I rubbed my eyes—my sinuses, my temples, my head, every muscle in my body ached.

Across the room on the dresser, I spotted a white lily tucked into a bud vase. A slip of paper was taped to the mirror.

I forced myself to my feet. Woozy. Nauseous. I took several deep breaths, then lurched to the dresser.

The flower smelled pure and wonderful, sweet and heavy.

I yanked the note from the mirror, and prepared to read something impossible and unexpected.

Darling Nikki. You wouldn't be the only woman in this city to go bonkers. Smooches, Mo

A harmless message from Monica, a living human being.

I scrubbed and lathered in the shower. The knots in my arms and legs loosened from the hot water and memories of my anniversary melted into the past.

One day, you won't be frightened. You won't flip out. You'll just expect to see Truman roaming the hallways, and then, his presence won't frighten you. And the two of you will live happily together. Just like The Ghost and Mrs. Muir.

Before stepping out onto the tile, I peeked from behind the shower curtain.

Steam covered the mirror, but no message had been written on the glass.

I pulled on a T-shirt and sweats, then I trudged down the stairs. I froze as I reached the last step—smelled grilled beef and garlic. My stomach growled, excited by the prospect of food.

A dinner plate sat on the breakfast bar. A rib eye steak, fingerling potatoes, and sautéed asparagus. I poked a potato: still warm. A gift wrapped box, this one the size of a pencil case, sat near the fork.

I slipped onto a stool, and stuffed a potato into my mouth. Cut a chunk of steak, and shoved that in with the potatoes. After crunching on asparagus stalks, I tore off the box's wrapping paper: a Mont Blanc fountain pen. Agatha Christie limited edition. 18-karat gold nib. A ruby-eyed, sterling silver snake wrapped around the black resin cap.

Awesome.

I searched through the wrapping paper for a gift card from Monica. Nothing.

I grabbed the telephone from the counter, and punched Monica's number.

"What's up?" she asked. "You get my note?"

"I did," I said with a full mouth. "And thanks for lunch."

Monica paused, then said, "What are you talking about?"

"The steak and potatoes," I said. "And the pen is beautiful." I rose from the stool to grab a bottle of water from the refrigerator.

The magnetic words on the fridge's door had found order again.

"I didn't cook anything," Monica was saying. "I left before nine this morning for a meeting at the Beverly Hilton. And I forgot to give you my gift after you gave me the Louis Vuitton. Who cooked—?"

"Okay," I said, absently, my gaze still on those words.

Never wish me away again.
You & I together

The last word hadn't come with the poetry journal. Someone—*Truman?*—had cut other words to make it.

DEAD.

Breathless, I reached for *DEAD* and plucked away *d*, and each letter that formed the word. Then, I snatched off another word—*rocket*—and then, another—*princess*—and tossed them both into the trash. I grabbed *glint* and *roar*, and shoved them in with *night* and *tender.* Soon, no words remained.

Flex D'Onofrio was cleaning scuba gear aboard the SS *Deep-Cee*, and preparing to go out on the Pacific. He smiled and held out his arms for a hug. "I was just thinking about—"

"Take me where you left him," I demanded as I stormed on deck.

He narrowed his eyes. "Nicole, honey. It's not that simple."

"I know the robot and all that fancy equipment searched for him, but *you* need to convince me, Flex, that he can't be alive. Take me there."

"With the current and drift, Truman wouldn't be where we—"

"I don't care. I need to see."

Like most Sunday afternoons, the harbor was busy. Multicolored sails snapped in the wind, and kayakers paddled out in groups of twos and fours. Sea lions sunbathed on buoys, only looking up to watch a passing boat.

Catalina Island loomed somewhere behind early afternoon haze. Truman and I had taken several day trips over to the island. Seafood dinners. Cheesy tours. Games of miniature golf. On the nighttime boat ride back to the mainland, we'd sit on the stern and make out like teenagers. Back in the parking lot, we'd climb into the car's back seat and make love. Those trips had stopped once he started climbing and diving—Catalina "bored" him.

"I don't understand," I said to Flex. "Why did you go out that day? There was a storm—"

Flex shook his head. "Truman's accident wasn't weather related."

"Was it her fault that he . . . ?" *Her.* I refused to say her name.

He paused before saying, "I don't wanna say *fault.*" The gray hair on his face and on his head now outnumbered the blond.

"Can we search again?" I asked. "The weather's still right for it. Things may have changed down there."

He said, "He may be twenty-five miles away from here. What's left of him."

I frowned. "What do you mean, *what's left?*"

Flex shifted his gaze to the ocean. "With the fish, and the waves, and rocks . . ."

"Oh." Dread rushed up my calves, and I shivered. "Can't we hire those engineers again? I know it costs, but I have the money."

Flex turned to me with a pained smile. "Sweetheart, it's not a matter of money. The ocean's huge—"

"We can chart it. Make grids or . . ."

"Nicole, I know you miss him—"

"Cuz what if he's alive?"

"He can't be."

"I've had dreams. I've seen him when I'm awake."

"You're grieving."

"How do you know?" I asked, wild-eyed. "You have no proof."

"What you're experiencing is similar to what wives in the whaling days—"

"I don't care about any of that," I shouted. "I need to see him. As he really is. What can I *do?*"

Flex stared at me with his smog-colored eyes, then slowly shook his head.

CHAPTER 11

Trish didn't notice that I stood at the reception desk. She was focusing on the computer monitor—sliding seven of hearts beneath eight of spades. "Winning?" I asked, trying to sound more cheerful than I felt.

The receptionist startled, and glanced at me over her shoulder. "Hey." She closed the game, and said, "Did you have an appointment today?" She started to flip through the scheduling book.

"No," I said, sliding $150 across the counter. "This is an emergency visit. This weekend was pretty painful."

"I hate hearing that," she said with crumpled eyebrows. "Well, you came to the right place. I'll tell her that you're—"

"Emma?" Zephyr, dressed in a green and gold caftan, stood at the entrance to the hallway.

"Would you mind seeing me last minute?" I asked, and tried to ignore that prickly feeling on the back of my neck. "It won't take long."

She hesitated before she nodded. "I'm glad you caught me. I was on my way out. But I always have time for you."

"How many clients do you see?" I asked as I followed her down the hallway.

"Oh. A few a day," she said. "It takes a toll on me, psychologically, so I limit my schedule. Many times, I visit people in their homes." She glanced back at me and added, "You know, your skin's changed since we've been seeing each other. It glows with the promise of life. From the inside. It's because you've been internalizing all that we've talked about.

I see that you even got a new haircut. Imagine how far you'll get if you come to see me twice a—"

"Excuse me, Zephyr?" Trish said. "The guy from . . . Umm . . . The man . . . Someone's here to see you."

A frown flashed across Zephyr's face, and quickly disappeared. She nodded toward her office. "Emma, I just brewed a pot of tea. Go on in and make yourself comfortable. This shouldn't take long."

A song by Enya murmured on the hidden stereo speakers, and the unicorn wind chimes tinkled above the open window.

I retreated to the credenza for a cup of tea—*this is the last cup I'll have here*—and glanced at the framed diplomas on the wall.

Yale University, Class of 1990.

Johns Hopkins Medical School.

American Psychiatric Association.

Each conferred to *Zephyr R. Tott.*

I wandered over to the window with my cup of tea and stared out at the tiny concrete patio: a white, wrought iron table with one chair, a small stone bird fountain, and a gray steel file cabinet.

The surface of Zephyr's desk hid beneath stacks of folders and newspapers. Swan and turtle paperweights assembled at the base of the computer monitor, and I picked up a crystal turtle—thirty-three dollars according to the price tag on its belly. I placed the paperweight on the stack of newspapers, and glanced at the top folder. Its handwritten label read NICOLE B.

Zephyr didn't know my real name. Had to be another Nicole B.

I sipped tea without thinking, and stared at that name written in thick, black marker.

What were the odds?

I drained the cup with one long gulp, then opened the file.

Credit reports from TRW and Experian for Nicole Porter Baxter. Magazine and newspaper articles about television executive Truman Baxter. Real estate documents detailing the purchase of our home in

Beachwood Canyon, and the sale of Truman's family home in Cerritos as well as Beryl Porter's condo in Culver City.

My life in paperwork.

I reached the final sheet in the folder: Truman's obituary. Someone had colored in his eyes with blue ink. I dropped the empty teacup, and it shattered near my feet.

"That *bitch*." I grabbed the folder, shoved it into my purse. *That bitch.* The only cohesive thought I could form.

Back in the waiting room, Zephyr was whispering to a middle-aged, chinless white man. "We just can't keep ignoring what's going on," he was saying. "Now—"

Zephyr turned to me and smiled. "I'm so sorry, Nicole. This won't take much longer."

I stopped in my step. *She said my name.* I glanced at the man's official-looking badge clipped to his shirt pocket. ART MORGAN, CITY INSPECTOR.

Zephyr said, "Nicole, maybe you should come back tomorrow. No charge."

The chinless man said, "Keisha, you're not taking the City seriously—"

I backed away from the couple, then raced to the exit.

American Psychiatric Association had no members named Zephyr R. Tott.

Yale University had no alumnae named Zephyr R. Tott.

Neither did Johns Hopkins.

I searched Amazon's website, and found one self-published book. *Losing Your Love, Losing Your Mind* by Zephyr R. Tott. Twenty misspellings on the first page.

She had lied to me. She had no connection to God or higher powers or anyone. She had taken advantage of someone in pain to gain influence and money.

Yes, I too had lied—my name wasn't Emma. But I *had* graduated from UC Santa Cruz. I had pledged Alpha Kappa Alpha my senior year. And my husband *was* missing and presumed dead. Nicole Porter Baxter existed.

My so-called spiritual adviser had fake diplomas, a fake name, a self-published book . . .

And my pride.

Monica was right.

I had been bamboozled.

I wandered back to the den, my mind muddled and exhausted.

The gun sat on the coffee table.

I eased onto the couch, my eyes never leaving the weapon.

Had I left it there?

Was it murder to kill someone who no longer existed?

Who are we talking about? You or Zephyr?

I slumped on the couch. So peaceful in the house. No rumbling. No creaking. I yawned, and my eyelids fluttered until they closed.

A cold finger stroked my cheek. *I'm dreaming.* I opened my eyes.

Truman stood over me, his face strips of purple skin. One icy hand caressed my cheek, and the other clutched the .22. Drops of water hung from his chin and nose, threatening to drip onto me but never falling. His arms were scraped and bruised. Tiny holes in his neck leaked seawater. He grinned as though he belonged there. "Come with me," he whispered.

I gawked at him, wanting to jump off the couch, wanting to scream. But I couldn't move. I couldn't speak.

He offered me the gun.

A part of my brain unlocked, and I said, "What do you want?"

He motioned for me to take the gun.

My eyes filled with tears. "I don't want to—"

"Liar," he said. "Tell me." His dank breath stank of rotting fish.

"Is this the only way you can get back at me?" I whispered. "Don't you—"

He grabbed my arm, and his sharp, cold talons pierced my skin.

I screamed, and fell off the couch as I wrestled out of his grip. I screamed again, then scrambled toward the door.

"Nicole!"

I threw a glance over my shoulder—he stood in front of the television, gun in hand. My face caught the edge of the door, and sharp pain zigzagged through my skull. I groaned as blood oozed near my hairline and in my mouth.

Truman wobbled toward me.

I forgot about my injuries, and I crawled down the hallway. Perfect beads of blood plopped from my head and mouth, leaving a crimson trail on the hardwood floor.

A few feet from the landing, I stopped. The stairs disappeared down into the darkness.

Truman took jerky steps toward me, his eyes dark with hate.

He's gonna kill me. His eyes told me that he would.

My head throbbed and burned. It hurt to move. And why move? He'd be there, wherever I escaped. "I was alone here," I shouted back at him. "When you were off climbing mountains, I was alone here."

Truman cocked his head. Water dripped out of his ear and dribbled to the floor.

Blood from the cut on my head seeped into my eyes. I blinked and the world tinged red. "I didn't mean to do it," I cried. "I just wanted to feel again, and you weren't around, and I was angry . . . I hated you, and I hated me, and I loved you . . . I slept with Jake Huston. I wanted to tell you back then, but I couldn't, so I'm telling you now—"

Truman lunged at me, leopard-like.

I reared back to avoid him, and tumbled down the stairs. After a final *oomph*, I stopped falling and lay twisted at the bottom of the staircase.

Glass shattered and a car alarm squawked. The clamor forced me out of a dark, quiet place, and I opened my eyes. I lay on my back, arms bent over my head. My spit was goopy and thick, and tasted metallic. I rotated my head, but the jolt of pain stopped me halfway. I resisted the urge to push my tongue against my teeth. I'd lose it for sure if a tooth was loose.

The car alarm continued to shriek.

I sat up. The room swayed. I focused on the rectangle hanging on the wall. Clearer . . . clearer . . . I blinked.

The Frazier-Ali poster hung on the wall across from me.

Impossible.

I blinked again, leaving my eyes closed for several seconds.

I left that poster in his office. It was there when I cleaned. I know *that.*

I opened my eyes: "Thrilla in Manila" written in blue. Ali and Frazier in red. September 30, 1975 . . .

No.

Nonononono . . .

The shrieking car alarm didn't help my headache or my attempts to think clear. I placed a hand against my sticky forehead, and groaned again.

It took several minutes, but I made it to my feet and limped to the kitchen door.

Outside, in the driveway, I saw that the lights on the Volvo were flashing.

I grabbed my keys, and steadied myself against the doorframe as the world rocked and rolled. I jabbed the car's "Panic" button.

One last chirp, then silence.

I opened the door, and stepped out onto the porch.

Glass from the Volvo's rear window sparkled against the concrete like diamonds. A cinder block sat near the front wheel. "WHORE" had been scratched into the paint of the passenger-side door.

Monica didn't believe me. "He *pushed* you down the stairs."

I nodded, even though she couldn't see me through the telephone. "Please come."

"At one o'clock in the morning?"

"Please?"

Monica said, "Fine," before hanging up.

Her anger ebbed once she saw my busted face and the vandalized Volvo. "What the hell happened?"

I said nothing as I trudged to the living room.

"I don't understand," she said, following me.

I plopped down on the couch and sipped wine from a mug.

"Who would do something like this?" she asked.

I drained the mug, then stood. Without a word, I limped to the staircase.

"So not only is he haunting you because you screwed the next-door neighbor," Monica said, "he's also attacking you in the hallway and trashing your car all while being dead?"

I climbed the stairs.

Monica followed me to the bathroom. "This makes sense to you?" She noticed the video camera's lens sticking out from the towels. "What the hell . . . ? No. I don't even wanna know what that's . . ." She sighed, then said, "Why do you have a camera in the bathroom?"

"For surveillance," I croaked. "I put them all around . . ." I considered the camera, then limped to the den. I grabbed the recorder from the bookshelf, sending Milton and Shakespeare to the floor. "It should be here. And I'll know. And you'll see."

"I'll see what?"

"Truman."

Monica peered over my shoulder as recorded video played in the camera's monitor: There I was, talking and screaming in the den.

"Who are you talking to?" Monica asked.

Anger burned in my belly. "Wait a minute . . . I don't see . . . He was . . . He was here."

Cory at Best Buy had assured me . . .

Monica said, "Do ghosts show up on video? Cuz you can't see vampires in mirrors."

I threw the camera to the floor. The body cracked, and the lens rolled beneath the couch. I stomped back to the bathroom. "Fucking Cory."

"Who's Cory?" Monica asked.

I retreated to the bathroom. Grabbed the Xanax vial from the medicine cabinet shelf and dumped two onto my palm.

"What are you—?" Monica slapped the pills out of my hand.

"*Hey!*" I dropped to my knees and searched for the pills.

Monica grabbed vials from the medicine cabinet. "Xanax?" she screeched, reading a label. "You just drank two glasses of wine, and you're taking . . . ?" She grabbed another. "*Klonopin?* You're on this, too? What kind of doctor prescribes—?"

Couldn't find the fallen drugs, so I grabbed the sink to stand. "I'm fine."

"You're seeing Truman because you're doped out of your mind," she shouted, grabbing every prescription medicine from the shelf. "You're hallucinating, Nicole. No wonder you're sleepwalking and seeing weird—"

"I don't wanna talk about it," I said, and moved toward the door.

Monica blocked my way. "Honey, you have to stop taking all of this."

"Don't talk to me like I'm some kind of addict," I shouted.

Monica shook her head. "It isn't your fault. I don't think that at all."

"Why did he leave me, Mo? Why did he have to go?"

"What do you want me to do?" Monica asked, her eyes pleading with me. "I'll do anything for you. We'll get you help." She reached for my face, but I slapped her hand away. "Are you trying to kill yourself? Is that what this is?"

"*Leave!*" I shouted, pushing my friend out of the doorway. "I don't want you here. Go!"

"Nic—"

"*Go!*"

Monica, crying now, stormed down the hallway to the stairs. Moments later, the front door slammed.

CHAPTER 12

Monica didn't understand. She had never lost anyone important to her. She had no clue what Leilani and I were now experiencing. *Screw her,* I thought, stomping down the hallway that led to my sister-in-law's apartment. I didn't need that kind of friend.

Back in the day, the Grand Towers had been one of the swankiest luxury apartment complexes Downtown. It boasted a swimming pool, a gym, even a concierge. But then, spoiled brats with trust funds moved in—including Leilani. These tenants acted as though they had never cleaned up after themselves as children, because now, as adults, they still didn't. Beer, food, and mud soiled the carpets. The ripped gold wallpaper hung like molted snakeskin. The corridors stank of cigarettes and spilled booze. People thawed meat in the swimming pool, and their dogs crapped on the gym floor. Grand Towers was now the most expensive slum in Los Angeles.

I knocked on the door to Unit 5D. "Lei," I shouted, "I know it's late, but . . ." I banged on the door again.

No answer.

I turned the knob—unlocked—and nudged the door open.

The living room lamp burned bright. Better to see the half-empty take-out containers and torn magazines covering the living room carpet and couch. Rotting food on the kitchen counters. Unwashed dishes in the sink. Squishy carpet that reeked of spilled beer. The constant buzz of flies . . .

Leilani had been taking care of me even as her life deteriorated.

I gagged, and tried to breathe through my mouth, but the stink had texture. "Lei, you in here?"

No answer.

On the refrigerator door, I noticed a picture trapped beneath a Tijuana magnet. Leilani and another woman wore bikinis and large sombreros. I peered closer at the tiny woman beside my friend. I knew that face. Zephyr Tott. *Keisha.*

Inside the fridge: beer, moldy strawberries, and a quart of Bombay gin.

I kept my hands over my mouth and nose, and crept to the bedroom door.

Stained sheets on the bed. The stink of sour milk. More take-out containers, more trash. Flies buzzed over a bowl of something I refused to identify.

Was this her apartment? Maybe, in my confused state, I had stumbled into the wrong unit. Maybe that picture on the fridge wasn't Leilani and Zephyr.

Because Leilani's place boasted creamy-white carpet, not this gray, smucky stuff. And the only constant sound had been the R&B radio station she kept on, not the buzz of giant houseflies.

I returned to the living room and pushed my foot through the litter of trash, glass vials, and little plastic baggies. This couldn't have been Leilani's apartment. Not Truman's sister. Not this crack den.

But then again, when was the last time I had visited Leilani at home?

Sometime in May. A group of us had come over for a "Passion Party"—Cosmopolitans and fancy hors d'oeuvres, and a woman named Trixie selling sex toys and soft porn for couples. Even in that mess of pink and feather boas and vodka bottles, Leilani's apartment had smelled of sandalwood incense and had been free of insects and garbage.

Not that she cleaned her place. A young woman named Celia came to Leilani's once a week. Looking at the apartment now, though, it was obvious that Celia hadn't visited in weeks . . . just as I hadn't.

A near-empty bottle of Acqua di Giò on the crowded coffee table. *Truman wore Acqua di Giò.*

I screwed off the bottle's top. Crisp. Citrus.

A mesh bag sat at the foot of the couch. Inside: a paperback copy of *Cell* and a package of licorice. A cell phone sat on the couch cushion. An icon of an empty battery on the screen—it needed to charge. *Leilani doesn't own this model.*

But Truman did . . .

My arms weakened and the Acqua di Giò bottle slipped from my hands. Cologne seeped into a small mound of white powder left on the table, and onto a Mach 3 razor, its blade thick with whiskers.

CHAPTER 13

I sped out of the apartment's parking garage, the images of all I had just seen storming around my head. Truman's cologne, the phone, the razor blade, all that filth . . . I remembered the smell of Leilani's place, and I gagged, and my skin felt oily, and the car stank of cologne and sour beer still wet in my shoe soles.

Could she have dumped the whiskers into the sink at home?

Did I smell Truman's cologne, not because of memories, but because she was actually sprinkling it all around the house?

Was *she* texting me?

But why would she do that?

Was I being paranoid again?

I didn't know what to do, what to believe. Because I *saw* Truman. I had *talked* to Truman.

Or was Monica right about that, too? Had the Xanax made me hallucinate more than what was normal for a grieving widow? Had the pills pushed my predisposition to freak out into overdrive?

The security video.

I almost slammed the car's brakes as I remembered the other cameras hidden in the bathroom and kitchen. The den's camera seemed to offer nothing, but maybe I hadn't rewound the recording far back enough.

The house was a sauna when I got home. I pulled off my sweatshirt and tossed it to the kitchen floor—back to bad habits. My head pounded, and my body felt like it had been trampled by a herd of wildebeest. Blurry-eyed, I grabbed the vial of Tylenol off the breakfast bar.

I dumped one of the last two pills onto my palm, then slipped it onto my tongue. I pulled the camera from between the chips and the box of cereal. I pushed "Rewind" and waited.

Maybe I am hallucinating because of drugs, because of grief.

Maybe I do need to stay at Rayo del Sol for a few months.

I pushed "Play." No sound. Empty kitchen. Just as I started to touch "Stop," the video showed a woman entering my kitchen. Wasn't Monica. Wasn't Leilani. And I had changed a lot since Truman's accident, but I hadn't lost four inches, become light skinned, and had my hair twisted into locs . . .

Zephyr.

The camera fumbled in my hands, and I caught it before it hit the floor.

The time stamp at the bottom of the video screen said JUL 21 11:58 AM . . . My wedding anniversary.

Zephyr walked closer to the hidden camera, nearing the refrigerator. She was so close, the lens could no longer see her.

What the hell was she doing here?

"Keisha, you finished?" a woman asked off-screen. "She's gonna wake up soon."

I knew that voice.

"No," Keisha answered.

The video showed Leilani standing in the doorway with a black Mont Blanc bag in her hand. "I'm gonna get the food out of the car. Can you handle everything?"

"You act like I ain't never been in this house before with her in it," Keisha said. "And what the hell is this supposed to mean? *Never wish me away again, you and—*"

The image in the camera's monitor twisted before me, and I narrowed my eyes to focus. The breakfast bar had moved thirty feet away from me, and I hadn't even moved from my spot. I squeezed my eyes shut, then opened them—my side vision was gone, and the kitchen seesawed before me.

Disoriented, I dropped the camera, and waggled my head. I pitched myself out to the living room. My knees gave out before I reached the couch, and as I stumbled, my teeth clicked so hard that I tasted blood. My abdomen tensed, and I puked onto the hardwood floor. The light in the room dimmed, and a cold breeze washed over me. A sharp pain jolted in my belly, and I collapsed face-first into the pool of vomit.

I opened my eyes to dim, golden light. Smelled pomegranate and sandalwood . . . and burning. I tried to move my arms, but something held them down. My legs were heavy, each limb sandbagged. Tried to swallow, but no spit came, and it hurt to swallow anyway.

Leilani was kneeling at the coffee table . . . three miles away. A billion burning candles sat on the table, on the computer desk, on top of the television, everywhere. She lit a final candle, then glanced at me.

I floated above the couch, cold air streaming beneath me. Angels, each the size of penlights, drifted over me like stardust. "Why we at church?" I muttered. Leilani had closed the gap between us, and now, she was so close, I could touch her. "Your head is huge," I said, snickering. "What's up?"

Leilani smirked and gazed at me with flat eyes. "You lit a bunch of candles like you do all the time. Then, you took too many pills like you do all the time. Tried to commit suicide." She shook her head and said, "If I had found you in time, you could've lived. But you stumbled over one of your stupid candles and started another fire."

I grunted, then glanced at the soaring angels. And those golden doves. And a tiny Nicole, naked and praying. *Fire?* "I started another fire?" I croaked. "Oh, crap. When?" Tried to move again, and this time, my hand flew before my face. But that couldn't have been my hand. This . . . *thing* was as large as a baseball mitt.

"Can you just . . . ?" Leilani looked to the ceiling. "Shut up for a minute. I'm thinking."

I lay back, turned to her, and said, "I'm glad it's burning. I hate that house, you know?" I shifted, and all 206 of my bones clicked. "Help me up. Wanna go home."

Leilani's eyes glistened in the light.

"Don't cry, Lei. It'll be ohhh-kaay."

Without looking, she knocked a candle off the coffee table.

"*Wait, wait, wait,*" I said. "Why you do that?"

She bit her lip, then said, "I need to start the fire."

"I'm a little slow right now. Lemme get out—"

"No."

I giggled. "This is a joke, right? An intervention or something? You talked to Mo, huh? Dude, I took a Tylenol, that's it."

"Open your mouth," she demanded, standing over me now.

I whispered, "Did you know there are angels in here? Ssh."

"Open it, damn."

"Why?"

She held out a blue pill. "To take this."

I perched on my elbow and glanced around the room. So many candles. "I took one of those already. It's made me a little loopy cuz it's a PM edition."

She frowned. "It's not Tylenol. It's Special K."

The ceiling looked like dancing sunset. "Special what?"

"Ketamine," Leilani said. "But you didn't take two. Why didn't you take two? Cutting back now? So you can adopt your stupid little crack baby?"

My muscles twitched, and my heart pounded in my chest.

"You know what I really think about that?" Without waiting for my reply, she turned and knocked another candle off the table.

The votive tumbled to the floor and rolled toward my quilt.

I sobered some, and said, "What do you want?"

"*Now* you ask me that?" she screeched. "*Now?* After Truman leaves you everything? After you tell me you're gonna raise some kid who will get my brother's shit before I do? How is that right? How do two strangers get all my family's money?"

I stared at the wax from the fallen candle dripping onto the hardwood floor. "The candle's messing up my—"

"It's always about you," she shouted. "Keisha told me about your sessions together. Just how damn whiny you were. *How can I go on? Why is he visiting me? Make him stop.*"

"She helped you do this."

"Hell, yeah, she helped me," Leilani said. "I'm too tall to sneak around this damn house, slamming doors and hanging crap on walls without you hearing me. And she got out of LA tonight before they could arrest her for fraud or some crap like that. America's so hostile to small businesses."

I remembered: the tape. *Keisha at my fridge. Leilani with that bag.* And then, the world had disappeared.

"My brother was a fool," Leilani said. "He shoulda divorced you as soon I told him about your ass."

"Told him what?" I asked, struggling to sit up.

Leilani narrowed her eyes. "That you were sleeping around on him."

I stopped moving.

"I saw you go into Jake's house, and I saw you and Jake on the living room couch. I saw the whole damn thing. And I drove to Truman's office and I told him that night. He went off. Screaming, cursing . . . He hated your ass." She wandered to the computer table and knocked over another candle.

Icy tears stung my cheeks as I whispered, "He came to my job in the morning. We made up. He told me he loved me. I was planning to confess that night. I swear."

Leilani stood over me. "Trust me. If he had lived, he would've left you."

"We would've worked it out," I said, my voice strained. "He knew I loved him, that I wanted to be married to him."

"Bullshit," she shouted, her face now just inches away from mine. "You loved what he gave you. And now, you get to be the saintly widow, right? Why oh why did he ignore me, right? I hate this house. If only I'd been a better wife *blah blah blah . . .*" She reached behind her and knocked over two more candles. "And there I was, having to take care of your lying, cheating ass, hoping that you'd give me what I deserved since you no longer did. I hated you every minute of the damned day.

"And I didn't want to do this," she said, flicking her hand at the candles. "I tried to scare you into doing the right thing . . . It was obvious that you were crazy as hell, that you felt guilty for doing what you did, so what was the harm? You needed to be punished by somebody since Truman wasn't here to do it himself. And you were gonna OD anyway, between the Xanax and that other crap. I gave you the gun, hoping that maybe you'd stick the barrel in your mouth and pull the trigger.

"Everything me and Keisha did around here worked cuz you were getting crazier and crazier . . . But you didn't OD. You didn't shoot yourself in the head. Don't know why, but bitches like you always live. So now I gotta be direct about it." She sat on my chest, and all the air in my body was forced out. "Open up."

I struggled beneath her, but only my legs could move. "Get off me," I tried to shout.

Leilani clawed at my mouth, but I whipped my head back and forth—she couldn't get a hold. She tired of struggling with me, and grabbed the .22 from the coffee table.

"We're friends, Lei," I said, gasping for air, noticing that my quilt had caught fire.

She placed the gun's cold nuzzle against my temple.

Smoke billowed up to the ceiling, and the smoke alarm started its screech.

Leilani glared at the plastic disk above us, and said, "Damn, that's loud."

Down the hall, the alarm box squawked. The female operator said, "This is APX Control Center. Is everything okay there?"

Leilani smiled as though the woman could see her. "Yeah," she shouted. "I just burned something in the oven."

"Hello?" the operator said. "Ma'am, you're gonna have to speak up. I can't hear you."

Leilani rushed to the doorway, and shouted, "I just burned something in the oven."

I reached beneath the couch cushion, and touched the machete's cold handle.

"You don't need the fire department?" the operator asked.

"No," Leilani said. "Thanks, anyway."

I slipped off the couch and stood—Jell-O had replaced the cartilage in my knees.

"That's fine, Mrs. Baxter. I need your code word."

I gripped the machete, and wobbled closer to the door.

"Code word?" Leilani said. "I don't . . . Hold on." She looked back over her shoulder and said, "Nicole, what's the—"

I swung the long knife through the air. It stopped its glide midway through Leilani's neck, and warm blood geysered from a violated artery, bathing my hands. Leilani's finger reactively pulled the trigger, and a shot blasted from the gun's barrel. My right thigh burned with heat, and I dropped to the floor.

Leilani, still clutching the gun, collapsed beside me.

I grabbed my wounded thigh, my sweatpants now soggy with blood. Icy pain sparked through my body each time I took a breath. I cried out as I dragged myself past Leilani's crumpled body and into the darkened hallway. But I stopped. It hurt too much to move. It hurt too much to breathe. Tears and spit pooled beneath me—I couldn't do it. I closed my eyes and hid my face in my arms.

The sky was cornflower blue. Soft wind kissed my cheeks and hair. Long blades of grass tickled my arms. I lay in a field of candy-colored poppies, and in the distance, colorful hot air balloons drifted across the horizon like dandelion seeds.

A man was walking toward me.

I narrowed my eyes, but still couldn't see his face.

He came closer . . . closer . . .

Truman wore khakis and a crisp white shirt. His eyes were bright, and his skin—the color of Maui earth—radiated in the sunlight. He smiled at me.

I trembled—so happy to see him—and held out my arms. "Let me touch you."

He sat beside me, then kissed my cheeks, my lips . . .

I nuzzled his neck. Citrus and sunscreen.

He held my face in his hands and whispered, "Live."

I nodded.

Truman kissed me again, then said, "Wake up, babe. You need to go."

My eyes popped open as glass shattered in the den. A sea of flames was sweeping over the couch. Fire chewed at the computer desk. The smoke alarm continued to shriek.

Wake up, babe. You need to go.

I grabbed at the doorknob and pulled myself to stand. I limped down the hallway, ignoring pain with each step. Thick, acrid smoke billowed from behind me, and I coughed as smoke filled my lungs. I clung to the walls for support, and made it to the staircase. I placed too much weight on my injured right leg, and crashed down the stairs, coming to a stop in the middle of the landing.

The smoke alarm in the bedroom had started its own shrieking. Every space of silence had been filled with noise.

I scooted to the second step. Then to the third step. The fourth . . . I reached the first floor, but couldn't see anything. I grabbed the banister and pulled myself to my feet. My left leg shuddered as I hopped through the foyer. I opened the front door and threw myself into the cold, moist air. I stumbled, and flopped onto the flagstone pathway.

The only sounds in the neighborhood were coming from my house—all that shrieking, all that shattering. Before I passed out, I heard the faint rumble of fire trucks making their way through sleepy Beachwood Canyon.

THE AFTERLIFE

January 2

After a December without rain, tar-colored clouds banished the sun to another galaxy and released a deluge Los Angeles hadn't seen since the El Niño storms years ago. The rain fell heavy all day and without pause. The sky was falling, and so was everything else. Newscasts showed reel after reel of trees falling on houses, houses falling down hills, hills falling into the Pacific Ocean.

I stood on the ladder in my renovated den, pushing a paint roller across the wall, listening to the storm.

"Scarlet's still a bold choice," Monica said, sitting on the drop cloth and chomping on a tempura carrot.

"Dr. Clark said that I needed to make bold choices to improve the quality of my life," I said. "Scarlet paint is just one of many." I glanced down at my friend. "I'm glad she hated Bolivia."

Monica smiled. "It's hard living without a Costco in your neighborhood."

I finished painting the last strip of bare wall, then winced. I sat on a rung and massaged my thigh.

"You okay?" Monica asked.

I nodded. My leg still ached even though the bullet wound had healed.

"You should eat," Monica suggested.

"After I finish the room."

Monica waggled her finger, but before she could admonish me further, the telephone rang.

I grabbed the receiver from the top of a paint can and plucked a tempura carrot from the container.

"Nicole, it's Flex."

"Hey," I said. "Happy New Year. What's going on?"

"We found him."

During the cremation service, I stared past the mortuary workers, stared past the draped pallet hosting the plain coffin. I didn't talk. Didn't cry. Dry-eyed and mute, emotion manifested on my tight mouth, and on chipped and chewed fingernails. Monica clutched my arm in case the truth hit me: *Truman was dead. The proof was in front of me.*

Two hours later, the kind-faced mortician handed me a silver box. "His ashes," she whispered, nodding to the container.

Close to thirty people had waited for Monica and me to arrive at the pier: Flex, Keith, Jake, friends and coworkers, even Dr. Clark.

Jake kissed my cheek, and asked, "You okay?"

I shook my head, and said, "Don't know."

He nodded, understanding all that I couldn't—or didn't know how to say.

I tried to smile as I jabbed his chest with my finger. "I haven't forgotten: You owe me dinner."

He chuckled and gripped my hand in his. "Of course. Just tell me when."

I clutched the box as Monica talked to Flex and to the bishop of her church. Glanced up at the clear blue sky—the storms had moved on.

Monica returned to my side. "Ready?"

People chatted softly as the SS *Deep-Cee* chugged 1,000 yards away from California's shore. Monica had carried out my wishes, and my guests sipped Moët and nibbled on brie and sliced green apples while listening to Truman's favorite Peter Gabriel CD playing softly on a boom box. *A few of Truman's favorite things.* Wished that I could've given everyone boxes of licorice and pints of Cherry Garcia . . .

I would always find empty Ben & Jerry's ice cream cartons hidden beneath our bed and left on his desk. Once, sugar ants had discovered the sticky-sweet container in the downstairs den, and Truman couldn't understand how the ants . . .

Monica touched my hand. "We're almost there."

I handed Monica the silver box.

She left my side, and passed the box to Bishop Turner.

During our second Christmas season together, Truman and I had bought a tree from Home Depot. After we had forced the noble fir into its stand, we discovered that the tree leaned left. "So it's not perfect," I said. "Who is?" Around 3:30 in the morning, our imperfect tree crashed to the carpet. The police came with flashlights and drawn guns. "We received a call about a break-in . . ."

The boat's engine quieted, and Monica whispered, "Ready?"

I nodded.

Keith talked about Truman's brilliance and his unwavering spirit as he climbed the highest mountain in the world.

Monica told the story of me bumping into Leilani's cute big brother at a New Year's Eve party over a decade ago.

Others talked about Truman's integrity, his sense of humor, his love of life . . .

Two days after returning home from our honeymoon, Truman and I had gone grocery shopping. We had filled our shopping cart, adding the prices of each item we had plucked from the shelves. Cereal cost four dollars, cheese cost three dollars. Bread, two dollars and fifty cents. "Gettin' kinda high," Truman said. Back then, he made only $26,000 a year and I made less than that. At POULTRY—six dollars for two chicken breasts—we gawked at each other, and without saying another word, abandoned that cart full of food and went to Denny's for dinner.

Bishop Turner clutched a basket Monica had filled with Casablanca lilies and white roses. Flex attached a thick line to the basket's handle.

Keith read Dorothy Parker's poem.

> I think no matter where you stray
> That I shall go with you a way . . .

The basket lowered and touched the foamy sea.

A sob broke from my chest. Someone wrapped their arms around me—Monica, Jake, I don't know—as that basket dropped beneath the ocean's surface, as Truman's ashes disappeared into the depths below.

Silence on the Pacific. Soft murmurs of the grief-stricken.

Lilies and roses bobbed on the waves, drifting farther away . . . farther . . . Until I could no longer see them.

Truman and I are sitting on the couch, watching reruns of Lost *and eating Thai. He tosses his plate of noodles on the coffee table, and says, "Well, that was nasty."*

I smile. "You say that every time we order from there."

"I do, huh?" He kisses me . . .

I opened my eyes. A dream.

This is not my bedroom. I sat up. *Santa Barbara. The Four Seasons.*

I climbed out of bed and padded to the suite's window.

The Pacific Ocean glistened beneath the moon.

I remembered my first trip here with Truman. *A three-hour whale-watching tour with no whales the entire time.* It had been forty-eight degrees that day. I caught a cold, and Truman developed an ear infection. We swore never to go whale watching again.

And we didn't. I smiled, then slipped back into bed and pulled the comforter to my chin.

Truman's spot in bed remained empty.

I twisted the rings on my fingers, then touched his pillow before closing my eyes.

ABOUT THE AUTHOR

Photo © 2023 Andre Ellis

Rachel Howzell Hall is the *New York Times* bestselling author of *What Fire Brings, Fog and Fury, The Cruel Dawn, The Last One, What Never Happened, We Lie Here, These Toxic Things, And Now She's Gone, They All Fall Down*, and, with James Patterson, *The Good Sister*, which was included in Patterson's collection *The Family Lawyer*. A two-time Los Angeles Times Book Prize finalist as well as an Anthony, International Thriller Writers, and Lefty Award nominee, Rachel is also the author of *Land of Shadows, Skies of Ash, Trail of Echoes*, and *City of Saviors* in the Detective Elouise Norton series. A past member of the board of directors for Mystery Writers of America, she has been a featured writer on NPR's acclaimed *Crime in the City* series and the National Endowment for the Arts weekly podcast. Rachel lives in Los Angeles with her husband and daughter. For more information, visit www.rachelhowzell.com.